WRITTEN IN BLOOD

Crime short stories by women from Wales

Edited by
Lindsay Ashford and Caroline Oakley

HONNO MODERN FICTION

Published by Honno
'Ailsa Craig', Heol y Cawl, Dinas Powys
South Glamorgan, Wales, CF64 4AH

A catalogue record for this book is available from The British Library.

ISBN/EAN: 978-1-906784-01-0

The publisher gratefully acknowledges the financial support of the
Welsh Books Council

Cover image: © Getty Images
Cover design: G Preston

Printed in Wales by Gomer

Contents

Introdtion.. ix

Man and Boy
Yasmin Ali... 13

Tailings
   Caroline Clark 31

The Wolf in the Attic
   Anita Rowe 47

Ten Little Londoners
   Joy Tucker 63

The Sound of Crying
   H D Lewis 77

Cherry Pie
   Kay Sheard... 89

China Doll
   Kate Kinnersley... 107

Bitter Harvest
   Val Douglas.. 125

Killing the Village Cat
   Jan Baker.. 139

The Emerald Earring
   Sue Anderson 155

Pork Pies
   Maggie Cainen 169

Christmas Present
   Hilary Bowers 179

Within a Whisker
   Beryl Roberts 199

The Visitor
   Delphine Richards.. 215

Without a Trace
   Imogen Rhia Herrad 233

Author biographies.. 257

Introduction

This is a collection of crime fiction, but not all the stories feature an illegal act. Death is present in every story except one – but not all the deaths are murders. What the authors have in common is a fascination with the dark side of human nature and the ripple effect caused when it manifests itself.

Women, in particular, seem to be drawn to the bloody, the sordid and the downright gruesome. This first struck me when I was a lecturer, teaching a module on serial killers. The female students far outnumbered the men and they wanted to know every gory detail of a murderer's handiwork. I was reminded of *les tricoteuses*, the women who sat knitting by the side of the guillotine during the French Revolution. Where does such fascination come from? Is it rooted in the fact that women have to endure menstruation and childbirth and are less fazed by the sight of blood than men?

Crime fiction is certainly one genre in which women are equally successful as men: some would argue that they are more successful, certainly in terms of their longevity. Agatha Christie, P.D. James and Ruth Rendell have all enjoyed prolific careers spanning many decades. And female authors seem to be able to write within any sub-genre of crime, from the 'cosy' to the gut-wrenchingly violent. *Written In Blood* brings fresh voices to an area of fiction that shows no sign of losing its power to captivate.

Lindsay Ashford

I've been editing crime fiction for the best part of fifteen years – and I've been reading it since I was ten (sitting on the end of my Grandpa's sofa reading the yellow and maroon Gollancz hardbacks he borrowed weekly from the library). This collection features almost all the variants I've come across, from British cosies to American noir. It's always good to hear new voices and find new twists on the old human frailties and I loved them all; from Maggie Cainen's *Pork Pies* (an oldie but goodie) to Caroline Clark's Tailings (an imaginative take on the *crime passionnel*).

Women have been writing fiction about crime, detectives and the evil that 'men' do for almost as long as novels have been around, from Mary Shelley to Ngaio Marsh and Val McDermid to Denise Mina. This collection brings together a group of voices from Wales that shows there are still new stories to be told and hints at a rich future for the genre and the women who love to both write and read about the rogues and misfits that stalk our streets and our imaginations. It was fascinating to see the ways in which these – often first time – writers got to grips with the tropes and fancies of the form, to look for those who took a new turn or turned expectation on its head – to wonder who might perhaps have enjoyed the experience so much that there's a novel now making its way onto paper or pc screen! I hope you enjoy them as much as I did…

Caroline Oakley

Man and Boy

Yasmin Ali

The sky spills like damp stuffing from a fly tipped mattress. The houses are not old; they are puny and scuffed with tiny gardens full of random, blighted vegetation and windblown polystyrene and cigarette butts. Some windows are chipboarded up. Others have curtains, but they betoken a fragile feminine resistance that would crumble easily before the threat of a matchstick or a brick.

This is where Lisa lives.

Mario doesn't live here. Lisa's his woman, so he says. To her. She likes it when he says that, but he scares her, too. What can she do about it? Men are like that, restless, absent. Lisa looks across at Danny, sitting on the settee with his sisters, eating from a bucket of KFC and laughing at the television. He's almost sixteen now. Some boys are already men at that age, big and impenetrable, forever on the edge of violence, but not Danny. He's sweet.

Mario came around last night. He was jumpy, jumpier than usual, his eyes red, his pupils wide.

'I want you to look after something for me,' he said. Mario wasn't really looking at Lisa as he said this. He was looking over her shoulder, though there was nothing behind her but a wire clothes dryer draped with children's clothes.

'What, babe?' Lisa had said, though she knew it had to be something she probably wouldn't want in the house, or else

Mario wouldn't have asked. She knew that what Mario wants, Mario gets. She didn't take it personally. It's just how things are.

He pulled the package from a Netto bag and put it on the table next to the loaf of bread and the jar of peanut butter. The cloth looked oily, grubby, but Lisa didn't say anything. She quietly removed the bread and screwed the lid back onto the peanut butter as Mario unwrapped the cloth, gently, as though he were changing a baby. Lisa, flinching, raised her hands to her mouth when she saw the gun.

'But—' was the only word she managed to say.

Mario looked at her sharply: 'It's protection. I need it for protection. But I can't keep it at my place. It'll only be for a bit.'

'Not in the house, please, babe,' said Lisa softly.

There was a small porch on the front of the house, with two doors. The plain one bore a latch and housed the wheelie bin. The door with the cracked glass panel opened onto a separate space that led to the interior of the house. It contained two small cupboards on the wall, the upper of which sheltered the utilities meters. The lower one, rarely opened, was a jumble of mildewed trainers and woodlice. This was where Mario was persuaded to conceal the weapon. Although it was chill in the unheated space, Mario was sweating slightly when he returned to the kitchen.

Lisa was washing up. Mario came up behind her and encircled her with his arms, trapping her against the sink, her hands still under the water in the basin. Lisa understood the embrace as a warning. She said nothing as Mario began to kiss her roughly at the back of her neck, and on her throat, his groin now pushing hard against her, slamming her thigh painfully against the handle of the under sink cabinet.

'The kids…please,' said Lisa. 'Upstairs?'

Keisha heard her mother and Mario stumble upstairs and into the bedroom, just as she had earlier heard Mario fumbling about in the porch cupboard. She slipped off the settee, surprisingly agile in the big furry slippers with the bunny rabbit heads on the front. Danny threw a cushion at her, which she caught and threw back, laughing. Jade looked up disapprovingly from her mother's copy of *Take a Break*. Keisha left the room.

A large spider was scuttling over the handle of the porch cupboard. Keisha knocked it to the floor with a piece of Jade's broken scooter, and opened the door carefully. A clear trail in the dust led her eye immediately to the corner into which a plastic bag had been stuffed. It rustled when she reached out to touch it; more so as she dragged its weight forward towards her. A shoe fell out with a thud, and Jade's voice rang out, 'What you doing, Keish?' Keisha hastily shoved the package back, shut the door, and returned to the living room. She climbed back onto the settee and leaned heavily into Danny.

'Pooh! You stink of smoke, Danny,' said Keisha.

'Leave me alone, I'm trying to watch *Heroes*.'

Danny reached for the remote control and turned up the volume, further muffling the sound of Mario, who had started shouting upstairs.

Lisa was pleased that Mario hadn't stayed the night when she woke at 5.00 a.m. to get ready for work. She preferred the early shift. Danny was old enough to get the girls off to school in the morning, and Lisa was home from work in time to get the kids their tea. She dressed in track pants and a T-shirt, and laced her heavy work boots. Lisa kept her overalls on a hook at work. She had a good job at Templeton's. They maintained and repaired supermarket trolleys. It was dirty work, but they paid more than the minimum wage.

'You've got to eat something, Jade.' Danny pushed the cereal packet towards his sister. She pushed it back. They repeated the action several times until a push became a shove and the box tipped over, spilling the contents across the table.

'Ha, ha!' shrieked Keisha happily. 'You're in trouble, Jade! You did that on purpose. I'm telling Mummy!'

'You dare tell on me, and I'll tell Mum what you did this morning,' said Jade slyly.

'I didn't do nothing,' protested Keisha, but she lowered her gaze defensively.

'What did you do?' asked Danny gently. His sisters hated it when he assumed a reasonable tone, like a grown-up.

'She's been messing with Mario's stuff. Like how dumb is that?' said Jade.

'Look,' said Danny, 'we'll all be better off if we keep out of his way, so don't go winding him up.'

The walk to school took its usual form. The girls walked ahead where Danny could see them. He sloped along behind, his hood pulled up, his shoulders hunched, in a manner calculated to pass beneath the radar of those of his peers who might be looking for trouble. But Danny's mind was only partly focused on not attracting attention. He was anxious about Mario, who had been round their house too often in recent weeks, turning up at odd times, wired and volatile. Danny had noticed bruises on his mother's arms.

Lisa was thinking of Mario, too. At first she hadn't thought of him as much different from any other man. He was good looking, it was true, but he didn't have the vanity that mars some attractive men. Mario wasn't life partner material, but Lisa had few illusions about finding one of those. Men and women led essentially autonomous lives in her experience, sharing sex and sometimes food, but rarely intimacy. They came, they went. Mario, however, didn't seem to be in any hurry to move on. Mario was becoming a problem.

'Can anyone explain why the United States was initially reluctant to enter the Second World War?' asked the teacher. 'Someone must have an idea. Danny?'

Danny flinched and dipped his head, anxious to avoid speaking.

'OK, how about you, Cass?'

'They liked the Germans?' chanced Cass.

Danny groaned inwardly. He'd read a lot about the 20th century, and bored his sisters with his compulsive viewing of the History Channel, but such pastimes were too perverse to acknowledge publicly.

'Danny, give it try,' said the teacher encouragingly.

Danny focused vaguely on his shoe until the moment had passed, but it had not gone unnoticed. Later three boys pinned Danny against a wall, the largest of them sneering, 'Tell us about the war, Danny...' It was the smallest boy who frightened him, though. That boy said nothing, but he raised the blade of his knife until Danny could feel its cold tip against his warm throat. Seconds later the boys had melted away into the throng. Such were the lessons Danny learnt at school.

Lisa's lunch break was at 10 a.m. Most of her co-workers were men, but their shapeless overalls streaked with oil conferred a kind of equality upon them as they huddled outside the workshops snatching a cigarette. Work was good, thought Lisa. It was safe, reliable, you always knew what to do, what to expect, at work. Even the gaffer was OK, most of the time. He leered at Lisa, and he always stood too close, but it was worth humouring him. If she needed overtime, or time off, he could be flexible. But her thoughts at that moment had only one focus. She had to do something about Mario.

'Have you heard?' said a workmate leaning against a wall close to Lisa. He said this as he carefully folded up his newspaper and slid it into one of his pockets. This distracted Lisa from her reverie.

'What you talking about, Dave?'

'Bob's going. Fat Bob. Everyone says it's between you and Gez… Who gets his job. And you've done the training, haven't you? Got to give you the edge.'

The rest of the shift passed quickly. Lisa looked much like any of the others in the workshop, pulling wheels from trolleys, sliding them down the chute, grading, stacking, sorting, junking – depending on the condition of the cart passing down the line. But her head was full of a tumult of thoughts, from the heady possibility of more money if she got Bob's job, to a sober assessment of her chances of getting Mario and his gun out of her house, permanently. Lisa needed to talk to someone who'd understand.

Later, when the kids had settled down after their tea, Lisa pulled on her parka and headed out to see her sister Claudine. Claudine lived on the estate, too. You could walk it in twenty minutes, but the light was fading, and Lisa knew better than to walk through the fortified block of shops they called the precinct, alone, after dark. She walked instead to the main road and waited for a bus.

'How long's it been?' asked Claudine. 'Six months?'

'More than that,' said Lisa, 'I met him last summer. You remember, at Stevie's party?'

'I told you he was trouble then, but you wouldn't listen,' said Claudine, drawing deeply on a cigarette to underscore her point.

'No, you didn't,' Lisa was laughing despite herself. 'You said he was fit and flashing the cash and that I ought to get in there before some other woman got her claws into him!'

'Yeah, but I still said he was trouble. But I didn't think he did guns. I mean, you can't have that, not with Danny and the girls around. If Mario needs that kind of protection, then you sure as hell don't want his enemies round your place.'

* * *

18

Back at Lisa's house, Danny was doing the washing up whilst Keisha dried.

'Danny…' Keisha's tone was both tentative and insistent.

'What?' Danny replied. His little sister could be seriously irritating.

'I heard someone pulled a knife on you at school today,' she continued.

'Nah,' said Danny, flicking soapy water at Keisha, 'not me.'

'Bet they wouldn't do that if you had a gun,' said the girl.

'Don't be stupid,' said Danny. 'You think your big bro's a gangsta or something? Those boys are losers.'

'Is Mario a loser?' Keisha seemed genuinely to be pondering the question.

'Don't talk about that guy, right?' said Danny. He hoped that pretending that Mario was nothing to do with their family might make it a reality.

'But Mario's got a gun. He left it here yesterday,' insisted Keisha.

Danny wiped his hands on his jeans and turned to face his sister. He took her hand and led her to the table. She sat, her stockinged feet dangling, her face grave. Danny leaned towards her, his elbows resting on his thighs, his hands cupped to support his face.

'I want you to tell me the truth, Keish. Don't talk about guns just because you've heard other people. Did Mario really bring a gun here?'

'I'll show you,' said Keisha, springing from her seat.

Danny reached out and grabbed her arm. 'No you don't! If it's true just tell me where it is.'

Mario didn't show that night. His absence was both a relief and a worry to Lisa. She did not want a gun in her house. It occurred to her to buy a padlock for the cupboard, but the kids would be sure to notice. It might be safer to do nothing than to draw attention to its presence.

Jade usually ignored Danny when she caught sight of him around school. At 14, slender and pretty, Jade drew the right kind of attention. The siblings' slight build was less of an asset to her brother, and his perpetually anxious manner rendered him conspicuous in the company of his big, swaggering peers. This time, Jade stopped to look down the corridor and caught sight of a group of lads jostling Danny. When he did nothing to react, one of the boys casually launched a kick boxing move at her brother's groin. Danny crumpled to the floor as the others moved on, apparently neither concerned nor amused by their actions. Despite herself, Jade quickened her pace and went to assist her brother.

'Danny,' Jade said softly, crouching down to where he sat, his arms wrapped defensively around his slim body.

He would not meet her eyes. 'Leave me alone,' he said miserably. Thin tear tracks ran across his smooth cheeks. Jade pulled a crumpled tissue from her pocket and pushed it roughly into his clenched hand. She shielded Danny from the view of passing students as he lifted himself back into a standing position, composed himself and began to make his way, late, to his class.

That it was a Friday had been a relief for Danny; two days' respite from his tormentors loomed. Friday was less welcome to his mother. Lisa felt certain that not only would Mario appear, but that he would want her to dress up and go out with him. What she hadn't expected was to see him at the bus stop as she made her way home from her last shift at just after 2 p.m. The car door that swung open as she approached the bus shelter was not that of Mario's usual vehicle.

'Get in.'

Lisa tried to smile as she got in beside Mario. She was self-conscious in her soiled and shapeless work clothes, all too aware of her lack of lip gloss and heels. Mario seemed not to notice. He was distracted, tense, his eyes darting everywhere despite the car's tinted windows. He pulled away from the curb and moved out into the stream of traffic without indicating.

'I'm going away,' said Mario. Lisa said nothing. 'A couple of weeks, maybe. I need to keep my head down for a bit. It's best you don't know where I am.'

'That thing...' Lisa began hesitantly, 'the thing you left at mine...'

'It had better be still there? It stays there, right?'Mario looked directly at Lisa for the first time as he said this. Again, she said nothing.

Shortly after this Mario pulled into a side road. The engine still engaged, he reached across and opened the passenger door.

'I can't take you any further,' said Mario.

'I know,' said Lisa as she got out, though she didn't. 'Take care, babe,' she said, as she slammed the door. Hitching her bag to her shoulder, Lisa crossed the road, rounded a corner and made her way to another bus stop.

The weekend was over too fast. On Saturday they all took the bus into town together – if together includes a teenager hovering two paces behind with a hood pulled up to obscure his face. Where Danny then went, Lisa knew better than to ask. Not that he would have told her the truth; that he had booked a session on the computers at the library. The girls disappeared into Primark, intent on all the glitter and sequins that their pocket money could buy. Lisa was only window shopping, but with thoughts of a possible promotion – and pay hike – to add a little lustre to her day dreams.

On Sunday it rained, Lisa cleaned the floors, and the kids lolled about like kids will. It almost seemed normal, Lisa thought, until she returned the mop and bucket to the porch and caught sight of the cupboard with its deadly secret. She felt certain that she would not be able to relax until the gun had been removed.

It was still raining on Monday morning. This week Lisa was on the 2 p.m. until 10 p.m. shift, the one she liked least. She got a lie in, and it wasn't the tedium of nights, but somehow 'two till tens' stole the whole day, rather than just a part of each 24 hours.

'Jade,' said Lisa, 'you will eat breakfast. Believe me, love, it's the fat girls who don't eat in the morning.'

'That is so not logical,' sulked Jade, but she poured herself a bowl of cereal anyway.

'And you, Danny,' said Lisa. 'It's not like you not to eat your breakfast. Are you all right, darling?'

Jade threw a significant look at her brother.

'I don't feel well, Mum,' Danny said.

'You didn't say anything yesterday,' said Lisa. She reached out a hand to test his temperature. 'What's wrong with you?'

An appalled look crossed Danny's face as Jade began to speak.

'He's been having headaches, haven't you Danny?'

'Have you?' asks Lisa, 'Why didn't you say anything?'

This was sufficient to secure a day off school for Danny. Lisa walked the girls to school, and called inside to report Danny's absence. On the way home she went into the GPs' surgery to get an appointment for Danny that afternoon.

Danny sat in the doctors' waiting room at 3.30 p.m., a knot of anxiety in his stomach. His life was a deadly enough process to negotiate without the complication of having to lie to people like his mother and his doctor. Posters on the walls publicised self-help groups, dietary advice, emergency contraception… A health information video about alcohol problems was playing on a small screen. The tone of the commentary was calm and sympathetic. It occurred to Danny that perhaps he ought to tell the doctor about his problems at school; perhaps there was someone who could help.

The receptionist called Danny's name and directed him into one of the consulting rooms. The doctor did not look up as Danny entered. Danny hovered before the GP's desk, uncertain of what was required from him as the doctor continued tapping at a keyboard.

'Sit down,' said the doctor, once he had finished his task. 'What can we do for you?'

Danny's fragile hope deserted him. 'I've been having headaches,' he said, so softly that the doctor had to ask him to repeat himself. Questions followed, to which Danny chose to give such vague and noncommittal replies that he felt certain that the doctor would order him from the room for wasting his time.

The doctor did no such thing. 'I'm going to take your blood pressure,' he said. 'Can you roll up your sleeve?' The doctor wrapped a band around Danny's arm and looked carefully at the reading.

'How did you get those marks?' asked the doctor, his tone even and matter of fact.

Danny hesitated. He could feel himself flush as he stumbled out a reply about falling over playing football.

'These are very distinctive marks, Daniel,' said the doctor. 'Did you make them yourself?'

Danny nodded, consumed with shame.

'I want you to see the Community Nurse, Daniel. She will be able to help you. Make an appointment with reception when you go out.'

Danny did a lot of thinking when he got home. He hadn't followed the doctor's advice and made an appointment with the nurse; the problem, after all, was not medical. But it did now occur to him that something could be done to make school less of an ordeal. Keisha, in her childish way, was perhaps right. Other boys had bulk, or they had martial arts, or they had knives. Danny had tried the knife thing before, taking a small kitchen knife to school, and when cornered in the toilets he had tried to produce it in self-defence. But his attackers had merely jeered in derision and disarmed him with casual ease. A gun was something else. Everyone knew you never had to use a gun; just to know where to get one brought you status. Danny knew that he had to see Mario's gun, to feel its weight in his hand, to be able describe its appearance in detail.

With a couple of hours to go before Lisa returned from her shift, Danny walked softly to the porch where Keisha had said that the gun had been hidden. The door hinge squeaked a protest as Danny tried to open the door slowly to avoid attracting his sisters' attention. Using a torch, rather than turning on the ceiling light, Danny probed the contents of the cupboard. He had no idea what size a gun might be, wondering whether it might have been concealed within a trainer, or in one of his mother's old handbags.

'It's in the plastic carrier bag,' said Keisha.

Danny turned in fright at his sister's voice in his ear.

'Go away,' said Danny. 'We don't need Jade to know.'

'You think I don't know everything that goes on in this house?' said Jade, walking into the porch and flicking on the light. Just carry the bag into the front room and look at it there. Then for God's sake put it back before Mum gets home.'

Despite his fear of violence, Danny found the gun surprisingly fascinating. It was larger, heavier than he had expected. He could not easily hold it with one hand, and the poses struck by movie actors seemed impossible to reproduce with a real firearm. The gun had a pleasing solidity, which curiously made it feel more real than the household objects in the room. The word Baikal was etched in an elegant italic script on the barrel. Gripping the gun firmly with both hands, his legs apart, his arms straight, Danny raised it up to point directly at his own image in the mirror. Danny rarely stood so erect, his shoulders square, his gaze level. He looked, for once, like a man. Even Jade looked a little impressed.

'Bang bang, I'm dead!' shouted Keisha, flinging herself back theatrically onto the settee.

'Shut up,' said Danny, suddenly serious. He re-wrapped the gun in its oily cloth, and placed it in the plastic bag, which he carried back to the cupboard where Mario had chosen to conceal the weapon.

Danny slept fitfully that night. The fear that Mario might turn up whilst he was examining the gun had sent waves of anxiety through him, yet something else had happened to him as well. He felt a sense of power, of being on a level with his peers, of no longer being a nobody they could push around.

At school the next day Danny walked a little faster, a little taller, than his habitual gait. He didn't swagger or strut, but the change was noticed.

'Where were you yesterday?' The boy who said this had Danny pinned against a wall, his spittle flecked mouth so close to his face that Danny could smell the boy's sour breath.

Danny usually dipped his gaze submissively in such situations. This time he did not. He looked directly back at the boy. 'I had business to do,' said Danny. His heart was beating fast in his chest, but he did not feel his usual shrinking fear. The boy stepped back as a teacher walked by, but did not resume his aggressive stance once the teacher was gone.

'What business?' he said, almost conversationally.

'I can't tell you. I don't know if I can trust you.'

* * *

After this the day did not proceed along the usual lines. The bumping and jostling were tempered by questions rather than taunts and threats. Kyle was the gofer of the group, whose allotted role was the gathering and the dissemination of information. It was a role he suited, being talkative without ever understanding much of what he said or was told. Kyle talked a lot to Danny that morning, seemingly oblivious to Danny's reluctance to give anything up in return. But Danny was interested in what Kyle had to say, especially after the morning break.

'I know what you're up to now. You've got a job. One of the girls saw you yesterday. With a bike and a really flash mobile.'

Danny didn't contest Kyle's words, false as they were. Nor did he suggest there was any truth in the claim. It was enough that people were talking of him as a man with connections, rather than a skinny nerd. That such a transformation in his fortunes might arise merely from handling a gun, the existence of which was unknown to his erstwhile tormentors, lent the weapon magical qualities. Danny's secret brought him an inner stillness that others began to perceive as superiority, arrogance even. It was a heady experience.

In history, Danny looked at the teacher while she spoke, rather than at the hems of his trousers, or at some point in the middle distance. He answered questions, and not just when asked directly, though he did not raise a hand once, but rather he interjected languidly in the smirking tone that other boys used to make trouble. The teacher seemed disconcerted by this change. Danny's contributions were intelligent, but his manner oddly offensive. His peers responded positively, noting only Danny's new style rather than his erudition.

On the way home Danny walked with his sisters for once. Jade was, after all, someone boys noticed and girls envied; together they could exude an air of superiority. In the past Danny had felt a burden of ridicule for his babysitting role, but now Keisha's presence was secondary.

After tea, Danny spread a newspaper out on the coffee table and went to retrieve the gun from its hideaway. He laid the cloth-wrapped weapon in the centre of the table and began reverently to peel back its oily shroud. He darted a glance at Jade, who was sitting on the other side of the room affecting a lack of interest. Keisha was in the backyard feeding the rabbit. Danny was uncertain of his feelings about the object before him. He could not deny its insolent power, or its capacity to transfer that power to any man who wielded the gun in his hand. Had he not himself been transformed by its alchemy, if only for a day? But Danny was also troubled by other feelings; the gun repelled him, it reeked of men with stunted emotions and puny ambitions, men like Mario. He tried to dissociate the weapon from its owner. Danny thought of warriors with causes, like the armies that fought Hitler, but somehow he couldn't see this Baikal in the hands of a uniformed man protecting children from barbarism. It looked defiantly unheroic, an object in its proper place keeping company with losers and lowlife.

Jade broke into Danny's thoughts. 'You didn't tell anyone at school about that thing, did you?'

'No,' said Danny. 'Not a thing, honest.'

'You're not planning to take it to school?'

It had not occurred to Danny to take the gun to school. He looked across at Jade as though waiting for her to make a suggestion. She looked back, daring him to answer her question.

'I don't need to take it to school. I don't need to take it anywhere. It's just interesting, that's all.'

From the kitchen they heard the sound of running water, followed by a slamming door. Danny and Jade sprang from their seats, Danny shoving the gun and cloth roughly into the carrier bag and thrust the package under a cushion. Mario usually arrived noisily through the back door. Jade walked across the room and opened the door, peering out into the hall.

'Is that you Keish?' she called. When there was no answer she moved towards the kitchen. There was no one there, but beyond the glass door she could see her sister refilling the rabbit's food holders. Jade opened the door and asked 'Have you seen anyone? Mario, maybe?'

Keisha, still concentrating on the rabbit hutch, said, 'No Jade. It's just me and Jackie.' With that she fed a dandelion leaf to Jackie through the chicken wire.

Jade went back to her brother. 'It's OK, Dan. No sign of Mario. But you want to be careful, you know. If he finds out you've been messing with his things I wouldn't like to be in your shoes.'

The door opened and Keisha bounded in. 'Oh, Danny! You got the gun out again without telling me! That's not fair!'

'It's not for little girls, all right?' said Danny, 'Never, ever mention this to anyone. I mean it, Keish, not anyone.'

'What? Not even Joella?'

'I might have known you couldn't keep your big mouth shut. You've told Joella, haven't you?'

'No,' said Keisha in a hurt tone, 'but even if I did, she wouldn't tell anyone if I made her promise.'

That night Danny did a lot of thinking. Keisha or her friend had probably been the source of whatever rumours had been circulating about him. If that's all there was to it, he thought he could handle it. The important thing was to hope that nothing got back to Mario.

If anything, the following day at school was even more of an improvement. The crowding, and jostling and pushing happened to other boys, but everyone seemed careful not to edge into Danny's space. Girls looked at him differently, too, as though they sensed his new status. Even Jade started nodding to him as they passed in the corridors, instead of acting as though he was nothing to do with her. Despite his ambivalence, Danny had to acknowledge that the gun – despicable Mario's damned gun – was in some indefinable way the source of his good fortune.

That evening it seemed the most normal thing in the world to unwrap the gun once more. Danny didn't stare at it, or run an awestruck finger along the barrel, or wonder at whose it had been and what it had done. He simply hefted it up, two handed, one handed, at ease now with its shape, its weight, its feel. As he looked at himself in the mirror, the gun comfortable in his grip, Danny sensed his emotions changing. The weapon was losing its association with Mario, and perhaps even transferring its allegiance to Danny. After all, what could Mario do if he walked in now? Danny was the one with the gun.

The door crashed open, and Danny swung around, braced, the gun steady in both hands.

'Oh, wow, you're playing with the gun again!' cried Keisha, tumbling into the room.

'Don't do that, Keish!' said Danny.

Keisha started bounding around, zigzagging behind tables and chairs, and bouncing off the settee.

'I bet you couldn't shoot me!' she giggled, and picked up a cushion and hurled it at her brother. He loosed one hand from the gun, catching the cushion and lobbing it back at his sister. She dodged it deftly, and it hit a shelf causing one of their mother's collection of porcelain shoes to topple over and fall to the floor.

'If you broke that you're in big trouble!' said Danny.

'You threw it!' yelled Keisha. 'I'll tell on you!'

With that Keisha hurled herself at her brother. Laughing, he thrust out a forearm off which she bounced, tumbling to the floor and landing hard on her bottom. Danny bent, holding out his free hand to help Keisha to her feet. She reached forward, but instead of grasping his outstretched hand, Keisha snatched at the gun he held by the barrel in his other hand.

'I want a go!'

Danny tried to tug the gun back, suddenly afraid for his little sister, the weapon being out of his control. The gun discharged its bullet with a crack and a deep low rumble. Keisha's eyes widened and her mouth gaped silently. Jade ran down the stairs towards the noise. She saw Keisha, rigid, frozen. She saw Danny, slumped against the coffee table, a growing red stain seeping through his white school shirt.

Danny looked up at Jade and parted his lips as if to speak. He made a sound like a gurgle, and a gobbet of thick dark slime slid out of his mouth and began to move slowly down his chin.

Lisa had just shrugged off her overalls and hung them back on the peg when the gaffer led the police officer into the changing rooms. She tensed with anxiety, suspecting that the police had come about Mario and his mysterious absence, but when the officer gently sat her down Lisa's mood became one of bleak despair. Within half an hour she was at Danny's bedside.

The nurses had covered his wound and removed the medical technology before Lisa arrived. She looked at Danny's body lying on the bed. He didn't even look 15, thought Lisa. He was so small, still a child. The skin on his face was smooth with the texture of matt silk, his upper lip didn't yet show even a hint of manhood. Lisa raised her hand, rough and calloused from her job, and laid it upon Danny's soft, delicate, perfect hand.

'Danny,' said Lisa, 'my little boy.'

Tailings

Caroline Clark

Under the eye of the circling kite, pine trees follow the ridge's shoulder. Below trees and spiny scrub are broken walls splashed with lichen; thorns hide a dark mouth choked with old poison. From the flat shelf beneath, a skirt of stark grey drapes the bank, tailing down towards the close-bitten sheep pasture. On a broader terrace the long white farmhouse of Cefncwmlas cwtshes into a cleft. The bedroom curtains, drawn against the low sun, give it a sleepy or a secretive look.

Pauline McKinnon, parking her little yellow Nissan in the farmyard, felt for a moment the chill of the wind, then she hitched her briefcase under one arm, her lap-top under the other, locked the car and fended off Meg the collie's muddy greeting. Mali Watkin held the kitchen door open for her guest. She was a tall, rangy woman in her middle sixties, wearing, as usual, several sweaters and an old coat tied with orange bailer-string. Pauline thanked her and struggled through to dump her burdens on the old settee. The dog skittered in across uneven tiles and Mali shooed her out.

'Any more lambs since I left this morning?' Pauline asked, knowing that would be uppermost in Mali's mind.

'A couple, ewe-lambs and sucking well, fair play to them.' The older woman pushed her white hair back and grinned: 'A good day. Mam's slept all afternoon. I'll put the kettle on. Tea, is it?'

'You bet!'

Pauline stretched her shoulders then reached out to the fire. She felt surprisingly at home now in this old-fashioned house, half a world away from her parents' sheep farm above the Bay of Plenty in New Zealand. When her supervisor had suggested that she lodge with the farmer on whose land she would be doing research it had seemed an ideal arrangement, both professionally and economically. He had also indicated that a bit of help around the farm would be welcome. Pauline, who had suffered terrible home-sickness in her first placement, in Liverpool, had longed for the familiar rhythms and routines of a sheep farm.

Her first impression of the household was less encouraging. The rooms seemed unbelievably dark and cluttered. Texts and gloomy sepia photos of chapel elders glowered at her. Dogs and chickens ran underfoot and the only recognisable article in the kitchen was the new microwave, looking as out of place as her own Nissan did in the yard. Tom Davis, her supervisor, had greeted Mali in Welsh and Pauline had briefly wondered if even language would be a problem but then Mali had turned to welcome Pauline and the warmth in the dark brown eyes had instantly reached and reassured her. Mali asked about the farm at home and Pauline found herself pouring out not only acreage and flock numbers but when she had delivered her first lamb and what her favourite dogs were called. Tom Davis asked briefly after 'the old lady', then said he would leave them to it and see Pauline next day. Mali, over their second cup of tea, explained that her ninety-year-old mother was now bed-ridden after a stroke. Her father had died only a couple of years ago, since when she had run the farm alone, with a little help from neighbours.

'A bit of company will be great for me,' Mali said, 'but you can set up your books and papers in the parlour. I hardly ever use it now. Your room is the other end of the house from mother

– not that she calls a lot but I wouldn't want you disturbed in the night.'

Pauline was introduced to Anwen Watkin; a frail, sharp-nosed figure, as pale as Mali was dark. Her one hand constantly reached and grasped the air, her eyes passed over or through Pauline. She did not speak. 'How long…?' Pauline hesitated, not sure which of them to ask.

Mali said gently, 'Mam had the stroke two years ago. She can hear us, I think, but she doesn't talk much now.' She moved closer to the bed, 'Pauline's from New Zealand. She'll be staying here a bit.'

The watery blue eyes wandered to rest on her for a moment, questioning, then closed.

Next day Pauline went over her research outlines with Tom. Cefncwmlas was a tenant farm on the old estate of Hen Plas, which had recently been bequeathed to the Grassland Research Institute. It was an area once famous for lead and silver mines, almost all of which had closed by the 1920s. Indeed many of the smaller mines folded in the 1870s when lead prices fell. The mine above Mali's farm was one of these. However, local councils had cleared or attempted to 'reclaim' spoil at many similar sites in the 1970s. The Watkin mine had not been touched. It could now be used as a sort of control. Pauline's aim was to sample the soils in the area of the mine and make a detailed record of plants, lichens etc. in the area, throughout the year, which could then be compared with sites which had been treated or reclaimed at different periods over the last century.

'Why didn't Mali's place get treated too?' Pauline asked. Tom shrugged,

'Not sure, possibly something to do with the estate, but the mine's not very big and it's not near a water source so they wouldn't be too bothered about poison leeching from the fine tailings. Probably it just got forgotten. Ask Mali.'

That evening, after tea, Pauline asked, 'Didn't anyone ever suggest any reclamation work on your mine, Mali? About thirty years ago?'

'Oh yes. The landlord sent a letter round, but Dada wouldn't have anything done. He and Mr. Williams, Hen Plas, went to the same chapel, so they left us alone. He told me some officials had tried to survey it a long time back, too; at the end of the war – when some of the old mines were opened up for zincblende. They had tons out of that one above Pontrhydfendigaid. But Dada wouldn't let them on the farm, took his gun to them. I only remember a lot of shouting and banging on the doors – when I was four or five.'

'Why didn't the landlord make him?'

'He persuaded old Mr. Williams that stirring up the tailings – the old dust – would poison the sheep. Nothing mattered to him like his sheep. A good shepherd he was, always.' She looked up fondly at the photograph above the fire.

Next morning was fine and dry. Pauline helped Mali feed and check on the ewes, then she set off with her maps, pegs, string and camera to make a first appraisal of the area and begin a trial quadrant. It was too early in the year for many plants to be visible but a good time to check on lichen. She took the farm track up towards the ridge then followed what might be the line of a leat along to the clear remains of spoil. She checked its position on her map, made a few measurements and then climbed higher to where thorny scrub had taken hold. It did not look as though there had been any large buildings. The walls that did remain showed clear signs of demolition and a small sheep-fold below in the field had probably been the beneficiary years ago. She made more notes, took some photos, then, pulling the hood of her Goretex up, she shouldered through rusty thorns to where the adit and shaft were marked.

The grooves where truck-wheels had cut into the rock could still be felt under the moss and lichen. Beyond was a dark, apparently dry tunnel. She could see grey-seamed oak and red-rusted metal – part of the under-frame of a truck, perhaps – wedged in the hole, but no other signs of closure.

Any further investigation of that would need a torch and some secateurs, if she decided to pursue it. As she emerged, being careful not to scrape the rock-sill, she was startled by the high keening of buzzards above the pines.

As Pauline had installed her books and computer in the parlour, Mali had a fire going and, after their meal, she brought their mugs of coffee in and sat down with Pauline. The parlour was even more archaic than the living-room. A stuffed owl gazed fiercely down at them from its glass dome, but on the mantelpiece was a much more recent photograph of Mali's father. He held a well-set lamb under one arm and a splendid silver trophy in the other hand.

'Something special?' Pauline asked.

'Very special,' said Mali. 'Best in breed at the Royal Welsh. He'd been close a few times and that year he got it. Oh he was jumping, and so was I,' she laughed at the memory. Pauline looked at the triumphant face, blue eyes sparkling; very different from his severe image in the other room.

'Were you very close?' she asked.

Mali paused, 'To tell the truth, not for a while. When I was little I was scared of him. He was very strict and silent, but after I started to help with the sheep and he saw that I took to them, we were much closer. Somehow, with Mam, it was the other way about, but I suppose that's only natural. Maybe she was one of those who are happiest with children when they are small, but she only had the one.' Mali looked sad.

Pauline asked, 'How d'you mean?'

'When I first remember her she was very lively, lots of fun.

35

She used to tell me stories, when Dada was out. Then the stories got sad and she hardly spoke. Oh, she worked as hard ever, but she faded, somehow. I never thought she would make old bones, to tell the truth.'

Pauline, a little uncomfortable, turned to the room: 'That's a lovely rug, such a pretty pattern, is it Persian?'

'Fancy you noticing that! I don't think it's foreign. They were fashionable in the big houses when Mam was young. She'd been in service up at Hen Plas as a girl and they gave it her as a wedding present.' She smiled fondly, 'I used to think it was magic.'

'A flying carpet?' Pauline asked.

'Yes, because of the story Mam told me, over and over, about a princess in a white tower and an eastern prince in silks and gold who fell in love with her. She was locked in, but he flew up and rescued her and they flew off together on the carpet to his golden palace in the sun. I used to think those long, thin clouds you get at sunset were magic carpets, heading into the sun.' She laughed, then shook her head, 'But when I was older the story changed, the prince forgot the princess and flew home without her. I always used to hope I would find a way to make the rug fly,' she laughed, 'but it's still here.'

After a while, when Pauline had documented quite a range of quadrats around the mine, she decided to investigate the adit again. Rare ferns and bryophytes had turned up on some of the walls on similar sites and she wanted to see if there were any inside. She borrowed some old secateurs and gardening gloves from Mali and took a torch out of the car. The weather had been dry; cold at night, but the sun was warm on her back as she climbed the fields.

Careful only to cut back enough bramble to let herself squeeze past, she examined and noted the lichen and hanging fern just beginning to show where watery light reached the rock entrance. Treading carefully she moved into the dark, her torch picking out splashes of colour on the grey ribbed walls she came up to the truck-frame, barring the way, and examined the surface of wood and metal, careful not to disturb it. Just beyond the barrier her torch-beam caught what she thought was a group of stems. She focused in, then almost grabbed the frame in shock.

Pale green, chalky, surely those were the still articulated bones of a hand?

She controlled the impulse to escape and angled the beam further into the tunnel. There was a machine shape, rusted like the truck wheels, but not part of the mine. A heavy motor-cycle was jack-knifed and rammed into the tunnel. Beneath it was something like a thick boot and from one side the outline of a sleeve ended in the cluster of bones.

Moving very carefully, Pauline backed out into the sunlight. She put down her torch on the grass and felt rather sick. Certainly the body might have been the victim of a crash, an accidental death, but then it had been hidden, in a place no-one had been allowed to disturb.

Even she, so recently on the scene, knew who had kept it that way – for sixty years or more. Surely she had no choice but to report it, even though the investigations might prejudice her research, but that hardly concerned her. It was the implications for Mali which appalled her. Whoever lay there had been hidden in her father's time, with his compliance or worse.

Pauline cursed her own thoroughness. She could have left the shaft undisturbed. The rest would have been enough for her study, but she had already discussed it with Tom Davis. He would want to know why she had changed her mind. Pauline pulled her coat around her and sat watching the sheep wander closer.

'A good shepherd,' Mali had said. Must she destroy the beloved memories of a lifetime for something so long forgotten?

But perhaps the body in there wasn't forgotten. Perhaps even now someone needed to know why their husband or father had never come home. She could not ignore what she had found. Stiffly she reached into her breast pocket and pulled out her phone. Tom Davis answered almost immediately:

'How's it going? Anything exciting?'

Pauline choked. 'Kind of, but not in the way you mean. Any chance you can come over? I... Well, I've found something that shouldn't be here. In the mine. I really need some advice.'

'Mystery's not your usual style, Pauline.' Tom sounded a bit disappointed, 'What is it?'

'OK, but please come and see. It's complicated. It's a body.'

'What!' The phone almost jumped out of her hand, then, more calmly, he asked, 'Recent? Or something from the mining period?'

'Not recent, but not a miner either. Please come.'

Pauline was crying now, the ice of the shock was melting. Tom Davis was suddenly more sympathetic: 'I'll come at once. Do you want to meet me at the farm?'

'No! I don't want Mali to know yet. Come up the fields from the bridge. Bring a torch if you can.'

He agreed and Pauline stayed where she was, watching the road below. After a few minutes she took out her flask and shakily poured a cup of tea. It warmed and steadied her. After all, she told herself, whoever 'he' was had been dead a long time. Perhaps no-one would really be interested. She was still very relieved to spot Tom's Land Rover pull in beside the bridge and to see him climbing up towards her. She waved and tried to pull herself together to discuss what should be done. At first he was more concerned for her. *Did she feel OK? Did she want to go back straight away?*

'I know we mustn't touch anything but I want you to see what's there, in case I could be mistaken.'

'But you don't think you are?'

Pauline shook her head sadly.

'I've cut the brambles away enough for me but you might need these.' She gave him the secateurs and gloves. 'There's a barrier, something from the mine jammed in the way but you can see through and, on the right, by the wall...' she swallowed hard, 'there's a hand.' Tom Davis took what she offered and edged through the curtain of thorns. Pauline waited, staring at the ground before her; trying to concentrate on the leaves, grasses, wisps of wool, dung and grit; trying not to see the pictures in her mind. In a short while she heard Tom moving down the slope. He sat down beside her, almost as pale as she was. She gestured towards the Thermos and he nodded.

'I'm sorry,' she said, when he had gulped some of the tea. 'I shouldn't have gone in there. There was no need.'

'Don't think that. It wasn't your fault, how were you to know?'

'I suppose we couldn't just leave it?' Pauline said, tentatively. 'I felt I had to tell you because we'd talked about sampling in there, but no-one else...'

'It's a crime scene, Pauline,' he said flatly. 'It can't be anything else. We have to report it. I know it was a shock but it's ages old. Nothing to do with us...'

'Not us but.....Mr. Davis, you know these people...Mali...'

'It can't be Mali's fault. I should think that motor-cycle's fifty years old at least.'

'Not her. Her father. She told me he wouldn't let anyone touch the mine; not even back in the '40s when some were opened up for work again. He drove the surveyors off with his shotgun; persuaded the landowner that it would poison the sheep. He must have known.'

Tom Davis sighed. 'I remember Gwyn Watkin. A stubborn old man, right enough. Oh Hell!' He turned away, rubbing his hands over his hair and eyes. 'It's no good. Whatever we think, we have to report it. Pack up your stuff. I'll take you down to the farm and speak to Mali. Then we'll go into town and report it to the police. I don't know, they might decide it is too old to bother with, but there will have to be an inquest. The other thing,' he straightened up 'is protecting the site. I'll talk to the police about that. I reckon I know their pathologist.'

Mali wasn't in the house when they got to the farm. Pauline was very relieved; she could not have faced her, thinking as she did. Tom drove off to town.

'I expect they'll send someone up for a statement but I'll try to get them to keep it as low-key as possible,' he said as he left.

Pauline changed, washed and tried to organise her notes and concentrate on them as she waited for Mali to come back. But her gaze kept wandering to the mantelpiece – to the triumph in the eyes of Gwyn Watkin.

The district nurse made her daily visit to the old lady and Pauline asked if there was anything she needed.

'No thanks, Mali always leaves everything ready – I expect she's busy with the lambing. Mrs. Watkin is quite stable; nothing to worry about.'

I wish, thought Pauline.

Mali had indeed been with the sheep. She hurried in just as the light was going, 'Sorry I am, Pauline. Tea will be a while yet. I've got to get cleaned up.' She ran water noisily into the tin bowl and splashed in some Dettol. 'I saved the ewe I think. If she sleeps long enough and it doesn't turn too cold, she'll do. But I had to cut up the lamb to get it. Dead and wedged it was, ach y fi! Sometimes, as Dada used to say, you have to make up your mind to cut and be quick about it.' She scrubbed her hands and the old horn-handled clasp knife she always carried for the sheep.

'I'll leave a message for the vet to come in the morning. She was too far gone to call him for the lamb.'

'I'm sorry, Mali. I wish I'd been around to give you a hand.

It's a horrid job to do on your own,' Pauline said, trying to sound normal and not think about something else 'dead and wedged'. Mali turned to look at her.

'What is it, Pauline? You look pinched, is there a cold on you? The wind's still sharp.'

'No, Mali. I went up to the old shaft today…have you ever been into it?'

'No. Dada always told me it was dangerous – and I don't like dark tunnels, I never even like going through them on trains. You didn't get hurt, did you?' Her eyes were full of innocent concern for Pauline; no hint of knowledge.

'I only looked in, but there was something there Mr. Davis felt we should report. I'm sorry. We would have told you first but you were out.' She took a deep breath, 'We think there's a body under a machine in there. From a long time ago.'

'Oh, you poor girl! What a shock for you. One of the miners, I suppose. Let me get dry and I'll get us some tea. I'll use that micro-thing. You'll feel better when you've got something warm inside you – and so shall I.'

Pauline was glad to let it pass at that. Pauline stoked up the fire, made tea and by the time they had eaten she had almost persuaded herself that Mali might be right.

They had a call quite early next morning to say an officer would come up to the farm by half-past ten. He would arrange access for the pathologist and team and take statements from them both. Mali decided to move the sheep down from the top pasture and set off with Meg leaping happily around her.

The young policeman was prompt. He introduced himself as Constable Hughes and had a brief chat with Mali about one of his relations who had bought a ram from her, then he took a statement from her that she had no personal knowledge of the shaft and believed that it had been undisturbed for the last sixty years. He turned to Pauline, 'Professor Davis said you have been recording plants on the rocks up there. I'll just make a note of when you went in and what you did, then, if you come with me, we could cover any sensitive spots before the team arrive. I've got some sheets of plastic in the van.'

'Thank you so much, I'll come at once,' Pauline said, smiling with relief. She hadn't expected anyone to care about her work, in the circumstances, but Constable Hughes seemed both interested and friendly. She even found herself thinking he was the best looking bloke she had seen since she came here. On the way they talked a bit about where she came from. Once on the site she quickly showed him the rocky areas that needed covering. He didn't think they would need to touch the old buildings.

'I'll need to cut the brambles away to give access to the shaft but I'll put a cover on the outer floor. You don't need to come.'

Pauline nodded and said she would get back to the farm.

'They won't need to talk to me again, will they?' she asked.

'I shouldn't think so. You didn't move anything. It was just your bad luck to find it first. I'll let Miss Watkin know about the Coroner when the time comes.' He paused. 'Are you likely to still be around?'

'I hope so, if it's ok with Mali.'

She saw him grin as he turned away, then he gathered up tools and plastic sheeting and scrambled up the hill. She checked her charts to make sure she hadn't missed anything, then walked back down the track.

Mali was scraping and chopping vegetables for a stew. Pauline offered to help.

'Nearly finished; but I'd be glad of a hand to clear out the caravan, if you're not studying. The ewes seem settled for now.'

They opened the slightly musty Sprite which Mali kept behind the barn and gave it an airing. It wasn't really a holiday let, but used now and then by visitors or workers on that or the neighbouring farms.

'Nice lad, that constable,' Mali said.

Pauline found herself grinning like a teenager, 'Yes, very considerate. He said he'd let you know how things went...the inquest and that.'

Mali sighed, 'Poor soul. Who'd have thought – all those years...'

Pauline nodded and applied herself to the cleaning. She watched Mali's slim brown fingers untangling a window-cord and thought, *Do two blue-eyed parents ever have a brown-eyed child?*

It was not many days before Constable Hughes re-appeared. Mali was sitting with her mother, so Pauline let him in.

'I came to tell Miss Watkin that the inquest is fixed for next Monday. She will need to be there and there are some things I need to ask her. It's going to be upsetting, I'm afraid.'

Pauline sighed, 'Well, even from what little I know I guess her father must have been involved in hiding – whoever he was. But I thought it would take much longer to discover anything concrete.'

'The benefits of war-time bureaucracy; the chap was a flyer – RAF Pilot Officer with his ID card on him in a wallet and certainly not a local; Indian, would you believe? In 1945! It seemed queer that no-one had looked for him. After all, the services are pretty hot on men going AWOL and he wouldn't exactly blend in. Apparently they thought he'd been killed in a fire. Not a bomb or anything – the place he was stationed had a fuel tank blow up, everyone sleeping there was presumed dead. What on earth he was doing out here we'll probably never know.'

'What was his name?'

'Something long with Yoga in it, it means he was a Hindu apparently, but the first name was like Harry, I expect that's what they called him.'

'I suppose there's no way to tell what killed him. I mean if it was a crash, an accident…'

Constable Hughes was about to answer then hesitated. 'I think I have to ask Miss Watkin a few things before I say any more. How's the work going?'

'Very exciting, I might even find some forked spleenwort later in the year, if I'm lucky!'

He looked unsure, 'That's good?'

Pauline laughed, 'Well, it would be, but it hardly compares with your investigations, does it?'

'I expect you're pretty busy though. I just wondered if you'd found your way to the Arts Centre yet, in town. They have some good films.' He went red about the ears. 'It's Mike, by the way, when I'm not on duty.'

Pauline said, 'I'd like to get to know the place. I haven't been anywhere much beyond the Institute and doing food shopping in town. Perhaps when we're really through the lambing… Mali can do with me around just now.'

'I'll keep in touch.'

He looked up as Mali came downstairs. 'Miss Watkin, I'm sorry to bother you again but I need to ask you a few questions. Some of them might seem rather odd.'

Pauline got up, 'I'll go to my room, Mali.'

'No, cariad, stay, unless the constable minds.'

Mike shook his head. 'Miss Watkin, we believe the body was put in the mine in 1945. How old would you have been then?'

'I was three in December that year.'

'Do you remember when there was first a suggestion the mine be re-started?'

'I think I was about five, I told Pauline, my father wouldn't allow it for fear it poisoned the sheep.'

'Do you have any knives your father used when you were little? Something that's always been here?'

'Well, there's the carving set, that was my Grandfather's. It's in the drawer.'

She took a long, old-fashioned 'carver' out of the dresser. The constable examined the perfect, well-honed blade but continued, 'Something shorter? Something he used on the farm?'

'There's the pocket-knife, I suppose, but I don't see...'

'Could I just look, do you think?'

'I'll get it,' said Pauline. 'It's on the kitchen window sill."

She picked up the horn-handled knife and brought it to the table.

Mike Hughes opened it and asked, 'Do you remember the tip of the blade being broken, Miss Watkin?'

'Duw, it's always been like that, we use it for rough work, you see, but it's handy. What's all this got to do with the miner?'

'I will need to take these with me, just for now, Miss Watkin.'

He stood up and Pauline said, 'I'll see you out.' She gave Mike a couple of plastic bags for the knives and opened the door for him.

'What was all that about?' she asked when they got to his car.

'The pathologist says there is no doubt what killed the chap. His throat was cut. The neck-bone is hacked into from the front and a piece of steel still in it.' He hefted the smaller bundle.

'I never thought it would still be around but who knows?' He got into the car. 'There's no use talking to the old lady, I suppose?'

'I'm sure there isn't. And it's so long ago, do you really have to go into it?'

'There has to be an inquest but I shouldn't think it will go any further.'

'Poor Mali!'

'No-one could blame her for anything.'

'But it'll re-write her life,' said Pauline, thinking more than he knew.

'Then I'm glad she's got you here for a bit.'

'I don't know. I stirred it all up.'

'Oh, that was just bad luck. Now the Institute has taken over it was bound to happen.'

She nodded. 'I suppose.' She watched him drive off then returned to the living room.

'Is there anything I can do for you, Mali? Shall I feed the ewes?'

'No, thank you, cariad. I'd better check them. If you've time you could get the tea on. Are you going out, tonight?'

'No, why?'

'Oh, I just wondered,' she smiled. 'It's a hard job but he seems a nice young man. Keep the fire in.' She pulled on her old coat and went out into the dusk.

Pauline was laying the table when she heard something from the room above. She went up quietly, not wanting to wake Anwen if she was still asleep. The old lady was lying quite still but her eyes were open.

Pauline hesitated, 'Did you call? Did you need something?'

She picked up the plastic mug and offered it. Anwen shut her eyes, then she opened them wide, questioning, her hand reaching out.

Pauline sat with her for a while then she began, very quietly, not sure if she wanted to be heard: 'Do you remember the story, a princess in a white tower and an Indian prince who loved her; a prince who flew on a magic carpet and had a golden palace in the sun.' She fancied the grip tightened a little.

'You said the prince went home alone, forgot his princess. It wasn't so, Anwen. He never forgot. He was coming for her but an enemy destroyed his magic carpet. He didn't forget! Maybe he's still waiting?'

She looked at the face on the pillow but whether Anwen heard, or remembered, or understood, Pauline could not tell.

The Wolf in the Attic

Anita Rowe

'...every hyacinth the garden wears
Drop't in its lap from some once lovely head.'
(Omar Khayyam, trans. Edward Fitzgerald, 1859)

You wouldn't think, to look at me, that I have anything sinister
to hide. I sit here in my creative writing class, a short, stout
middle-aged woman in twinset and pearls, the epitome of
Welsh middle-class respectability. Retired nurse, empty-nester,
divorcee living alone, carefully nurtured pretence of total
celibacy – now threatening to become reality – dabbling in
a little creative scribbling to while away all these new-found
leisure hours.

But really, it's not like that at all. I joined this class with the
express purpose of making a confession in safety. Like Midas's
barber whispering into a hole in the ground:

'King Midas has ass's ears... King Midas has ass's ears...'

'Enfys Williams is a—'

No, I'm not going to spit it out just yet. It gives me secret
amusement to think of you, my tutor and co-students (probably
the only ones who will ever read these lines), imagining that
what I read out in these workshop sessions is fiction. Even
when I read out those last few sentences I've just written, you'll
never take it for truth. You'll think I'm just indulging in a clever

bit of post-modern authorial self-consciousness... A carefully thought-out fiction... Whereas, in reality, I'm scribbling down everything that enters my head.

'King Midas has ass's ears.' (Ancient Greek Myth)

'I sometimes think that never blows so red
The rose as where some buried Caesar bled.'
(Omar Khayyam, trans. Edward Fitzgerald, 1859)

Does everyone who commits a crime and gets away with it have an urge to confess sooner or later? I feel this urge grow stronger every day. Perhaps the very effort of keeping a secret, the need to hide something, the urgency of that need, engenders the paradoxical drive to disclosure. A drive – yes, that's what I feel. Driven. I feel driven. That's what the nightmares are about. This recurring dream in which I'm driving my car... Trying to drive it, that is... Because the car has its own agenda. I turn the wheel. It has no effect. The car turns in the opposite direction. I press the brake. The car goes faster. Still sitting in the driving seat I am no longer the driver. Being driven by a mindless or malignant machine I can only wait for the crash.

Soon, very soon, I must stand up and say, 'My name is Enfys Williams and I am a—'

My name was given me by my Welsh father, my real father, who was killed in the war. It's a pretty name (pronounced Envis, for those who don't know), Welsh for 'rainbow'. But it also sounds rather like the English word 'envious'. Am I envious? I was once very envious of my little half-sister, Perdita. Her name was chosen by my English stepfather, Oliver Crawley. I was allowed to call him Oliver instead of 'Dad' and they said I could choose to keep my own surname or change it to Crawley, like theirs. I chose to keep my own, and I've also chosen to revert to it after my divorce. Something to do with preserving my fragile sense of identity, I suppose. Although I was glad about keeping my true father's name, it did make me feel an outsider. At times it felt as if the three of them ganged up against me. I envied Perdita having her own father still alive, still there to love her and take care of her. With hindsight I see that her name was ironic: 'the lost one'. Because I really did lose her... Literally.

When I was very young, before my mother met Oliver, people used to say, looking at me sideways and lowering their voices, 'She's lost her father, you know.' As if I'd carelessly dropped him or left him behind on a bus. Later I realised he'd fallen out of his plane in the sky and been smashed to bits on reaching the ground, like Humpty Dumpty. So I could stop feeling it was my fault. But I really did lose Perdita. And it was my fault.

I took her out to play one Saturday, as usual, and came back without her. 'We were playing hide and seek,' I told my mother. 'She hid and I couldn't find her. I looked for ages and ages. I looked everywhere I could think of. I kept shouting her name. Then at last I went back to the place where I'd stood hiding my eyes and waited. I thought she might get tired of hiding and come back of her own accord. But she never did.'

It was a lie. I've never told anyone the truth. I don't know if my mother believed me or not. She gave me a long, sharp look, asked a few questions, and marched out, with me in tow to show her exactly where we'd been playing in the woods. We searched and called and searched and called. We didn't find Perdita. No surprise to me, of course. I knew we weren't going to find her there.

By the time Oliver came home from the football match and subjected me to an angry and lengthy interrogation, the police were already on the case. Local people joined in the search.

National radio appeals were broadcast on the BBC Home Service. Over the next week the woods were tooth-combed, then several areas in and around our little Welsh seaside town. Areas where people claimed to have seen us. For instance, two women told the police (several days later) they'd seen my sister wandering around town on Saturday afternoon, and she'd stopped and asked them if they'd seen me.

'Whyever couldn't they have just brought her home? Or told a policeman at the time?' My mother asked in tearful bewilderment, over and over. 'She's only four, after all.'

At other times she said to me, 'You're eight years old. You were supposed to be taking care of her.' This pierced my guilty heart and made me cry, but Oliver's tirades left me stony faced.

People had seen her, or both of us, in all sorts of places, they said. One man said he'd seen us playing on the beach, where we were absolutely not allowed without adults. This was as untrue as my own story. Possibly he'd confused us with some other little girls.

'We never went near the beach,' I insisted, 'cross my heart and hope to die.' And I meant it. This protestation was grimly ignored by my mother and stepfather, who eventually concluded, like the police, that I'd left Perdita to her own devices, which I often did, in pursuit of my solitary games or book-reading; that she'd wandered too near the treacherous winter waves and been swept out to sea. Naturally her body never came ashore. Before that conclusion a lot of people were questioned by the police, apart from me and my parents. My mother's three boarders, for instance… She kept visitors in our big, Edwardian house near the sea front, a house she'd inherited from her parents who had both died young. We were open all year round, but few people came in winter.

I knew that Perdita had not sunk below the green-glassy waves, but after a few months had gone by I stopped protesting and let them think what they liked. Perhaps it was safer, I thought. I was very scared of my mother finding out what had really happened, and as for Oliver – to say I was terrified of him would be an understatement. He had loved Perdita so much, calling her his little darling, hugging and kissing her. Now morose in his grief, he barely spoke to me. He had never laid a hand on me, either in love or anger, but the disapproval and resentment that replaced his previous indifference chilled me to the bone. The way he glared at me, it was as though he knew. My mother still hugged me now and again, and kissed me goodnight, but there was a new wariness in her attitude to me as well as a deep, deep sadness, deep as the sea. We continued living to the rhythm of that sea as it beat on the nearby shore, in tune with the mournful wail of the gulls. My mother lost interest in her housekeeping, the boarders left, and I frequently came across her weeping quietly into a little lace handkerchief. We didn't celebrate Christmas that year, but I was given a few presents by distant relatives.

My little sister wasn't on the sea bed with the crabs and fishes. She lay still and silent under the gravel, and later below the green turf. In my nightmares she rose up from all these places to accuse me. As well as from places where she couldn't possibly be, such as the eaves cupboard in the attic of our house… Though it was impossible that she could have been there, I became frightened to open this cupboard, then became scared to go up to the attic on my own at all.

'I sometimes think that never blows so red
The rose as where some buried Caesar bled;
That every hyacinth the garden wears
Drop't in its lap from some once lovely head.'
(Omar Khayyam, trans. Edward Fitzgerald, 1859)

Perdita's head was beautiful, with its bright blue eyes and

blonde hair curling onto her shoulders. She took after her father – my mother and I are both dark. Old ladies used to smile at her and say, 'Gai gyrlan gen ti, mach i?' (Will you give me a curl, little one?) No one ever said that to me, not even when my mother had pinned up my hair in rags overnight to make ringlets, which was before Perdita was even born.

'I sometimes think that never grows so green
The grass as where Perdita was last seen.'
(Enfys Williams, aged 13, 1953).

My childhood scribbles were always derivative. This Khayyam imitation was inspired by the fresh green of the lawns at the Coronation Garden, planted in 1953 in honour of our new Queen. Not planted by the Council, mind you, but by the women who lived in Lôn Llygod Bach (Little Mice Lane). This was near the centre of town, a half crescent of fewer than a dozen tiny terraced cottages dating back to the eighteenth century, curving around the ruin of what had been a fine Victorian hotel that burned down in the 1930s. Nobody knew who owned the ruined hotel, so the Council couldn't demolish or rebuild it. It remained an eyesore and a danger to the children who played among its crumbling masonry until 1952, when the women of Lôn Llygod Bach organised a petition to the Council to have the area made safe for their children.

They nagged and badgered the Council into taking all the ruin walls down to two feet and making them good. Then, determined to make a garden in time for the Coronation, they persuaded a builder to give them, gratis, a lorry load of topsoil to cover the whole area between the walls. Every day when it didn't rain, weekends and after school on weekdays, they and their children, plus one or two husbands, armed with borrowed spades, marched out to the country lanes surrounding the town to cut neat little squares of turf from the overgrown verges and carry them home in sacks. The turfs were then watered and carefully set down edge to edge. The area to be covered was so large and the squares of turf so small that at first the task reminded me of a story in the Children's Encyclopaedia about a squirrel trying to move a lake by dipping its tail in it then shaking its tail in the area of the intended new lake.

As the project grew and prospered, however, the women carefully watering the new lawns and weeding the rest every day, more volunteers from other areas joined in, impressed by the team's determination. More fortunate ladies with lovely gardens donated plants for the borders. I too joined in with enthusiasm, going out with them to cut turfs every evening before going home to do my homework, seeing it as a kind of penance and reparation. It was good to think of my little sister's resting place being turned into a beautiful garden.

By that time Oliver was long gone. Only a few months after his daughter's disappearance he went away with that waitress from the Gwynant café and we never heard from him again. But now I'm getting ahead of myself. I've rushed along to 1953 before telling you what really happened in 1948. This is the kind of thing we beginner writers do, isn't it? You may think I'm avoiding the confession I claim to be so eager to make. You see, I don't just want to confess. I want to explain. I want you to understand what I was like as a child. And why what I was like has made it impossible for me to confess later. I did consider it, you know, after my mother died, when I was forty and single again. Then I thought of my childhood reputation as the biggest liar in town, my adult breakdown, psychotic episode and spell in the mental hospital. I looked at the prestigious new complex of flats and shops that now stands where the Coronation Garden used to be. I could imagine the police's reaction. And what would my grown up children say? I reconsidered and kept quiet.

After Perdita's birth my mother continued to walk me to

school and back. I used to make a big fuss of my new little sister in her pram, as my friends did. As soon as I was five, however, my mother said I could walk to school and back with the big gang of older children who came and went from the estate of council houses near the sea front. Some of them were rather rough but my mother didn't seem to notice and I soon got used to them.

As my little sister grew older my parents stopped treating her as if she were a basket of eggs. They even shouted at her sometimes if she did naughty things as she toddled around. When this happened I felt warm and protective towards her. She was too little to understand much, after all. But if I came home from school and found her and my mother cosily absorbed in some game or looking at a picture book together I'd feel jealous of their intimacy. I would then start some game I knew Perdita loved, like 'wolf in the attic', and so divert her attention to me. 'Wolf in the attic' consisted of me lurking on the attic stairs making howling noises, while she tiptoed up to peek at me. As soon as I saw her my howls would change to snarls and I'd run after her growling that I was going to eat her up for my dinner. She would toddle round the house screaming in delight while my mother sighed and grumbled, 'It was nice and quiet till you appeared.'

What I really hated was the fuss Oliver made of her. He would say things like 'Where's my little darling Perdy Pussykins today? Has she gone away?', while she hid behind the settee, giggling. Sometimes she'd hide by just covering her face with her hands, thinking he couldn't see her because she couldn't see him. Then he'd say 'Aha, here she is!', pick her up and smother her face and neck with kisses, making silly baby noises. It was disgusting. He always read her a bedtime story in her bedroom and he was in there as long as an hour sometimes. I could hear her giggling through the wall from my room next door. Me he just ignored. He never even asked what I'd done at school that

54

day as any grown-up would. I grew to dislike him more and more. Always on the lookout for any minor misdemeanour on his part, such as stubbing out a cigarette on the kitchen worktop instead of an ashtray, or forgetting to wipe his feet when he came in, I would shout, 'I'll tell Mam of you, I will!'

One morning during the school holidays my friend and I, walking past Gwynant café, saw Oliver kissing one of the waitresses. The café was next door to the estate agent's office where he was manager, and he often popped in for a coffee. My mother was annoyed when I told her about this, but he denied it and my friend was too scared to back me up. He succeeded in persuading my mother that I was telling lies. So, feeling I might as well be hanged for a sheep, I really did start to tell lies about Oliver. If I were feeling really mean I would make up some fictitious peccadillo. These fabrications grew more and more outrageous. I told lies about him to neighbours and teachers as well. My mother grew heartily tired of this and forbade me to tell any more tales about him. Perdita was beginning to copy me and say, 'I'll tell Mam of you!' to her father as well. At other times she would say, 'Don't tell lies about my daddy, you bad girl,' in imitation of the grown-ups.

Perdita loved to get my attention and was always wanting me to play with her or take her out to meet my friends. Sometimes this pleased me, but mostly it was a nuisance. If I got cross with her I'd give her the slip and hide somewhere to bury my nose in my latest library book in peace, or my friends and I would run away to play on our own, leaving her crying, 'Emis, Emis, where are you?' But before we went home I'd be nice to her again, soften her up a bit, promise her things, so that she wouldn't tell on me. And mostly she didn't, only sometimes other people did; adults who had witnessed my callous behaviour.

On that fatal Saturday it was just the two of us. She wanted to play hide and seek in the woods but I wasn't in the mood.

'Maybe later,' I said. I had some pocket money to spend, and some sweet coupons left, so we walked into town and bought a comic and a packet of Smarties from a newsagent, who later reported seeing us to the police.

'Let's go to Lôn Gygo' Bach to eat them,' suggested Perdita.

I shook my head. I didn't like those ruins at Lôn Llygod Bach. I thought they were scary. Some years ago a local man had committed suicide in one of the ruined rooms by drinking rat poison, and people said his ghost still haunted the place. The walls of the old rooms were still quite high so nobody could see you in there though it was in the centre of town, and sometimes bricks would fall off. As the adults were always warning us, you could get knocked out by a falling brick and lie there unconscious for days before anyone found you. But for some reason my little sister had taken a fancy to the place.

'Come on, we'll go to the park,' I said. 'We'll share the sweets and I'll read some of my comic to you, then we'll go on the slide and swings.'

She nodded happily and trotted along. The park in our home town is tiny, hardly deserving of the name. It has a few benches sheltered by bushes, and we sat on one of these. After playing 'lipsticks' with the red, brown and orange Smarties, admiring ourselves in a little mirror I carried in my pocket, we ate all the rest. Then I read some of my comic to Perdita. But she soon became bored with that and started tickling me. Then I tickled her back and she lay on the bench giggling, then screeching with laughter.

'Tickle me again!' she cried, 'Tickle me there.' She lifted up her short, grey pleated skirt and pointed to the little triangle of pink knickers between her legs.

'No, I won't!' I retorted. 'That's very naughty. It's rude. You shouldn't lift up your skirt like that. Mam and Oliver would be very cross if they saw you.'

She pouted. 'No, they wouldn't! My daddy tickles me there.'

She always used to say 'my daddy', emphasising the 'my' as if to taunt me with my fatherlessness.

'I don't believe you.'

And I didn't at first. Until, irritated by my indifference and lack of reaction, she went on to say more in a defiant little voice. About how it was their secret and she wasn't supposed to tell me or Mam. How he did these things to her every night at bedtime and it was great fun. And sometimes he did things outside as well, when it was just the two of them in a secret place. In the sand dunes at the beach, for instance. I remembered a time when Perdita had been having a tantrum, Mam had a headache and was busy with visitors, I was curled up with a book and refused to go out. Oliver had put his daughter in her coat and taken her out for a walk, just the two of them, and they had returned in half an hour with her happily licking an ice-cream. Mam said they might have brought one back for me too, so I had just smiled sweetly and said it didn't matter. I remembered the long, private bedtime sessions in the room next door. And I thought how little she had mixed with any other children who could have told her such things. She had not yet begun school. When she realised I was listening with a horrified expression she carried on, enjoying the attention. She was probably silly and innocent enough to think I was jealous.

'And one day Mam taked you to the dentist. And my daddy taked me for a walk to Lôn Gygo' Bach. And we went in the ruins to a secret place with high walls all round. And there's a blackberry bush growing through the wall. And my daddy gived me his handkerchief and he tells me to go like this.'

She took out her own little handkerchief with a teddy embroidered on it, pressed it against her nose and mouth and made an exaggerated pantomime of breathing in and out very deeply. 'And my daddy's handkerchief smells very funny. And then I had a funny dream. And then I waked up. And then we went to Gwynant café and you and Mam was in there and we

57

all had fish and chips. And I was sick. I was sick all over the floor. That wasn't very nice.'

I remembered that day. It had only been about two months previously. Perdita had looked really ill in the café, pale with dark circles under her eyes. I recalled occasionally noticing an odd pong when Oliver took out a handkerchief to blow his nose. A sort of heavy, chemical, sweet smell. I now believed every word she had told me and a shiver ran down my spine. I'd known about children doing naughty things like that but I'd never heard about adults who did. I knew it was very wrong, although I knew nothing about the facts of life. My mother would be very angry with Oliver if she found out, I was sure of that. She would be more angry than about him kissing the waitress. But if I told her she would never believe me. Not in a million years.

'You must tell Mam about this,' I said.

She shook her head. 'No, I not tell Mam of my daddy. My daddy loves me and he doesn't love you because he's not your daddy. It's a secret. You mustn't tell Mam and I mustn't tell Mam.'

'She won't believe anything I say about Oliver. You have to tell her.' I wasn't thinking about protecting my sister. I don't really think I cared about that. I just wanted to get him into trouble. I felt self righteous about all this bad stuff being true. I'd been right all along not to like him. I could stop feeling guilty about hating him now. But she just shook her head again and smiled. 'I love my daddy,' she said. That made me angry with her. And this time I felt I had a good reason to treat her badly as I'd so often done before.

'If you won't tell Mam I'll never play with you again. I'll never share my sweets with you or take you out with my friends. I won't even talk to you.' And with that I ran out of the park as fast as I could.

On reaching the end of the road I turned back to see her

trying to run after me on her little legs and crying, 'Stop, Emis. Please wait for me. Don't leave me alone. I'll tell...'

I ran faster still, all the way to the woods, climbed up into my favourite tree and curled up to finish reading my comic. That sight of Perdita from the end of the road is now etched into my memory like an unwanted photograph I am powerless to destroy.

'I sometimes think that never grows so green
The grass as where Perdita was last seen.'

'That every hyacinth the garden wears
Drop't in its lap from some once lovely head.'

The comic finished, my anger dissolved, I climbed down from the tree and decided it was time I went to find my sister. This time I wouldn't try to get back into her good books before taking her home. If she told my mother what I'd done I'd look at her coldly and say,

'I think she has something else to tell you as well.'

But of course, that's not the way it turned out. I went back to the park, thinking to find her curled up on a seat with her thumb in her mouth, waiting for me to change my mind and come back for her as I always did. No sign of her. I didn't think she would have walked all the way home on her own. Probably she had gone round the town centre to look for me. I went up and down all the streets several times in vain. I even stopped one or two people, saying my little sister was hiding from me, and had they seen her? They hadn't. Could she have gone to the ruin, I wondered? Back I went to Lôn Llygod Bach, which was deserted, and crept down to the ruined hotel. I hated this place. If she'd gone in here on her own she had more guts than I did. A scratching, scraping sound came from one of the old rooms, the high walled one with the brambles growing through. Was she in there? Or was it the ghost? Biting my lip and trembling, I tip-toed over the rough ground till I reached the nearest of the three tall walls and peered through a tiny hole in it. What I saw was totally unexpected. It was Oliver, in his shirt sleeves, his tweed sports jacket and grey overcoat flung over a pile of bricks, digging with a garden spade. Although his sleeves were rolled up he was still wearing his tan pigskin gloves.

He seemed to have dug a large hole in the weedy ground. Rubble, weeds, gravel and fresh earth were piled up next to it. As I watched he straightened up, put down the spade and turned to his jacket and coat. He pulled them back to reveal, not a pile of bricks as I'd thought, but Perdita asleep and very pale. Had he been playing the handkerchief trick again? He picked her up and carefully lowered her into the black hole. Then he picked up the spade again and began shovelling the pile of fresh soil on top of her. At first I wondered if it was a kind of game like burying people in the sand on the beach. Then I realised that he was pouring soil all over her head as well as the rest of her and that she would not be able to breathe. I felt very, very frightened. And puzzled. Oliver loved her so much. Why was he treating her like this?

I think I must have realised at some point that she was dead. I don't quite know what I thought. I do remember that at no time during Oliver's shovelling did it occur to me to jump out and try to save her. What I do remember, very clearly, as I watched him flatten the grave and sprinkle it with rubble and gravel so you wouldn't know it was there, is my overwhelming fear of him. If he could treat his little darling like this, what would he do to me?

So I never told anyone what I saw, never even hinted that he couldn't have been at that football match. And as far as I know the police never checked. He was a forty-year-old bachelor when he met my mother and we discovered little of his past or subsequent history. I don't even know if he's still alive. Ironic, isn't it? After all those lies I'd told in the past I didn't dare tell about the real wolf in the attic.

My name is Enfys Williams and I am a coward.

Ten Little Londoners

Joy Tucker

Once a year the invitation arrives. The same all-girls-together kind of words, different postmarks – I think they take turns to send it – and each year, I know the feelings it will engender. It's there now, on the notice-board in the kitchen, pinned amongst the family jumble of dental appointments, raffle tickets, special offers. The card is of good quality, creamy-white with a sheen. The print is stylish, with curlicue letters, always in black. The invitations have followed me to two different addresses. The message never varies. *Do come – relive old times, those memories – a chance to let your hair down – no friends like old friends.* And until the date on the invitation has passed, it will catch my eye and I will tell myself to go, to do as it says, relive the old times. These were my friends. Remember the fun we had.

There were ten of us then, living together, and all in one room. It sounds like squalor, but it wasn't. The room was a large, Regency drawing-room, with a frieze of fat, plaster roses all round its high ceiling. At one end, long, elegant windows opened on to a balcony above a leafy London square, where chestnut trees changed the seasons for us, and a circle of grass gave space for sun-bathing. At the other end of the room was a conservatory, a graceful creation of glass and wrought-iron. Inside, it was not so graceful, draped continually with lines of drying washing, its corners cluttered with boots and sandals, tennis racquets, occasionally a bicycle wheel with a puncture to be mended. It was part of a girls' hostel, and the ten of us accepted it as home. Ten beds, ten wardrobes, ten lockers and as much female companionship as anyone new to London and a young, carefree, independent life could need.

It was a melting-pot of a place. Anything could be learned about women there. Anything could be copied, or lost, or modified. Attitudes, fashion fads, hair-styles, morals – so much was interchangeable. There were so many of us, good, bad, indifferent, nasty, nice, beautiful, not-so-beautiful, mousy, clever, cleverer. And the first lesson I learned was that no one was all good, or all beautiful. Loyalty was another lesson – and the way some people can change theirs. But it can take a while to learn new lessons. Multi-faceted was the cover-all word I chose to describe my room-mates.

Living in a group of ten young women was also a multi-faceted experience. You could see it all ways. It was a hot-house of femininity, a web of intrigue, an open confessional, or just somewhere cheap to live while waiting for the next rung on the career-ladder, the next exam pass, or marriage. One of the ten had already left, for marriage, when I arrived. I had her bed, in a corner, next to Marietta's.

The temptation to answer the invitation, to go to the reunion, is strong when I remember the fun we had. There was always someone to go out with, someone who knew the required bus route, someone who played tennis, or was going to a party, or had a boyfriend with a spare for a blind date. London could have been so lonely. I might have been lonely for the first few weeks if it had not been for Marietta.

She was the first of the group I met. Strangely, it was her reflection I saw first, as, breathless from carrying my suitcase up a long, curving stone staircase – I was too nervous to use the lift – I opened the door of the room and stood on the threshold. Opposite the door was a large gilt-rimmed mirror – with Marietta in a pale-coloured dress, standing before it, gazing at herself in the worn, watery glass. And when she spoke, without turning, for a moment it was as if I were being greeted by some ghostly figure. Her greeting, too, was unusual. 'I'm glad you've come' she said. 'I've been lonely. The others' – she gestured towards the rest of the room, which seemed to me at that vulnerable time like a mysterious cavern of semi-darkness – 'have gone somewhere.' So I welcomed her words. What a welcome.

If only it was possible to rewind the convoluted tape of our memories.. Stop – just there – before I opened the door. Quick edit – back to where I was thinking about the pleasant times, then fast forward to the next morning, to a room full of bright young people, the sun coming through the window, filtered by the wide green fingers of the chestnut trees, morning music on someone's radio, a voice singing along, and someone else calling out about borrowing a red cardigan. Why can't we choose our memories?

I met the other girls the next morning, and was welcomed, but, even by then, Marietta had taken charge of me. Much of her takeover was helpful, telling me the routine of hostel-life, the do's and the don'ts of communal living, the quickest way to get to where I was to begin my first job. But before I had properly settled in, to the hostel or to my new office, she had also taken charge of my spare time. I had a slightly ungrateful feeling from time to time that I wasn't doing what I wanted to do, but rather what Marietta wanted me to do. I didn't seem to have a chance to get to know the other girls, to make more than one friend. Before I fully realised what was happening, before I had time to separate out the Margarets from the Marions, the Penelopes from the Patricias and Genevieves and Elizabeths – don't worry, old friends, I've changed the names – I had been given a run-down on all of them, and had learned a list of sins and foibles which I didn't want to know or hadn't even heard of.

At the same time, I found myself being questioned and cross-questioned in a way that I first dismissed as friendly curiosity, but soon began to feel was making me wary and uneasy. Straight from school and a comfortable home life to London had not left much time for having anything to hide. But after a few evenings with Marietta I was beginning to doubt myself. Why did Marietta need to know so much about me: my parents, my brothers, my life? She spoke of herself sometimes, slipping sad snippets of a lonely childhood into our conversations, turning the talk back to me whenever I questioned her. Maybe there is always a Marietta, waiting for a newcomer, preparing to capture.

One of the girls – a Margaret – tried to rescue me, early in my time with the Ten.

'Avoid her like the plague,' she said. 'Don't get involved.'

'Maybe she's lonely?' I countered.

'Be careful – or you'll be lonely too,' she warned.

I think it was resentment I felt at that moment. Why should yet another near-stranger tell me who should be my friend? I know it is resentment I feel now when I look at the invitation again. Why can't they leave me alone? Why stir up these feelings year after year? Aren't they happy too? Can't they just get on with their lives, raise their families, hate their bosses, love their husbands – forget? Or was it all in my imagination? Am I the only one who cannot forget?

I saw Margaret a few years ago, not at the re-union. I never go to their re-unions. But on one occasion, when an invitation was – as now – hanging on my notice-board, and – as now – I was re-living the range of emotions it raises within me, I travelled to the place where they were meeting. I hid myself behind a pillar in the foyer of the hotel. I felt stupid and gauche, rather as I had when Margaret had warned me that first time, as if acting badly the part of a stage private-eye. But

I wanted to see them. Margaret was the first to arrive. I would have known her anywhere. Tall and slim, despite the years, the only signs of ageing were the grim lines around her mouth. Still warning? Perhaps, but there was enough of grimness there to make me turn and flee through a side door, not waiting to see the others. I should not have gone. I resent the resentment they have given me. I resent the fear.

Funny that Margaret should still look the same when she has changed so much in my imagination. She was very attractive in the days of the Ten, though not as attractive as Marietta. That was another part of the problem as I saw it then. Marietta was too attractive. It wasn't only her hair, black and silky, with the ability to suit whichever style she chose, or her pale skin – which didn't seem to be affected by the weather – which made her beautiful. There was a depth of blue in her eyes which seemed to glitter, and an aura around her, a waif-like attraction – before the waif-look had become fashionable. And in those early days, when it began to be obvious to me that the other girls did not like Marietta, I hazarded a guess that they were envious, even jealous. Marietta's hints made it sound that way, and there were also her stories of how none of our room-mates seemed to be able to keep a boyfriend for long. And Marietta knew what nice boys they were. She had been out with several of them. And she wouldn't be able to come with me to the theatre next week, as she had just met someone – she thought Patricia knew him – perhaps Patricia could use her ticket?

Patricia did not only warn me about Marietta; she spoke plainly, telling me several things about myself – silly, secret things – that I couldn't believe she could know. Too late I realised how Marietta had embellished even my more cautious answers to her questions, and passed them on. Other things could only have been known by reading my diary, and Patricia was ready to swear that they had been part of Marietta's briefing to the rest of the room.

'She could quote from that diary,' she said. 'She's a bitch, you know, or sometimes I think she's a witch!'

Another lesson learned, a little too late. Don't trust too easily; another emotion discovered, excessive in its strength when felt so young, the pain of betrayal. The result was for me to turn away from Marietta's proffered friendship, into the waiting welcome of the rest of the group. And oh, how they were waiting. Enthusiasm, entertainment, interest and empathy – it was warm in there and my happier days in London began. I still can feel gratitude. They introduced me to so much: a love of London and its variety of life – of opera and concerts when groups of us would queue together in turns for gallery and promenade tickets – the eternal shopping quest through stores, boutiques and markets. I could feel myself changing – from country girl to little Londoner in ten easy lessons. Work became more interesting as I became more confident. I bought new clothes, followed fashion, read more newspapers, had boyfriends. Rocketing from my friendly base, I flew higher and higher.

I became multi-faceted too, and felt that I could even forgive Marietta. Perhaps Patricia's stories had been over-motivated by jealousy. I tried to draw Marietta in to the warmer circle where I felt sure she would eventually be welcomed. Sometimes it seemed that I would succeed, but she seemed to delight in spoiling the situation, making a gibe at the wrong moment, and if I did not turn against her with the others I could quickly feel the cooling of the welcome fires of friendship. When I did manage to set up a situation to include her, one in which she managed not to exclude herself, a Penelope or Genevieve would take me aside and tell me of the latest betrayal – another lie told, another blossoming romance withered. And I would shrink away with the others, leaving Marietta alone.

I suppose guilt is a multi-faceted emotion. There are so

many aspects of it that I still have not sorted out. Is the guilt of knowing, of saying nothing, worse than the guilt of saying or doing? The invitation is inlaid with guilt. It quivers at me from the notice-board today. I shut my eyes to it and move on.

I knew that Marietta was lonely. No matter how many boyfriends she stole to go out with, no matter how often she admired her reflection in the ornate mirror which was so incongruous above the one gas fire which attempted to heat our cold shared room – I knew she was lonely.

I kept thinking of what she had said on one of her favourite evening walks by the Thames. The river was high at the time, waves slapping against the wall of the Embankment. We had been talking about families, and she had told me that she had no family. Her upbringing had been in an orphanage, her living had always been communal. Her voice, when I tried to sympathise, had turned harsh and bitter.

'You don't know what it's like,' she said. 'When I am really lonely, I often feel I would be better down there.' She pointed at the black water, and, as I followed her gaze, a rat scurried up over the wall, and disappeared. I jumped back, startled, and as she leaned over the wall, pulled her away.

'Don't be so silly,' I said, trying to laugh. 'Think of the rats you would meet.'

'There are worse things,' she replied, then changed the subject.

Of course I knew she was lonely. My bed was closest to hers. I could hear her sighing as she slept. I knew how often she cried herself to sleep.

Dear old pals, chums every one, do you ever weep tears for Marietta? Or am I the only one who ever did? Am I the only one who ever knew? Who knows? Maybe I should go to the reunion. Gin and tonics all round, and after we've toasted each other and old times, remembered this, remembered that, said how wonderful it is that each and every one of us has hardly changed at all, come out with it, straight from the shoulder. Surely this is the sisterhood – the sharing and the caring. Come on girls – let's talk about Marietta – tell me the truth.

We played 'Truth or Dare' occasionally, when we were the Ten. Gathered around the gas fire, faces flickering in the old mirror, with a few bottles of wine and someone making toast while we grilled mushrooms on an upturned iron (no cooking in rooms allowed), we lost our thin layer of recently-acquired sophistication and were schoolgirls again, feasting at midnight. The frisson of satisfaction when nine rounded on Marietta for truths was a palpable breath of evil. Or did I imagine that too – and the tears which followed when the others were asleep? I can't remember now. The morning after one of those occasions, the wine and mushrooms – or something – had left a bad taste in my mouth. I resolved not to get involved in such games again, and when I heard plans being made for more midnight feasting the following Saturday, decided it was time to make a long-promised visit to cousins in Sussex. Suddenly I'd had enough of so many sisters. I needed a breather.

I said as much to Marietta when we were alone in the lift on the Friday evening, and immediately regretted my words, knowing they would somehow be twisted and repeated against me. I did not want to become detached from the main group again.

Marietta looked ill that evening. Each delicate feature seemed etched on the drained white oval of her face, as she pushed back a dark cloud of hair and asked me directly not to leave her with the Ten. I was flippant at first, and just a little taunting.

'One went off for the weekend and then there were nine. Don't play their silly games if you don't want to.'

The lift stopped, and Marietta held her finger on the door-open button, barring my exit. Her voice became pleading.

'Please, please, don't go.'

'But Marietta, I've promised. I told you I need to get away from London – it's only for a couple of days.'

It was Patricia's 'witch' who faced me then. Her stare was hard, blazing blue. 'You'll be sorry if you go,' she said, as I pushed her aside.

I was not sorry. But it was a weekend that would change lives. Of all things, I fell in love. The cousins had a friend, a young doctor who was, in the phrase we used then, *just my type*, and I soon knew, with a sure, clear certainty that my life was about to change. Fortunately he seemed to feel the same way. We floated back to London together on a slow train, making plans for the future, and I was only sorry that I was too late to tell my friends the news. The room was in darkness and everyone asleep. In the morning there was no time to talk and, in any case, I overslept.

I was ready to break the news that evening but I had forgotten about Marietta. She wasn't there, but the cool, rather distant atmosphere told me everything. Or I thought it did. I could imagine her whispering the words I had spoken in the lift to the other girls, elaborating, embroidering with barbs. There was a tension in the room. They were not quite ignoring me. It was as if a layer of mist hung there at eye-level. No one was actually looking at me – but rather gazing off into eight separate distances. When I grumbled about the wine bottles littering the corner of the conservatory and added some comment about 'Truth and Dare bottles', Margaret was quick to tidy them away, her voice sharp.

'We didn't play – don't worry, you didn't miss anything. In fact, we drank a little too much and went to bed early.'

I was angry by then and ready to sort things out. I wanted their friendship. I wanted them to hear my good news. More than anything I was angry with Marietta for having spoiled my moment.

'Where is Marietta?' I shouted down the length of the room.

Eight heads came out of their mists and turned towards me.

'What do you mean?' asked Patricia.

Margaret's voice cut across hers quickly. 'She's gone. Didn't you notice?'

'Gone? What do you mean?'

'She left on Sunday – early in the morning before any of us were awake.'

'But where did she go?' I asked.

'Back home, wherever that was.'

'But she didn't have a home…'

'Wasn't there something before about her mother being ill?'

'She told me her mother was dead,' I insisted. 'And I believed her.'

'Oh you believe anything!'

I was confused, puzzled. Everyone began to speak at once.

'Off with one of her boyfriends perhaps?'

'One of ours, don't you mean?'

'She didn't tell us.'

'She didn't even tell the warden.'

'She probably owed a month's rent.'

'Good riddance.'

The chorus ended. It left an air of relief in the room, an undercurrent of excitement. I could feel their warmth returning and I remembered my wonderful news. By the time they were planning what to wear to my future wedding, I had almost forgotten about Marietta. I didn't want to be sorry.

In a strange way I missed her for a while, the empty bed reminding me each night, and I hoped in my happiness that somewhere she had stopped being lonely. Once I woke suddenly from a nightmare, thinking I heard her sobbing but the tears were on my cheeks.

Time passed. There was still no news of Marietta. Margaret said she had spoken to the warden and although she had expressed surprise at such a quick departure, there was no rent due. Patricia, who had started getting up early enough to go to church each morning before work, told me one day in the lift that she often prayed for Marietta.

'*You'll* be going soon,' she said, 'and then we'll be eight.'
As the lift stopped, I shivered, suddenly remembering my words to Marietta. *And then there were nine.*

'I'll pray for you too,' said Patricia.

The camaraderie in the room was still warm and comforting, but I no longer needed it. Kenneth and I became officially engaged, and began to make plans for our wedding. My room-mates said they were sad to see me go; they threw a party in farewell; we did not play 'Truth or Dare'. Before I left I asked them to let me know should they hear anything of Marietta. They promised they would and that's when Margaret, so often the leader, came up with the idea of an annual re-union, so that we could always keep in touch.

Saying goodbye to the warden, I mentioned Marietta, asking if she had heard from her. She hadn't, but added that one of the girls, she couldn't remember which, had seen her and said she was fine; also that her rent was paid up, and that she herself had answered a query from Marietta's employer, putting his mind at rest.

'These things happen, dear,' she said, 'some young girls can be flighty, you know. And this is London. Do have a nice wedding.'

At the wedding I even remembered to ask again for news of Marietta. Patricia said she knew someone who had seen and spoken to her, so not to worry. She would try to make contact with her before the first reunion. We ate cake together and drank champagne. They threw confetti and rice, standing in a lovely line to wave goodbye, my multi-faceted friends. And on that day of days I loved every one of them.

Their invitation is fading on the notice-board. We have had a spell of hot weather since it arrived. Its crimped edges have curled like those of an ancient parchment. It will soon be time to take it down, tear it across and try to forget about it. It is as easy as that to lose touch with some old friends.

I went back to the hostel once more, to see them in the long room with its silvery mirror of girlish faces. It was several months after the wedding, on a warm, sultry afternoon. I had been lunching with Kenneth at the hospital where he had trained and now worked. My office was close by and we met for lunch whenever we could. I had seen most of the medical school by then, the lecture theatre, the gym, the labs with all their equipment. It was really too hot to be inside, but I was quite happy to see another part of the building when Ken offered. 'You're graduating today,' he said, taking my hand and leading me along a corridor which felt dank and cold in comparison to the rest of the building. He had pushed the double doors open before I had time to realise that I was in the anatomy department.

What happened next was my own fault. I had expressed an interest in all aspects of his work and his early studies. I knew this was the room of cadavers, the dissection room, where medical students learned the intricacies of anatomy. I would have been all right. I would have walked around amongst the tables and tried not to think about real people. And I knew that these were bodies. I knew that doctors had to learn from bodies, even young bodies, if they were available. I knew that the smell was formaldehyde and not the smell of fear. But I had looked too closely. Next thing I knew I was stretched out on a leather couch in the cold corridor with Kenneth and several other people leaning over me.

You can recover quite quickly from fainting: forget that drifting feeling, that urgent need to escape from the world, to leave reality. I recovered quite quickly. Kenneth apologised for taking me there. I said I was fine and that it must have been the heat. We went to the refectory for a cup of tea before I had to get back to work. Kenneth was still concerned about my faint.

'I'm sorry. I should have warned you. Hadn't you ever seen a dead body?'

'No. Never.' I paused. 'Where do these bodies come from?'

'Some are donated. Some never claimed. From the river sometimes – as long as they haven't been in the water too long.'

It was time for me to go.

I went back to work, told my boss I was unwell, and took the rest of the day off. Then I sat under a heavy grey sky in the leafy green square beside the hostel, looking up at the balcony of the room until the time when they would all be there. My heart was pounding as I climbed the stairs. Somehow I did not want to share the lift, nor to be alone in it to remember the pleading words, the sudden claustrophobic fear, the threat. I could hear the girls laughing and chattering in the room – a familiar, happy sound. I threw the door open, not knowing what I was going to say. There was the ghostly mirror, and there were ten faces turned towards me. They were complete strangers. I had seen none of them before. I looked at them, and at the mirror and the fat, plaster roses and the lines of washing hanging in the conservatory.

'I'm sorry,' I said, 'wrong room.'

I shall not go to the reunion. Tomorrow the invitation will be unpinned, cut into pieces and thrown away. I will try not to think of these things for another year, try not to see a pale, pretty face and a cloud of black hair in my nightmares, try not to see a mutilated body stretched on a cold metal table. And if any of my dear old friends read this, and have reason for concern, they should know that I have never told anyone where I saw Marietta – until now.

The Sound of Crying

H D Lewis

Can you hear that?

Listen.

Crying.

My baby is crying. She needs me. Her cot is empty, there's a warm shape of her still left sleeping on her mattress, but she's gone. I can't breathe in fully, she's gone. In the spare room, I'm running, her cries piercing me, nothing. Louder and louder she's screaming for me. Missing stairs and footing, tumbling into the living room, her voice roaring inside my skull, the sweet scent of her new skin drenched on the air I gulp.

I can't find my baby. I can't find her...

The alarm thunders through the chaos storming round my subconscious. It's morning. It was a nightmare. Just another nightmare. Not much different from the one on Wednesday night, or Tuesday night or Monday night or every other night since then.

Since my baby died. Baby and died, two words that should never be in the same sentence. Two unendurable extremes of pain: the need for a baby, the loss of one. Two places a human soul should not visit: the longing hunger for month after month and the slow excruciating death that stillbirth brings.

I have another day to get through. I have reached the point now where I can think in days. I graduated from an hour at a time a few months ago. Maybe time was cleverly healing or it might have been the clocks going forward, more daylight, longer evenings, as a well-meaning neighbour suggested. Longer evenings, more time to grieve, I wanted to say, but I only had the energy for a smile.

Downstairs, I think about breakfast, a thought that passes unexplored. Coffee will do and some plastic news from GMTV. It's a bad habit that's on its way to compulsion, the need to fill each room with noise to drown out the silence. I can hear her in the quiet. My baby, she cries out to me, but I can't find her.

The news is trivial and fluffy, wrapped up for the brainless, transmitted into my kitchen to mock and torture me gently. Brangelina pregnant again, Kerry Katona is expecting for the third, fourth, fifth time. I'm being stoned by other people's fertility. 'Who fucking cares!' I scream at the screen.

I do.

'And police are appealing for witnesses to come forward after the discovery this morning of a 32 year old woman's body. The victim was discovered with fatal head injuries in the front garden of her home in Brently. A police spokesman said that information on the whereabouts of Mr Daniel Simons, the victim's husband, is urgently sought.'

I can't stomach any more of the outside world's misery. Brently is too close to home, the stop before here if you're travelling by train; the next ugly urban blur, ten minutes down the road if you drive.

And I do. I have to drive. I have to button up some normality, paint on a sunny 'Don't feel sorry for me!' smile and pretend that I really mean, 'Hello, can I help you?'

'Hello, can I help you?'

'Mrs Wheeler, for Doctor Jenkins.'

'Thank you Mrs Wheeler, would you like to take a seat?'

Mrs Wheeler the widow doesn't have a husband to moan at any more so comes to see Doctor Jenkins instead. Same time, same day, first week of the month. I hate this. And this hates me, too, as it throws up a million little problems that are too pathetic to deal with. A dead end job I reversed into when I thought life was taking me somewhere amazing. The real joke is that I was a midwife - a thousand tiny lives all safely delivered thanks to me. But that was in another world, another town, hundreds of light years from the agony I now claw my way through.

I file the old, the confused and the really annoyed, collecting their precious jars of piss and shit and play-act interest and concern until 10.30. 10.30, the sacred hour of coffee and false bonhomie. Today the staff room is bursting with intrigue and forged concern for the body in the front garden, GMTV's only bit of proper news. How marvellous that Bridget actually spoke to her yesterday! What luck that Joan's husband works with the body's husband. And it's too tragic that Ellen's daughter teaches the eldest son. These are the people who cause the five mile tailbacks on motorways, taking photos on their mobile phones of the overturned lorry and severed body parts.

Interestingly, the body is the third person on Doctor Jenkins' list to meet a sticky end this year. We're only in March, maybe I should warn Mrs Wheeler.

Doctor Jenkins passed his medical degree with flying halitosis, specialising in general practice and specific groping. His list is overflowing, his trousers are too tight. He slept with the two women doctors the practice struggled to employ, destroying both their marriages and leaving our smear clinic in uproar after they both hastily resigned. There is a Mrs Jenkins; she is beautiful, expensive, and fertile. There are four small Jenkinses with flamboyant Shakespearian names that can be shortened into something cute and catchy. He is idolised by the rest of the reception coven, who simper over his babies when they graciously make an appearance and forgive his every filing misdemeanour.

'Looking lovely again today Sarah. Good to see some colour finally in those cheeks.' He storms into my personal space invading every inch that should be mine alone. He talks into my eyes, places an unnecessary hand on my upper arm, allowing his thumb to whisper imperceptibly across my breast. It must be revulsion that snarls in the pit of my belly making my shoulders shudder and his hand drop. He wants to know if I'm available for supper on Saturday, has a close friend he knows I'd find fascinating. I brush my forehead to check that my gullible light is not flashing and fake an excuse.

'You shouldn't be on your own Sarah, you're too young, too attractive to lock yourself away.'

'Thank you.' I manage, swallowing the raging bile.

I am on my own. Some joke of a God decided that one. He dangled David, a fairly attractive man, under my nose, who, like the coach in Cinderella, turned into a pumpkin on the last strike of our marriage vowels. And as a punchline to the gut left us childless and hunting frantically for somewhere to bury all the love we couldn't spend on each other.

At last the clock lazily ambles its way to five. I have been summoned to my sister's for supper. She lives not far from the Health Centre, in the right kind of house with the right kind of husband. The man I dated first, the man who first broke my heart. But we don't talk about that because it was a long time ago, too long for my sister to remember.

They are both waiting for me when I arrive, nervy and over-caring. I know what's coming next. I want to leave before she says it, because if I don't hear her say the words then I can pretend it's not happening.

'...Bit of a surprise, just thought it was the change, and a bit of over eating! Can you believe it, it's due in two months. Say you'll be Godmother Sarah.' I contract the muscles on either side of my face hoping the result will appear as close to a smile as I can manage. We laugh and joke about the impossibility of the whole situation, imagine…a baby at her age! And share disappointment that the Australia trip will have to be postponed till next year. We pay homage to my bravery, I am a rock, and convince ourselves that I will play a major role in this new being's life. It is only 5.45, we haven't even eaten; the food will be ready by 8.00 she says. I make it three hours to hold down the scream that is blazing in my throat, to keep my eyes open widen enough to stop the acid tears falling.

I am perfect. I am Oscar winning. I manage not to run out of their front door. I drive forwards, that's all I'm capable of, to somewhere that's not outside their house and stop and scream until I think my throat bleeds. It is enough to bring me back to earth. I put the car in first and go through the mechanics of making it move forward. I don't notice the dark puffa on top of a pair of jeans stepping into the road until the last moment. My tyres screech 'watch out!' He freezes in the force of my headlights. I see him floodlit, he sees only blinding white. An outside interference releases the pause button; Dr Jenkins makes a surrendering gesture and moves out of my laser beams on across the road. I thought he lived on the other side of the town.

Home waits up for me but has forgotten to keep the heating running or turn on any of the lights. Feeling sorry for me, the postman has pushed junk mail through the letterbox so I have something to trip over as I open the front door. I drop my bag and coat and drag my heavy feet up the stairs. I don't care that I'm fully clothed, that my teeth are furring; I seek only the oblivion of sleep. I pull the duvet over my head and search for some peace.

The doorbell is ringing, it's shouting and stamping to be answered. But the pull of the warm water I am lying in is too strong to move from. My toes poke out the end just under the taps. I gaze wondrously at the perfect swell of my belly. A ripple under my skin answers as I stroke the skin there. I have found my peace, but the ringing wants to spoil it.

It's the policeman. I know it will be him. This time though he has the face of Doctor Jenkins. He is sorry but he's brought bad news. I think fleetingly that I will shut the door, then he can't give the bad news to me, he will have to take it to some one else. He carries my husband David's holdall, the one that should be with him. He tells me the news that I know. The train. David's nausea, forcing open the window. The tragic accident. Death was instant. I push the door shut but the strength of his brutal news won't let me. I can hear crying, my baby is crying…

The alarm is not sharp enough to knock away all the crumbs left from my nightmares and I sit a while in bed contemplating instant death. Wondering if he had felt anything. Isn't death only instant for the heart that stops beating? For those of us that suffer the spread of grieving decay its presence is permanent.

It's the weekend, a paperboy, angry to be up this time on a Saturday morning, throws some news at my front door. I sit down with my coffee and spread the paper before me; an ugly headline catches my eye. Another body, another front garden. This time I recognise the name, I recognise the address.

Another patient. Not much older than myself, Friday 10.45 for Doctor Jenkins. I thought she'd looked anxious, she rolled her hands over themselves as she queued at the desk. Mrs Roming – Nancy. The paper describes her as a local high-flyer with a now devastated husband. I recognise the shock in the words he hands over to the paper. He borrows the ones I used when the same journalist came to steal my feelings after David's death. Vocabulary shuts down to a limited selection of heavy words. They are all the shocked brain can assemble: shattered, distressed and, the favourite, distraught.

Nancy Roming, like last Friday's girl was found in her front garden with a blow to the head. Except that Nancy Roming was discovered by her husband just minutes too late. She had gone to answer the front door, to welcome her murderer.

Nancy Roming lived in the same 'right kind of house', in the development that my sister lives in. As I had sat with my ecstatic sibling, a killer had been walking past her house deciding from which front door the perfect victim might emerge. I wonder what made him pass by number 8, inside which we were eating, what made him carry on down the road, turn right and choose number 3, The Gull Wings.

The murderer had opted for prime time TV hours as opposed to the early ones favoured by burglars. I thought of all the people I drove past from the Health Centre to my sister's address. I thought of the gang of hoodies by the bus stop where I had screamed out the cruelty of my evening. I thought of the man frozen in my headlights.

I'm shoved from my thoughts by the sound of crying. I hold my breath; my ears search my empty house, nothing. Josh, the little boy next door throws something heavy at his brother, his scream rips into my house filling it with the noise of pain. I need to find peace, I don't want to share the air with families. I spend the rest of the weekend out, nowhere in particular.

Work is upended when I arrive on Monday. Gossip runs around heedlessly, hand in hand with panic. Nancy Roming lives on posthumously, her life, her possibility of becoming the victim, her husband. Fear is filed as an addendum to each set of notes. Doctor Jenkins is late. Patients spill out of the waiting room and into the entrance hall. It is 8.45 and my head is pounding, a baby is crying. I want to go home.

When he does arrive, Doctor Jenkins is crumpled and grey, he's forgotten to bring his charm along and left his lunch at home. He goes to his room shutting out any further contact and calls for his first patient. At the end of morning surgery, Doctor Jenkins appears coated in a new veneer of charisma, his grey washed away. He sweet-talks Bridget into getting him some alternative lunch. I look up at the wrong moment and am left holding the chore of giving his room a 'quick once over'. Just another one of the perks this position offers: collector of bodily fluids, controller of crowds, cleaner of consulting rooms.

The walls of his room are papered with violent, childish splashes of paint each signed 'I love you Daddy'. His desk, a photo gallery dedicated to the loving husband and his beautiful family. I tidy the pens, shuffle paper, stack post. His middle drawer is half-open. Half-closed? I can see the top part of three folders of patient notes. My job is to file patient notes. I give the correct notes to each doctor at the beginning of surgery, they return them to me at the end, I refile them. Do I take these notes? Do I shut the drawer? I do neither, I pull the drawer open a little further, I check the names of each set of notes and write them down on a piece of his Mr Tickle note pad. If these notes are needed I will know where to look first. But I don't think they will be needed, dead people don't tend to make appointments.

I pull the liner from his bin; it's full of used rubber gloves and tissues. As I'm staring at his debris the door opens.

'You're a treasure Sarah. What would I do without you ladies! How about we take these sandwiches to the park, have a chat, feed the ducks?'

My tongue gets stuck around ums and ahhs, but for the first time I'm grateful to Bridget as she burst into his room with an urgent house call, child with a rash.

'Bloody patients,' he mutters under his breath, and leaves, ripping his coat from the wall.

There is a short time to eat something before the invasion of the antenatal clinic at two. The real high point of my week. I herd the expectant through to Jane, who runs the clinic, one at a time; weighing them, listening, offering the information that I can remember from my days at the coalface. Hating each and every radiant one of them. The first woman today looks ready to explode as she rocks towards me. The greedy bitch is expecting twins. She is anxious about the Caesarean that will be performed on Friday.

'You'll be fine, won't feel a thing, all over in few minutes,' I say. I pretend that I am on the set of a Hollywood blockbuster, today I am Julia Roberts, these are the lines I have learnt.

'Have you had one?' She catches me off guard; I don't remember this line from my script.

'Sorry?'

'A Caesarean. Have you had one?'

'No. I used to be a midwife, so I've seen quite a few. Could do them in my sleep if I had to.' She's convinced. Somebody's baby needs feeding, its screams pull the air. I move onto the next woman but the bell is calling from reception.

Mrs Jenkins is stood head to toe in fury; she throws a large case at me.

'Give this to the cheating bastard, tell him not to bother coming home.' She turns, storming out through the wrong door; it gives in unlocked by her anger. The collective gasp of Bridget, Joan and Ellen, who witness the event from their desks, melts into delight at the scandal. I want to stay, I want to relish his downfall, but a roomful of swollen women sit uncomfortably waiting their turn. As I leave the room Joan is proudly announcing.

'Another affair! And you'll never believe who. Nancy Roming!'

My eyes hang with the weight of the day. I put the radio on in the car to keep me awake on the drive home. The local station is buzzing with the latest on the Door Step Killer.

Chantel Owens, claims to be the luckiest woman in Brently this evening as she explains:

'It was about three months ago, just before my son was born, didn't think nothing of it at the time. Thought it was kids from the estate messing about. I was just going up to bed when I hears this noise, sounded like crying. Like someone had dumped a baby on the doorstep. When I opens the door there's nothing there, but I can hear something in the hedge. I called Brian, my husband, and he went out with a torch but he could find nothing. Like I say, we thought it was them kids from the estate.'

'Thank you Chantel Owens. Sounds like you've had a very lucky escape! If there are any more of you out there who have had similar experiences please call or email us, you know the number. We will be passing on all information to the local police. We need to act now, catch this evil guy before any one else gets killed. Let's go over to the news room for the latest.'

'Thank you Mike. Police are warning local people to use the safety chains on their front doors after reports that the Doorstep Killer may have been hunting more victims in the area. Inspector Vincent, of Brently CID, said this afternoon they have had several calls from women saying that they have heard babies' cries outside their doors when they're home alone at night. Inspector Vincent also said that local GP Julian Jenkins has been helping with their inquiries…'

The light on my answerphone is flashing when I get home. It's my sister. Rick is going away for two weeks, a business trip, she doesn't want to be on her own in the house, killer might attack, baby might come, can I come and stay? 'No!' I shout at the little machine. I pick up the phone.

'Yep not a problem, I'll be over tomorrow night straight from work.'

When I arrive at my sister's house the next evening, she twitters and flutters like a trapped bird so convinced is she that she will be the next victim of the Doorstep Killer. She has read every newspaper inch, collected every radio syllable on the gruesome progress of the investigation and hunt for the murderer. I have already overdosed on the subject, the police having spent the day at the Health Centre, searching, dusting, probing. Doctor Jenkins continues to help Inspector Vincent, but is allowed home. All his appointments are transferred to the other three GPs. We are angry, fascinated, appalled.

My brother-in-law dutifully calls, and my sister spends the evening snatching at the corner of the curtains convinced she can hear crying on the doorstep. At 9.30 a deep crack splits its way through my patience, I excuse myself and go to bed before I scream something unretractable at her. I climb under the covers, close my eyes allowing the sound of my baby crying to soothe me to sleep. Tomorrow will be one whole year since that policeman rang my doorbell. One whole year since the shock ripped a pain across my abdomen, frightening my little daughter, who fought her way into the world four months too early.

At something dark o'clock, my sister shakes me awake.

'Sarah, it's coming, the baby's coming!'

'Can't be. Too early,' my half conscious mouth murmurs. But I'm pulled from the warm water of my dreams by her deep animal groan.

I get her to the bathroom. I get water into the bath. I get her into the water. I tell her I'm going to call the ambulance.

'Just drive me there,' she pleads

'Not enough time,' I say heading down the stairs. I sit on the bottom step listening to her agonies, pulling me back to help her take the pain away. It takes every cell of strength to go back into the bathroom. I can see immediately she's in trouble, I tear the plug from the bath and as the watered down blood drains away I can see the baby's head. With the last of her power the baby appears. I grab a towel from the rail. I cradle the little life. It beats. She breathes. I can hear the sound of her crying.

My sister will need medical help. I pick up the phone and dial Doctor Jenkins' home number.

The Graveyard at St Michael's is set high above the village; I can even see the roof of our old cottage. The wind moans around the crooked stones, mourning the sleepers beneath. My daughter sighs peacefully, but frowns as a gust catches her cheek. I take her back to the car and fasten her seat carefully, leaving the car door open so that I have a clear full view of her. I don't have long, but it is important that I come to say goodbye.

Theirs is the newest stone in the row where they rest, David and our first daughter. They are buried together to keep each other company while they watch over the village below. I have brought them a rose each and lay them by their headstone. Grace cries out from the car, pulling me back to now and away from a year ago.

'Goodbye.' I leave them to sleep peacefully.

I get into the car and gaze down at my daughter, she has my sister's eyes, but then my sister's eyes are my eyes. She sleeps. All I can hear is the sound of her breathing. I start the car; we have a ferry to catch. I pull out of the church car park and turn on the radio.

'Police have arrested local doctor, Julian Jenkins, for the murder of five local women. The murders, which started in January, have become known locally as the "Door Step Killings". Last night Jenkins was picked up in the area close to where the body of a 42 year old woman was discovered in the front garden of her home. Unconfirmed reports claim that the women were all patients of Jenkins and had attended his antenatal clinics. Inspector Vincent of Brently CID said that they had strong evidence linking Jenkins to the murders. Items found at the murder scene, including a surgical rubber glove, carried a direct DNA match to Jenkins…'

Cherry Pie

Kay Sheard

There was only the sound of the rain, deadened by the hood of her coat. Nothing more could be heard. It drummed from a sky of lead onto the sedge and the grey waters of the lake.

It wasn't a lake. It was a reservoir. Amy always had to remind herself of that. Yet it seemed to fit so well in the landscape, as though it had always been there. Llyn Llwyd – that's what they called it, and on days like this it was easy to see why: llwyd – not just grey – Welsh grey. The grey of slate and the sea; the grey of mists, and storms gathering on the mountains.

She raised her head a little, her face sheltered by the wide brim of her hood, and gazed out at the lake through the veil of rain. Thirty years ago that same day, it had not been raining.

Thirty years ago, it had been warm and sunny. The reservoir had been new then, the waters trembling in the sunlight with the novelty of new being, as if aware they should not have been there at all. Some of what remained of the hillside above the water survived as grazing-land. Pines had invaded the rest; row upon row of regimented infant trees, as though a child had meticulously painted hundreds of dark green triangles onto the sun-scorched grass. A chalk track, newly gashed in the hillside, blazed in the sun like a coronet of white fire. Only on the southern edge did it vanish, hidden by a stretch of natural woodland which pre-dated the reservoir; a copse of oak and mountain ash, blackthorn and beech, marching against the presumptuous shore and surrounding a quiet inlet. Mocked by lapping water.

Thirty years ago, the reservoir had been alive with day-trippers. Cars were dotted along the track, their paintwork shining in the sun – people could take them right to the edge of the lake, back then. From this same spot, where the track left the lakeside and ran behind the ancient woodland, they had resembled gaudy plastic beads strung on a child's necklace.

A happy day. Children paddling in the shallows, playing with boats, splashing, laughing. Flip-flops and plastic sunglasses. Nylon fishing nets on canes. Jam jars filled with sticklebacks. Some people venturing further in, ignoring the warning signs. Some even swimming right out into the centre of the lake; deep, cold water. Everyone lulled into the false sense of security engendered by a Saturday afternoon in the school holidays. Nothing bad could happen to any of them. Not there, not that day. It was too benign, too convivial, too lovely…

Years later, everyone fated to be there that day could remember it as though it was yesterday. None were ever able to forget the shock they felt when they learnt that that afternoon Llyn Llwyd claimed its first life; a little girl. Seven years old. Lisa Jones.

'Amy.'

The voice was patient, kind. It came from the rain. Her back straightened perceptibly, and she took a deep, sharp intake of breath as though nudged from sleep.

'Amy, you'll catch your death. It's time to go back to the car.'

She turned. He stood a few feet behind her, a beacon of colour shining in the unrelenting grey: his long hair, the colour of fox fur, loosely tied back, cotton trousers the palette and pattern of a child's paint-box, a baggy green jumper under a big red umbrella.

She said nothing, only met his eyes; gentle grey eyes – they were the only thing about him which matched the landscape in which he stood. Then she nodded and stood. In silence they cut across the limp tussocks away from the lake, back to the car park along the eaves of the old woodland. Alone in that landscape, the wood was unchanged by the passage of thirty years.

'Take your coat off before you get in, you daft woman!' he said fondly as she opened the car door and prepared to slump inside just as she was. She looked up; he was putting the umbrella down, tossing it in the back. She opened the back door and did as he said, slipping quickly into the passenger seat, deftly picking up the folder on the seat as she did so, closing the door swiftly behind. Slightly breathless, her eyes fell on the windscreen, a wall of glass and water, so drenched in rain that all beyond was lost. An otherworldly study in grey.

He jumped into the driver's seat. She felt him looking at her, but still said nothing. The rain beat down, loud now, rhythmic, unrelenting; a womb of rain. Already the glass wall of the windscreen was starting to mist over, stealing the outside away like a half-forgotten dream or a childhood memory. She glimpsed herself, fading in the wing-mirror, her face distorted by the rain-drops: bedraggled brown hair, pale skin, eyes as black as mourning. The mistiness made her ageless, unreal… She had become one of the Tylwyth Teg – the fairy folk – not truly living at all.

Her hands clasped the edges of the folder on her knee. Her knuckles were white.

'Are you all right, Amy?'

Tensely, she nodded. She felt his hand on hers, warm, alive.

'You're freezing.'

'I'm okay.'

His hand moved to her thigh. It still felt warm even through the fabric.

'Your jeans are soaked through. Let me take you home.'

'No.' She spoke firmly.

'Just to change—'

'No.'

He gave a heart-felt sigh. 'Do you want some water?'

She shook her head.

'Something to eat?'

'No.'

The windscreen had completely fogged over, as though the car had been enveloped in a dense cloud. She remembered that time they'd been at the seaside, in the rain, eating fish and chips in the car. 'We've been stolen by the cloud fairies,' Mum said. 'And they'll only put us back if you eat everything up. Every last crumb. So, eat up, Cherry Pie, while they're nice and hot.'

She could still taste the grease. The memory of the salt and vinegar made her feel hungry.

She opened the folder and stared at the first page – the photocopy of a news clipping. A copy of a copy. Smudged. Distorted. Yet from the hundreds of black dots, a little girl still managed to stare out: wide, innocent eyes, a big smile, neat bobbed hair, held neatly back with a plastic slide. The slide was printed with a daisy pattern. It matched the daisy print of her dress. Amy knew that the dress and the slide had been pale blue. She knew too that the eyes of the daisies had been orange, not yellow. The headline: Schoolgirl Drowns in Tragic Accident.

Amy had read the article a hundred times and more. She didn't read it now, but words and phrases still floated up to her from the page. Family mourn death of their 'darling little angel'...popular with teachers and peers...loved reading... promising ballerina...family holiday at local campsite...picnic at Llyn Llwyd...walk along the dam-bank...just paddling in the shallows...mother had just driven to public toilets...father fell asleep...body found floating face down in middle of the lake...

'Amy?'

She had turned to another plastic envelope. The clipping in this photocopy was small, in the centre of the wedding-white page: *Jones-Pendry*, it read. *Kathleen Jones, of Tavistock Road, Garston and Keith Pendry, of Wood Avenue, Speke, married at Liverpool Registry Office, June 19th*. And the next page was just a piece of lined A4, on which were scrawled two lines in pencil: 22 Lavender Avenue, Llandudno.

'I want to see her,' she said.

He said nothing.

'Jay, I want to see her.'

It had stopped raining by the time they reached Llandudno, though the clouds still lowered. Lavender Avenue was a genteel road of spacious inter-war semis on the hillside. Solid, respectable, each with views of the sea and the Great Orme snatched on tiptoes through corners of upper windows.

'Are you sure?' asked Jay.

Amy gazed at the house for several moments. She had been there before – more than once – but she hadn't told Jay. She nodded. 'Wait here,' she said.

She opened the gate and walked up path. The front garden was impeccable; a small lawn surrounded by flower beds filled with roses and dahlias – plasticine yellows and pinks. There were gnomes in the rockery under the window. They were laughing at her. She turned her gaze to the reeded-glass door, and knocked.

Moments flickering past. A figure broken, distorted through the pane like a fractured ghost. The door opened. A woman stood there: short, plump, wrinkled. Eyes, brown, a little wary…a dislike of strangers…memories she'd rather not recall.

'Yes?'

Can't she tell? Can't she see it in my eyes?

'Can I help you?'

'It's me.' Amy was surprised how high and thin her voice

sounded. It didn't sound like her voice at all.

'Pardon?'

'It's me. Lisa.'

The woman blanched. Her eyes – the irises a faded blue, the whites creamy, a little bloodshot – widened. Lips parted. Bloodless.

'What...what do you mean?'

'Lisa, I'm Lisa.'

'What? I'm sorry, you must have got the wrong person.'

'You're Kathleen Pendry? You used to be married to Gareth Jones? You had a little girl – Lisa... Born March 11th 1971—'

Her voice cracked. 'What do you want from me?'

'Nothing... I just... It's just... I'm Lisa.'

Her face twisted, a battle between horror and disgust. 'Go away, or I'll call the police! My Lisa's dead... you must be mad or sick!'

'I'm neither... I know it's hard to believe, but it's the truth. I'm Lisa. I'm your daughter.'

The elderly woman just stared. Then, a moment later she slammed the door in Amy's face.

Amy bent down and called through the letterbox.

'Mrs Pendry, I swear, I'm not lying. I know it's incredible... I've struggled with it all my life... But it's true... I'm Lisa... Please, will you just hear me out?'

'Go away!' The words were choking her. 'Go away.'

'Remember when we went on holiday – somewhere down South with a pier? We had fish and chips and ate them in the car because it was raining. The car steamed up. You said we'd been stolen away by the cloud fairies. Every night we used to sing Oranges and Lemons, but you changed the last line from here comes a hatchet to chop off your head, to here comes a big hug and a kiss for your ted, because the original gave me nightmares.'

The door opened. The old woman looked as though she

had just witnessed the town sliding into the sea. 'How can you possibly know those things?' she asked, her voice now barely a croak. Her hand was at her throat. 'Who have you been talking to? What do you want?'

'I know it because I remember it. I've talked to no one. No one who knew you. I know it is almost impossible to believe. I struggle to believe it myself. But I am Lisa.'

'You're insane.'

Amy shook her head. 'I've been close to insanity. I've tried to take my life more than once. I am twenty-five years old, Mrs Pendry – and for all those twenty-five years I've been haunted by what happened. But I found someone who was able to help me; to take me into my past lives. And in my last life, I was your daughter. I need to find closure. I need to move on with my life… with this life. That's why I had to find you.'

'What was my pet name for y— for Lisa? Tell me that!'

'You used to call me all sorts of things. Lambkin, Duckling, Apple Blossom… But most of all, you used to call me Cherry Pie.'

Amy sat at the kitchen table, cradling a cup of tea in her hands. Her eyes kept being drawn to the photographs crammed on the wall around the glazed double doors to the dining room. Mostly they charted the progress of two boys from infancy to adulthood, but there were three of a little girl. Just three: a plump, startled-looking baby in a white dress embroidered with tiny forget-me-nots, a toddler in pink gingham with gaps in her toothy grin… and the third was the original of the picture in the newspaper clipping. The dress and the slide were pale blue, dotted with the tiny eyes of the daisies – orange, just as Amy remembered them. The background was blue too – the hazy blue of a summer sky. She had forgotten that.

She had also forgotten to mention that Jay only drank herbal tea. He hadn't said anything himself, nor had he refused what he was offered. They were all on their second cup. Mrs Pendry had spent the last forty minutes telling Amy about the years which had passed since the day Lisa drowned in Llyn Llwyd. Her marriage to Lisa's father hadn't survived long after. It had already been on rocky ground, and their daughter's death had been the last straw. They had separated within six months and divorced shortly after. She had remarried within weeks of the Decree Absolute to a colleague at the primary school where she'd worked as an infants' teacher. They'd had a happy enough marriage, blessed with the boys. They had both left home now, both working in London. Her second husband had died of cancer two years previously, not long after retiring. She'd been retired herself for five years now. Did volunteer work to keep busy. Raised funds for the hospice. She had met someone too – a widower. Early days, but time would tell. But fulfilling as her life had turned out to be, she had never been able to forget the little girl stolen from her so suddenly on a summer day so long ago.

Amy shared her story too. Her mother had been only sixteen when she'd been born. She'd tried to make a go of it with Amy's father, but it hadn't worked, and Amy had no recollection of him. He'd joined the army not long after leaving her mother, and been killed in Northern Ireland before Amy's third birthday. Her mother had had a string of relationships after that, three more daughters, each to different fathers. She'd had times when she couldn't cope and Amy and her sisters had ended up in foster homes. Eventually Amy had been adopted, but her new parents had split up a few years later too. She'd remained with her adoptive mother, but as she hit her teenage years they'd clashed as she got drawn into drink and drugs.

She'd run away from home for the first time when she was thirteen, and left for good at sixteen, when she'd moved in with her boyfriend. He'd been a waster. They'd wasted together. After a couple of years, shortly after breaking up with him, she'd found herself at a festival where she'd met Jay. Jay was a herbalist and hypnotherapist. He'd used hypnosis to help her get clean of the drugs. Guided her in past life regressions. Started her on the road to healing.

'But...but even if this is all true...even if you really were my...my Lisa. What is it that you want now? What is it that you want from me?'

'I... I don't know,' said Amy. 'My old life... Lisa's life... It ended so suddenly, so traumatically... I just need to find some resolution, before I can really start to get on with this life. I think I just need to say a proper goodbye to those I loved...to you, to Dad... then I'll finally be able to move on – as Amy.'

Mrs Pendry looked at Jay. 'Do you do this sort of thing a lot?' she asked. Her tone of voice was noticeably cooler. 'Get people remembering past lives? Is that how you make a living?'

'I help people if I can,' he replied. 'With past-life regression, and hypnosis, and...other stuff. But I don't make any money from it. I don't charge.'

'What do you do for a living, then?'

'I'm a gardener.'

'How did you get into it?'

'I went to horticultural college.'

'I didn't mean that,' she snapped. 'I meant, how do you get into doing those "past life regressions" and all that.'

'Oh, sorry. Just through the people I hung out with, I guess.'

Amy knew more. And she knew why Jay was so vague. People like Kathleen Pendry tended to feel uncomfortable when they learnt they were entertaining a modern-day druid. She'd found it a bit strange herself, until she'd got to know him. Begun to understand him. Jay was like a flat calm on an ocean – or the velvet blackness of a moonless sky glittering with icy stars. He knew the secrets whispered to the wind by yews which were old when the henges were built... She'd never met anyone like him before. She knew she never would again...

Silence. A clock ticking. Amy watched Kathleen. Distrustful eyes fixed on Jay. Mouth hard. Coffee cup held so tightly she could see the knuckle-bones.

But the picture of the little girl in the daisy-print dress drew her back.

'What about my... Lisa's dad?' she asked at length, her eyes lingering on the photograph. 'Is he still alive?'

'As far as I know,' said Kathleen shortly. 'It's many years since I had any contact with him.' She glanced at Amy, and softened. 'I don't know,' she said.

'Do you have an address for him? I've tried to find one, but had no success.'

'When last I heard he was still in Liverpool. In Knotty Ash.'

'Do you have an address?'

'There's no point contacting him.' Dismissive. Impatient. 'You could come out with something that no one on earth could possibly know but Lisa, and he'd never believe you. Even if he's still alive.'

'Please. At least allow me to try.'

Amy searched her face, begging her with her eyes. Kathleen frowned, and pursed her lips. 'Oh, very well,' she said. 'You can have it, for what it's worth. But you'll be wasting your time if you contact him. He won't believe a word.'

It was several weeks before Amy acted on what she'd learnt. She'd been all for driving straight to Liverpool from Llandudno, but Jay discouraged her. Said he didn't think it was the right time yet, so she'd bided her time. Visited Kathleen Pendry again. She marvelled at how well they began to get on. One time, though, she'd almost talked about that day at Llyn Llwyd. Jay nudged her ankle gently with his foot under the kitchen table. Cast her a warning glance. 'Not yet,' it said. 'Not to her.' Amy bit her lip.

Every now and again, Amy would raise the matter with Jay

again. 'I'm ready, I'm sure I am.' But every time, Jay shook his head. 'Not yet. It takes time, Amy. Give it time.'

Autumn came, the nights drew in. Winter began to bite. On Christmas Eve, Amy told Jay she really wanted to visit Gareth Jones. And this time, Jay said okay. If that's what she wanted, he thought she was just about ready.

They'd had to leave the car some distance away, next to a public park, as there wasn't a space on the street itself. It was just like a hundred other streets in Liverpool, a relentless row of brick terraced houses, all charm they might once have possessed knocked out of them when the sash-windows were ripped out and replaced with polyvinyl chloride. Many were drenched in Christmas lights, garish glowing Santas, reindeer, stars and icicles. Trees stood like watchful sentries in windows. Electric candles flashed like warning beacons.

But not number eighty-four. Number eighty-four was bleak and bare. Amy stared at the door. Somewhere nearby a dog was barking. A chill wind gusted down the street, blowing her hair into her eyes. She was acutely conscious of her own breathing.

'It's not too late to turn back,' said Jay quietly. 'You don't have to do this today. You don't ever have to do it.'

'No. I want to. It's time.'

She pressed the doorbell. They heard Westminster chimes ringing in the hall. Muffled footsteps approached. The door opened. A smell of boiled cabbage wafted into the street.

He wasn't as tall as Amy had expected – though perhaps that was because he was so much fatter. He was bald and ruddy-cheeked, and he eyed them with suspicion.

'Yeah?'

'Gareth Jones?'

'Who's asking? What do you want?'

'Can we come in?'

'Why? You collecting for something? Or are you Jehovah's Witnesses?'

'Neither – I'd... I'd just like to talk to you about something. It's about your daughter – Lisa.'

Just a flicker in his eye – that was the only indication at all that he'd even heard the name before. 'What about her?' he asked gruffly. 'She's been dead thirty years.'

'I know. Would you mind if I came in?'

'Are you police or something? What could you possibly want to ask me about?' She could see the vapour of his breath; a thin, spectral mist, glowing orange in the glare of the street-lamps.

'No...no, we're not police... and it's not so much something I want to ask you, as tell you.'

For several moments he just eyed her coldly. Amy couldn't bear it for more than a few seconds. It disturbed her too much. There was something about them she found deeply unsettling. They were calculating eyes, clinical eyes...devoid of all emotion...devoid of love...devoid of life.

'What's your name?'

'Amy...Amy Pierce.'

The sitting room was harshly lit by a ceiling light. It was sparsely furnished with tatty, ill-matched furniture. The carpet might once have been green – now it was dirty grey. The curtains were burgundy velvet, faded and threadbare in patches. In the corner, a television blared. Canned laughter. The floor was strewn with old newspapers, empty takeaway boxes and crumpled beer cans. The smell of cabbage was particularly strong here – but not strong enough to mask the stench of damp. There were no pictures of any kind.

'Well? What is it?' he said, picking up the remote control and switching off the TV.

'I'm Lisa.'

At last, a reaction in his face. 'You what? Are you mental?'

A strange sort of peace settled on her heart. Peace and

strength. 'I'm Lisa,' she said quietly but confidently. 'And I want to talk to you about the day you killed me.'

'What?' A bead of sweat broke on his forehead. 'What are you talking about?'

Amy took a step towards him. 'You murdered me, didn't you?'

'You're off your trolley.'

'You drowned me. You'd been abusing me, told me not to say anything, but you were afraid I'd tell anyway. So you waded into the shallows, pulled me down under the water, held me down, and drowned me. I didn't tell, Dad, I haven't told anyone, I promise.'

'You're mad… you cannot know—' His pupils were dilating, his brow glistening.

'I struggled, I broke the water, gasping for air. Gasping for life. But you pulled me down again. You stole my life away.'

'You're mad… You're…' Gareth clutched at his chest. 'You're…' But with a sickening groan, like bagpipes filling with air, he began to keel over, grasping the back of a chair for a moment. 'Help me!' he rasped, and promptly vomited. His arms gave way, and he fell to his knees. 'Call…ambulance… can't breathe…weak heart…'

Amy just stared at him. Frozen.

'Did you listen to Lisa's pleas?' asked Jay quietly, stepping forward. 'Did you care for her suffering?'

Gareth collapsed on his back, his breathing laboured, drowning in air. Impassively, Jay watched him. He noted the sweat on his brow, his face, smeared with vomit, growing paler by the moment, his eyes popping. 'Help me!' he rasped. 'Please! Lisa!'

Amy snapped alert, as though an enchantment upon her had been broken. She turned to Jay. 'Where's the telephone?' she said urgently. Her eyes scanned the room – she saw the stand on the windowsill, but the handset wasn't there. She plunged her hand into her pocket for her mobile, but Jay put his hand on her arm.

'No.'

She looked at him in surprise. 'But...but we must do something!'

'No.'

The surprise mutated to shock as she realised what he meant. 'Jay, we have to!'

'No.'

Her eyes searched his face wildly, then fell upon Gareth again. He convulsed for a moment – and then he stopped. He lay where he had fallen, perfectly still, perfectly silent.

'Oh God! I think he's dead!'

Jay said nothing. Did nothing. His eyes were fixed upon Gareth's face. He would not have recognised him after all these years, had he not known. Thirty years had passed since the day he'd last seen him, when Jay had been barely five years old. Gareth Jones hadn't been old, bald and fat then. He'd had no broken veins or blotchy skin. He had been quite skinny, bandy-legged, his flesh the white of raw pastry.

He did not look as though he had the strength to do what he did.

He'd wandered away from his parents, tempted by the wood. He was bored of paddling. His dad had been asleep since lunch; his mum had grown drowsy in the sun. First she'd continued to read her magazine lying on the rug, then she'd put it over her head and gone to sleep. 'I'll just have a little nap, Jay. Read your book. Don't wander off.'

But he'd finished his book. He sat there for a little while, watching the other families around them. So many people, swarming on the shore. A radio blared nearby, tinny pop music. Something inside him said it wasn't right. This lake wasn't right. These hills weren't meant for this. His eyes fell on the wood at the bottom of the lake.

That belonged; it was the only thing in the landscape which did.

No-one paid him any attention as he drifted down the white road, scuffing up the compacted chalk with the toes of his grubby plimsolls. He left the track, picked his way through the withered sedge. The further he went from the track, the fewer people there were. Instead of voices, he started to catch the sound of water lapping, a light breeze in the grass...and, at last, the wind moving through the trees, speaking secrets in the leaves, a language he yearned to understand.

The wood was cool. Quiet. Enticing. He followed a path, leading him away from the reservoir, towards the inlet. There was no-one there but him, and the trees were trying to tell him things... he was certain of it. He stroked the bark of one, the rough grain, and felt the decades of growth, the ebb and flow of the seasons... soft summer rain, and the bitter snarl of winter storms...year upon year... But then he caught sight of people again – a lone family at the water's edge of the smaller lake. He watched them resentfully, peering through a gorse bush so they couldn't see him. After a few moments, he realised it was the family who had the pitch next to his at the campsite. Jay was jealous of their tent – it was one of those big, modern trailer-tents: sunny orange canvas, big plastic windows and proper beds. His parents didn't approve, said it hardly counted as camping, but Jay thought they were cross because the orange tent had been pitched barely two feet from the wall of theirs, and Jay and his parents could hear almost every word they said.

The mum and the girl were all right, though a bit drippy. The mum fussed a lot, called the girl silly things like 'lambkin' and 'cherry pie'. Sang lots of stupid songs in a thin voice, and was always talking, reminiscing. It had poured down the day before, and still Jay could hear them. 'The windows are all steaming up!' complained the mother. Wipe them down with a tea-towel, then,' said the dad. 'It's probably the cloud fairies after our lunch again,' piped the girl. 'What, Lambkin?' said the mum. 'Don't you remember?' said the girl. 'When we went to Brighton, and ate some fish and chips in the car because it was raining? The car all steamed up and you said it was the cloud fairies.' The mum laughed. 'You shouldn't fill her head with such rubbish,' said the dad.

He didn't like the dad. It wasn't so much the things he said. He didn't really speak much. When he did, it was always harsh and critical. He said nasty things to the mother, and things Jay didn't understand, but which made his parents exchange disapproving glances. What Jay liked least, though, was the way he stared, especially at the swimming pool…the hungry sort of look in his eyes…the way they roved… Jay noticed he spent most of his time at the pool, swimming and watching…

The little girl had taken off her blue dress with the funny orange-eyed daisies and was now in a pink bikini. She was paddling in the shallows with a green fishing net and an orange bucket. The man lay on the rug. He looked asleep. The woman – short, plump – stood up. 'I'm just going to drive to the toilets, Lisa, love. Do you need to go?' The girl shook her head.

'Back soon, Cherry Pie.' She waved, then walked away. The sound of a car engine some distance away to the right, the drone fading until the lapping water drowned it out.

When it had gone, the man sat up. For a moment he watched the little girl. Then he stripped off his clothes – all his clothes – and lay them carefully on the rug. The little girl turned. She suddenly looked scared. 'Dad, please, don't,' he heard her say. 'Mummy will be back soon.' He said something – Jay didn't hear what. He watched in innocence. Jay saw his dad naked all the time. But the little girl was backing away, cowed. 'I didn't tell, Dad,' she said. 'I haven't told anyone. I promise.'

He didn't seem to hear her. The girl turned and tried to run, but her legs were thin and weak, and the water impeded her. The father was tall, his legs sliced through the water with ease. The lake was his ally. He grabbed her arms. She shrieked – a shriek of

104

*terror, high, like the cry of a bird – but short, so short. For within
a second he had pulled her beneath the water, fallen to his knees.
His body had vanished in the water up to his neck.*

*Transfixed with horror, Jay watched. The child thrashed, like
a caught fish, thrashed and thrashed. Her head broke the water
once, a desperate deep snatch of air, desperate spluttering 'Please!
Please don't—' But he'd embraced her round the middle, pulled
her under again...splashing, thrashing...then the water was still.
For a few moments nothing seemed to move at all, not the man,
not the water of the lake, not the trees, not the clouds... Then the
man ducked his own head below the water. For a moment, Jay
thought he was drowning himself too. But as the horror within
him reached a crescendo, he saw the girl, limp now, like a rag-doll,
moving, face down out into the lake, into the deep, cold water.
Then she moved no more, just floated on the surface, just a doll. Jay
sat rock-still, his eyes racing over the water, searching – then, with
an audible gasp, the man broke the surface again, right by the
shore. Breathing heavily, he stepped from the water, dried himself,
dressed again, lay down, closed his eyes...*

*Llyn Llwyd basked in the sunshine, sleek, content, oozing
satisfaction like a feasted cat. But the old trees wept; Jay heard
their broken sighs.*

*He ran, wanting to scream, but swallowing it down, deep
within, sealing it there, burying it with black earth, piling stones
on top – a cairn to mark the burial, to keep the dead within the
grave...the man mustn't know what he'd seen. The girl...she had
said she hadn't told something, but he hadn't believed her...that's
why he'd killed her... If he said anything, he'd kill him too...he
mustn't know...he mustn't know...he mustn't ever know...*

*And he'd kept that silence till he was twenty, keeping a lonely
vigil by the cairn within himself. But when he was twenty, even
that cairn could contain the scream no longer. It burst forth one
day – and he'd gone to the police, confessed what he'd seen. But
they accused him of making it up. Took one look at his long hair,*

the Celtic patterns tattooed on his arms, and said he'd probably hallucinated the whole thing on a bad trip. Why hadn't he said anything before? There'd been no evidence at the time that the girl's death had been anything other than an accident – and why was that then, eh? Because that's what it had been – an accident...

'Oh, God!' she blurted suddenly. 'Oh, God – I've killed him!'

'No. It wasn't your fault.' He took her hand and squeezed it. His other hand went to his pocket. Fingers closed around a tiny bottle, cold to the touch – but nothing to the icy death it contained, carefully prepared. Unused. He that is born to be hanged will never be drowned.

'Now,' he said, 'we can live.'

China Doll

Kate Kinnersley

1

Someone once said my job was to straighten out life's bananas. I guess that's about right. This particular banana walked into my office clouded in a scent I shall never forget: jasmine, light but lingering.

It was one black night and I was sitting at my desk listening to the rain pelting down onto the city streets, beating a tattoo on the sidewalk beneath my window. The moving traffic swished past, everybody heading home to their loved ones and I was thinking I might as well go down to Lennie's when there was a light tap on the door.

Through the glass I could make out the outline of a figure of eight, slim legs and high heels and a hat with a tall feather or something in it. Obviously a dame or one of my less than masculine male friends. I let my chair ease forward from its tilted position and with my pen I pushed my trilby up from over my eyes.

'Who is it?' I grumbled, wondering why Roxy, my secretary, hadn't come in to warn me. Opening my desk drawer I let my hand rest on the butt of my piece, just to be ready, and waited. The door opened and in she walked – if you can call it walking – that languid, liquid gait made you want to follow her just to watch.

She was a tall willowy blonde, the kinda babe you always wish would come into your life on a cold, wet, lonely night. The kind who always ends up bringing trouble along with her, but you don't care. She took off her fur wrap and slung it on the chair facing me. She was some broad, a waist you could wrap one hand around when you held her close and a chest that came to meet ya before she did.

'Are you Daniel Charles?' she asked. Her accent was like glass breaking on my Bronx born ears. Foreign, English and high toned but with the appeal of a diamond glinting a threat from black velvet.

'You have something I want,' she said and produced a small silver gun from her pocket. She had guts, I had to give her that. The piece she was threatening me with was about as lethal as a bad cold on a summer's day.

I took the china statue out of my desk drawer. Her eyes fastened on it and I knew I had guessed right. I stood up and took a step towards her, holding the figure out in front of me.

'Blow me away baby and the cutie goes too.' The gun wavered and she pressed the trigger. I flinched expecting a pellet as big as a pea to maybe make a hole in my jacket, but a tiny flame burst from it.

'Give me a cigarette, then,' she whispered, her shoulders drooping as she gave up the fight. I reached for the crumpled pack on my desk, but when she saw them she shook her head and opened her purse. Taking a tipped from a slim gold case she lit it then looked at me through the smoke, after taking a long pull and breathing it out, slowly, deliberately, filling the air with a sweet foreign scent.

Her gaze moved to the china statuette I held. It was an erotic, arty sculpture of a nude babe on her knees, head thrown back with long hair falling over her slender shoulders, breasts thrust forward, delicately pointed. The face was precisely drawn and was a dead ringer for the face I was looking at.

'Now park yourself and tell me just what's going down,' I said, kicking the wooden chair towards her. I lounged against the wall and listened while she told me some fairy story and then I smiled sardonically. 'Nice, very nice,' I drawled and slamming my fist on the desk I snapped at her. 'The truth. I want the truth, not something you just dreamed up.'

Her eyes flashed, then a glimpse of humour lightened them. She crossed her legs, taking her time, pulling her skirt up towards her thighs so that the cross came high not spoiling the lovely long line of them. The plain black shoes had thin glass heels, so high they looked great, but how could she walk in them I wondered?

Musing on this and feeling my skin tingle as I reacted to the shimmering of her stockings and the noise they made as they whispered together, made thinking hard. I saw her eyes mocking me, taking in the bulge in my trousers and I got a grip, remembering why I was there.

An hour ago, a guy had been sitting just where she was now. Angry and impatient and not the kinda guy I would usually spend time with, he had employed me to find her. Instead she had found me and I was curious.

I licked my lips. 'Tell me everything you know and don't leave anything out then, maybe, I'll decide to help you.'

'Very well, I'll tell you the truth. I have a problem. I need someone strong, single-minded and very discreet to solve it,' she said and sat down to regard me, amusement in her eyes while she waited for my answer. 'Are you that man?'

I coughed and tried to shift my gaze from her luscious body. 'Could be,' I said. 'What's he done? Is he cheatin' on you, beatin' on you, or worse?' Though Lord knows, I was thinking, any man must be crazy to do either with a dame like that at home. Where would he find anything better?

'Neither,' she said, lifting a sculptured brow. 'It's not him, it's my sister. She's missing. I want you to find out what has happened to her, what she has been mixed up in.'

I watched as she tapped the ash from her cigarette into my overflowing tray (courtesy of Lennie's Bar). I hesitated in replying and she pursed her beautiful lips questioningly.

'That is what you do, isn't it – find people?'

She smiled and I looked her over while I thought about what she had said. Her general air was expensive, upper class and discreet. Well cut designer clothes, tailored to fit her like a second skin, though she would look good in a sack. Good shoes with high stiletto heels, clean and well cared for, no doubt by staff.

Her slim elegant fingers looked as though they had never encountered anything dirtier than a cigarette lighter. Framing her lovely oval face she wore elegant droppers from each ear, diamonds with a ruby at the end of each one. I was to remember their blood red glow long after this case was over. Her lips matched the colour exactly and their fullness pouted sulkily as she waited for me to speak. Who was I going to work for, the greasy Italian or her? No contest.

'Okay, tell me about your sister and why you think she's in trouble.'

'Do you have all night? It's a long story,' she said. 'Why don't we go somewhere more comfortable and I'll tell you everything you want to know.'

'Sure, why not,' I agreed. She sure as hell didn't belong in my dingy office and it was getting cold.

The rain was pelting down and I was regretting not grabbing my coat as we left but she had a smart two-seater parked in the no-parking zone right outside. Had it been dry I might have whistled in appreciation but as it was we both dived for cover and settled into the luxurious leather seats. This baby had cost more than my apartment and office put together.

'A present from him?' I asked. She gave me a hard look.

'I worked for it, and bought it myself. Some women do that

you know.' Her cut-glass smacked me as if she had used her hand. The third finger on her right hand, nearest me, sported a rock as big as a peanut.

'That, too?' I said, dryly. 'Or was that for being good?' (Meaning bad.) I could have bitten my tongue out as soon as I said it, but this dame was getting to me and I hate that. It clouds my thinking and gets in the way of my job. And I had a job to do.

2

'I suppose Jake put you up to this.'

I was supposed to let the guy know as soon as I found her, but here I was in her car, going who knows where and liking it. Without thinking, my decision had been made. Jake – that's what she called him – would have to find another private eye.

I hadn't answered her, but she had guessed right. At first it was just a job, the kind that pays the rent and buys me the odd bourbon down at Lennie's. Wealthy 'Joe' buys himself a trophy babe and then starts treating her like a wife, leaving her home nights while he lives single with the boys.

So the wife gets bored, leaves, taking with her a suitcase full of expensive baubles he's paid for along the way. When I'd asked for a photo he'd taken the china doll out of his deep coat pocket. 'I don't have no photo, she don't like having her picture took,' he snarled. 'This is her, the bitch.' He traced the line of the figure with his stubby finger in such a way that I reached for it and took it from him before it made me feel even more uncomfortable.

'What's her name?' I asked. He started and for a fraction he looked old, much older than the forty or so years I judged him to be. 'Mandy,' he said bleakly and then the rage came back. 'Find her and let me know just where she is. Oh, by the way, she's English and frosty…frosty, that is, until you get to know her and then she burns and it kills you.'

He shook his head, a man with big trouble. 'Find her fast,' he said, and walked out. He'd been gone less than an hour when the frosty English lady had walked into my office and pointed the gun-shaped lighter at me. I could've asked her to take off her clothes and pose like the figure on my desk, but she had that no-nonsense look about her that warned me off. And here I was in her car speeding out of town, to a place I don't like being a Bronx guy.

'Where are we going?' I asked, surprised that I had put myself in this position. I liked being in control and I should have taken her down the block to Lennie's. Damn the rain and damn her. She didn't answer, just kept speeding along the shiny wet blacktop. The car purred, a big cat at ease, loping along at well over the speed limit.

After a while, I recognised the area we were in. It was where the rich and famous chose to hide away behind electric gates, where Rotweilers and Dobermans reigned at night, and anybody looking for trouble was bound to find it. Me, I just wanted to get back to the city.

We turned in to a wide tree-lined driveway, waited for the gates to open, then approached an old mansion stopping at the bottom of wide stone steps. I eased myself out of the low slung animal and would have helped her out, but she was out and up the steps to the huge oak doors in seconds, moving with the ease of a panther in her own habitat.

'The door's open!' Her voice was shrill with panic. I was up the steps and pushing her behind me before she stopped speaking. Reaching for my trusty Magnum, the one that couldn't light a cigarette but could knock a man off his feet without even having to aim right, I stepped into the hall.

I could feel her clutching my jacket and it felt good. We were in danger and I felt good – what was I thinking? There was a light on in one of the rooms off the hall. 'That's the library,' she whispered. I nodded and gestured to her to stay where she was while I investigated.

Minutes later I called her in. 'Who is he?' I asked, looking at the stiff sprawled over the desk. The gun was still in his hand. His head lay in a spreading pool of blood. A typewriter was pushed back in front of him, the letter still where he had left it in the machine. I knew what it said, but I wanted to know if 'My darling daughter,' was the dame who was staring at him. 'Is that your father?'

She nodded, covering her mouth with both hands. 'Is he dead?'

I didn't see the need to answer that. Who could be alive with the back of his head missing and his brains spattered all over the wall. 'I gotta call the cops,' I said, reaching for the phone.

'Wait, I must talk to you first. I have to find something before the police arrive.'

'Baby, this might be suicide, it might be murder looking like suicide,' I growled. 'Either way, I'm calling the cops now.'

'Please…. Oh, please, you don't understand. I need your help. Just give me half an hour and then we can call the police.'

Those large hazel eyes were brimming with tears and suddenly I felt like a heel, torturing a helpless kid. 'Okay, but then you gotta tell me everything, and I mean everything lady. This is serious.'

'Of course I will,' she whispered, and leaned towards me. I caught her in my arms and she pressed her luscious body against me. 'I need you to help me. Please take care of me.'

With her soft hair against my face and the subtle scent of jasmine teasing me, I forgot the bloody scene yards away and tilted her face up and kissed her on the mouth. Her lips were full and I bruised them in my eagerness. My tongue touched the tip of hers and every inch of me wanted her.

She responded, and before I knew what was happening we

were hungrily kissing and embracing in a storm of passion. My hands went inside her blouse and found her braless, her full breasts falling into them. Her nipples stood hard and I bent away from her kisses to give them my attention.

She shuddered and I would have gone further, I would have gone all the way, but she stopped me. 'Later, darling, later,' she murmured breathlessly, pushing against my chest. 'Let's do what we have to do first. Come with me.'

She led me through the house to a room decorated with animal heads and shotguns, a rich man's den. Daddy's study, she called it, I guess on account of the giant bookcase covering one wall. She touched a book and a door opened in the bookcase.

Behind the door was a room I could only describe as a dungeon, except it wasn't below ground. It was painted black and was full of the kinda things you find in a place run by a dominatrix, a 'fun room' but not my kinda fun. Pain goes with my job sometimes, but it sure ain't fun.

I should have gone in first, I know, but she was messing with my head and I wasn't thinking straight. The first thing I knew was a loud explosion and a blast of hot air as a bullet sped past my ear, then another followed and she fell backwards and crumpled against me, protecting me from another two shots.

The Magnum was in my hand firing past her body at the dark shape across the room. As I said, nothing escaped its power and that close to the target it was a cinch. The shape fell and I turned my attention to the babe in my arms, oozing blood all over her fine clothes. She said something and I bent to catch the words.

'You don't even know my name,' she whispered. Blood followed the words as she spoke and her life dribbled out of her in a stream of pink tinged bubbles. She went limp and I laid her gently on the floor then went over to kick the body of the man who had killed her. It was Jake, and he was still alive, just.

All round him were reels of film. One was still showing on the machine, the one he must have been watching when we surprised him. There was a girl of about fifteen, a girl who was now the woman lying dead across the room. The man slumped across the desk, the man she'd called 'Daddy', co-starred in the picture and they were doing things no man should do with a girl that age, never mind his daughter.

I switched the movie off and looked at the containers holding the others, and the empty ones that had been thrown aside. They had titles that told a sordid story. 'The First Time', 'Birthday Girl', 'Daddy does it Better', 'Puppy Training'. The sad story was all there, but I still wanted an answer to one question, so I removed the film from the machine and instead threaded in the one entitled 'An Oscar for Mandy'.

There it was, the china figure that Jake had somehow gotten hold of and given to me. In the movie it was presented to the girl who lay cold and bloody on the floor. She was older now, though, and this flick had been made within the last year or so.

She took the figure from Daddy, sat on a chair facing him and spread her legs. I switched the machine off, sickened, but not before I had seen something that caught my attention. They were not the only people in the room when the movie was made. At one point a shadow fell across Mandy and her daddy turned and said something to whoever it was.

I wanted to know who else was in the movie, but a Magnum makes a powerful noise and if I didn't call the police soon, some neighbour might do it and I would be in the middle of a mess I could be fitted up for. I'd seen such a situation scores of times in films and knew just what could happen. The cops don't like private dicks and I was no exception.

Gathering up all the tapes I could find into a box, I gave Mandy one long last look. Even now, with the life gone out of her, she looked beautiful. What a waste, we coulda made it good together. Then I got outta there and walked a few blocks

115

before I called Roxy, my sometime secretary and past lover, to come get me. I was still too close to the murder scene and a cabbie would remember picking me up.

3

'Vicious slaying of millionaire Joseph Bellini and his daughter, Amanda.'

Murder is not unusual in New York, but this one made the headlines. Some newshound had managed to get in before the cops. He described the scene in detail, which would have made them real sore. They wanted us, their readers, to think the motive was robbery. The article said the safe had not been discovered by the thieves, but several valuable objets d'art and irreplaceable pieces of jewellery were missing.

No mention of suicide and nothing about a third body. A few trinkets were missing, so it was a robbery. Daddy and his favourite girl were dead and Jake had crawled back under his stone to lick his wounds or die. Who cared? Me. My curiosity, which was not always good for my health, but which had kept me in Strikes and Bourbon for years, was, as Frosty would have said, piqued. In other words, I had that feeling I get when I can't let go of something until I have all the facts.

There was nothing pressing for my attention, nothing Roxy couldn't handle well enough without me, so I read the papers and waited for something to kick in, something that would set me on the track. I found it at the end of the gory sections, a few important words. 'Mr Bellini leaves a grieving wife, another daughter, Alexandra, and a son, James.'

Where were they, I wondered, when Daddy was redecorating the library with his blood and brains and all hell was taking place in the 'fun room'? I had to find out.

As I said, the cops don't like dicks, but there was one I could rely on since I knocked him out of the way of a bullet one night

116

in a shootout. We kept it light and I only called on him when I needed information I couldn't get any other way. He told me old man Bellini had made a fortune in the business of fancy ornaments and jewellery. His wife was an English society dame who ran away to the States when her aristocratic husband was found in bed with a boy.

Distraught, vulnerable and hounded by the British press, she'd run straight into Joseph Bellini. A minor player in the Mob he still had enough clout to deal with the newspaper boys and he had that Italian charm that seems to excite attract dizzy dames like Lady Antonia. In no time they were married and had been together for fifteen years.

I asked if there was anything on record and Joe looked into it and came back with nothing. The business was mainly import export. Maybe he was carrying drugs in and out but the cops never had enough to do a search and had left him alone. They had bigger more important boys to play with.

The cops were still keeping the murder scene under wraps and Lady Antonia was somewhere the news boys couldn't find her. After a coupla drinks together Joe slipped me the address where I might look for the mourning wife and kids. Time to go out of town again, to the beach this time, where what was left of the Bellini family were holed up in a palatial white stucco.

Modern and sleek the stucco had curves in all the right places, like a classy dame. Every window and door had a rounded balcony. Wide semi-circular steps led down to a figure of eight pool, and the gardens were lush, tropical, sheltered by thick tall hedges. In the summer it would be a holiday paradise, or a swell place to live.

I gave my card to the maid who put it on a tray and took it through, leaving me to wait in a silver and white room that made me want to hold my breath in case I stained something. Crumpled suit, whisky breath and me, we didn't belong here.

But when I followed the maid to where Lady Antonia was reclining in a glass fronted room that looked out on the pool, I stopped worrying. She was out of it, the glass she was holding spilling liquor onto the marble tiles.

The maid left us together and I sat down, after taking the glass from her drooping fingers and placing it on the table between us. Despite the stretched skin from too many facelifts and the dyed auburn hair, there was still a resemblance to the daughter I had laid on the floor as she breathed her last. A hint of the beauty that was hers fifteen years ago, when she first met Joseph Bellini, was still there. But this was the one who should have died if life was fair, I thought, as she peered at me through slitted eyes.

'And what do you want?' she slurred. 'If it's a drink, you'll have to help yourself.' She gestured loosely towards an array of bottles on a fancy gold-rimmed table. 'I'll have a gin-and-it. I suppose you know what that is? Mostly gin, oh forget the rest.' Her attempt at humour was sad and her eyes were bleak.

I obliged and poured myself a scotch, leaving the rocks where they glinted in a silver bucket. The atmosphere was cold enough and I took the scotch mainly to keep her company. Bourbon didn't live in this house. I sat in the chair alongside her and looked out at the beach. It was winter and the place was deserted. The sky was grey and rain was falling steadily into the pool. Anyone wanting to jump outta life might find this a good day to do it and this lady shouldn't be alone in a cold empty house.

I decided to talk straight. No point in being easy, she would just go back to sleep. 'Mandy came to see me yesterday, before she was killed. She wanted me to find her sister,' I said. Her reaction was surprising. She laughed, a dry croaking sound then the tears came pouring out of her. It sobered her up and she pushed herself upright in the cushioned bamboo chair, brushing the straggles of hair out of her eyes.

She looked for her glass and I handed it to her. One long swallow and she was ready to talk. 'I don't know what you are talking about, Mr...?'

'Charles,' I supplied, 'Danny Charles, private investigator. Your daughter Mandy came to my office. She said she wanted me to find her sister.'

Lady Antonia gave me a sharp look, half surprised, the rest suspicious. 'I don't know why she did that. It doesn't make sense, but I do understand. You've come to me to be paid. Well I'll give you a cheque, if you'll pass my purse, then you can leave and I can carry on drinking.' Her face crumpled. 'You do know that my husband and daughter have been murdered...'

'That's why I'm here,' I said, gruffly. 'Mandy said her sister was in some kinda trouble. Next thing I know, my client and her father have been murdered. That don't rest easy with me. I don't like leaving a job unfinished and it ain't the dollars I'm after.' I guess folk like the Bellinis always think it's about the dough, but it made me sore.

'If it's about Amanda's sister, you can forget it, Mr Charles. She is in London. London, England that is, far away from here, and thankfully out of this sordid mess. Alexandra stayed with her father Lord Hartford when I came here. I brought Amanda with me, more's the pity. By the time I knew something was wrong it was too late.

'I wanted to send her back home out of harm's way, but Joseph wouldn't allow it. I was helpless. It took several broken ribs and more beatings than I can remember. I tried but, God forgive me, I couldn't do anything to stop what was going on.' The tears came again and she closed her eyes, waving me away.

I didn't ask why she hadn't left him. Nobody leaves the Mob except feet first in a wooden box. I could see I wasn't going to get any further with her so I decided to leave and do a bit of investigating on my way out. I found what I was looking for on a desk in what looked like a study, a phone book with a load of numbers I knew were going to be useful.

I slipped it into my pocket just as the maid came to see me out. The cops were arriving as I was leaving. I tipped my hat but I didn't stay around to talk to them. They knew me and knew where to find me anytime they wanted to.

Back at the office I found Roxy on her knees picking up papers. The place had been ransacked while I was out. Roxy had wisely backed out as the thugs had walked in. I guessed they had been looking for the tapes and the china doll Jake had given me. I was sitting looking at it, my head still full of the girl who had been so hot and willing in my arms, when the phone rang.

'Is that Mr Charles?' It coulda been Frosty, same cut-glass accent, except this was a man.

'Yeah. Danny Charles.'

'Oh, thank goodness. You don't know me, Mr Charles. My name is Julian Stokes. I'm calling from London, England and it's about my wife.'

'Yeah.' What's with these English? I thought. Do they think we don't know where London is, or maybe we just seem stupid to them and what about his wife?

'She left here a week ago and was intending to make an appointment to see you Mr Charles. The trouble is I haven't heard from her since and I'm getting worried. Her name is Alexandra Stokes. I just wondered if she had been to see you. It was about her sister, Amanda, I believe.'

I did a double take and took a deep breath. My head was doing rapid sums. Who was dead, Alexandra or Mandy? Lady Antonia thought it was Mandy, I was sure of that. Something heavy was going down. I said the only thing I could.

'Mr Stokes, I think you'd better get yourself over here. Let me know when your flight is arriving and I'll meet you at the airport.'

He didn't argue. 'I'm already booked on a flight today.'

He told me the time and I settled down to do some serious thinking.

4

I was waiting just inside the doors at the airport when I spotted Julian Stokes. Taller than the rest of the dishevelled crowd, he had white hair, the soft kind that fell over his forehead, and blue eyes. A thousand years of English breeding walked towards me with a grim face but an outstretched hand. I was aware of my trilby dripping rain onto my old trench coat and his firm smooth hand made mine feel like a bear's paw.

'Awfully good of you to pick me up, Mr Charles. I hope you haven't had to wait long. Very pleased to meet you.'

'Yeah, likewise,' I muttered. 'Car's waiting.' What could you call a guy with a name like Julian, in New York, I wondered. Julie? Jules? I decided to take Stokes to the beach house and his drunken mother-in-law as soon as I saw him in the crowd of travellers at the airport. As clean-cut and English as Frosty, he woulda drawn too much attention in Lennie's.

We could see the beach house from half a mile away. It was lit up like the fourth of July. Outside a posse of squad cars were standing in the drive. I cut the engine, parked the car across the road and led Julian through the gate into the garden. From there we approached the house by the pool. The cops were just fishing Lady Antonia's fully clothed body out of the water. I could see that she was as dead as her daughter but there was no blood in sight. Joe was the first cop to spot us and sauntered over. 'Looks like suicide, Danny. The maid called us, gave us your name. You were here this afternoon. Maybe the last to see her alive. Want to fill me in before the Chief hears about it?'

'Yeah. I guess I don't have any choice, Joe. I was here asking about her daughter. She was a client before she got bumped off. This is Stokes. He's the English sister's husband, just arrived. I picked him up at the airport.' Joe gave him a curious once over and led the way into the house.

'Your wife's in the house, Mr Stokes. We found her locked in a bedroom. She's been roughed up but we disturbed the bum who did it so she ain't too bad. The guys are out looking for him now. It seems he was asking her about a statue, but she claims she knows nothing about it.' We followed Joe into the white and silver room and there she was, the girl I'd dreamt of last night, except this one was alive.

'Julian, dahling, oh thank Gaard you are here.' And I thought the dame in my office had a cut-glass tongue. This baby could scale the Empire State with hers, but it had a cold edge with no soul. Inside Frosty's icy skin there had been a volcano smouldering.

I remembered the warmth of her body, her skin under my hands and the sweetness of her tongue as I touched it with mine. I walked out of the room, my feelings burning me. I had to know about that statue, which was now hidden away in the secret compartment in my car.

It felt cold as ice in my hands and as I turned from closing the trunk a voice I recognised spat in my ear. 'I'll take that.' It was Jake, come back from near death to claim his prize. 'When I gave it to you, I didn't know how much it was worth but now I do and I want it back.'

I was looking into the muzzle of a gun, but I was in no mood to be beaten. 'Here, take it, punk,' I snarled and as he reached for it, I let go of the figure and knocked the gun up as it fired, then dropped to the ground. The statue smashed into a million shards and among the pieces were a dozen or so large, brilliant stones, diamonds, enough to build a small skyscraper with; the secret that three people had died for and another been lucky to escape with her life.

Before Jake had time to aim again a dozen shots took him down, down to the fancy tiled sidewalk where he came face to face with me. Dying for the second time, he still managed a grotesque twisted grin. 'A thousand bums balled her before me and you never got there, you sad schmuck.'

Luckily the blood spewed out of his mouth and he was dead before I could get my hands round his throat or I woulda had some explaining to do to the cops as they arrived. I got to my feet and strolled back to the house letting my anger go with the smoke from my cigarette and the satisfaction that he was out of my way.

The case was closed – at least for the cops. Jake had wiped out the Bellini family over a diamond racket that they had all been running along with the import export business. I tracked down the real story when the missing Bellini boy, James, came to my office. He wanted my help in escaping the Mob, who had decided to be rid of the only surviving member of the business the Bellinis were involved in.

Although drugs and prostitution, fuelled by murder and extortion, were the foundations on which the Mafia had been built, the Family frowned on anything to do with sex in the underage market and when the Bellini's flourishing business in child pornography had been discovered, they had sent Jake to clean up the mess. Jake had happened on the diamond racket and decided to take it over himself.

That the statue held a fortune in diamonds meant for Amanda's legacy was something Lady Antonia had told him just before he held her head under the water in the pool for the last time. After listening to his story, I did the only thing I could and turned James Bellini in.

In return for giving State's Evidence, James was given a new identity and is now in England somewhere. And living well enough on some of the diamonds I lifted before the cops swept the rest off the sidewalk. The ones I kept just about paid me enough to keep Roxy and myself in work.

My name is Danny Charles. I'm a private dick, and on black nights I sit at my desk and listen to the rain pelting down onto the city streets, beating a tattoo on the sidewalk beneath my window. I think about the night a dame with a figure to give you sweet dreams walked into my office and pointed a toy gun at me. And I wait for the next long-legged broad to walk in.

Bitter Harvest

Val Douglas

It was obvious at birth that Ifan was not wholly normal, thanks to his exceptionally large head, quite out of proportion to the rest of his body except his hands which were also particularly big.

Cassie, however, born in the same week on a neighbouring farm, was the complete opposite. She was perfect in every way. Her mother had longed for a daughter and, gazing at the beautiful child snuggled in her arms, thought she was the luckiest woman in the world. But it was tragedy rather than good fortune that came her way, for five days after Cassie's birth her mother collapsed with a pulmonary embolism and died within minutes.

Ifan's parents, Cynan and Ffion, already had four children and thought their family was complete. They were approaching middle age so it came as something of a surprise when Ifan arrived on the eve of his mother's forty-ninth birthday. His birth was traumatic, the child stuck in the birth canal for hours then, eventually, dragged out with forceps. There was some talk of a lack of oxygen resulting in brain damage and it became clear, as he grew older, that the child had some form of mental handicap.

He was a difficult baby to breast feed, resolutely refusing his mother's milk so that she was in agony with swollen breasts, frantic for the child to suckle. Then came news of her neighbour's sudden death and it seemed only sensible for Ffion to become Cassie's wet nurse. Ifan, meanwhile, took eagerly to the bottle as long as it had a large-holed teat to enable him to swallow maximum milk with minimum effort.

By the time Cassie was weaned she had developed a strong attachment to Ffion, who in turn loved the baby girl dearly. Looking after two infants took little more effort on her part than caring for just one and there was no way Cassie's father, Sean, could cope with a small child, so his daughter came to live with Ifan's family, while Sean repaid them by helping out on their farm. Inevitably, the two children became like siblings growing up side by side.

Ifan, unlike Cassie, was slow to walk, slow to speak, slow to become continent but all these things developed in time, even if later than usual. When the little girl started school Ffion could not see the point of sending Ifan. He would become the butt of cruel jokes, teased about his big head and funny ways, so his mother preferred to keep her last born at her side. She loved him and hardly noticed his loose-lipped drooling mouth, his odd eyes – one set wide open, the other permanently half-closed as if on the verge of a wink. Ffion saw only her gentle little boy with his wide smile and his uncanny affinity with animals.

Even as a small child he was helpful around the farm. At a difficult lambing Ifan would cradle the ewe's head and speak softly, soothing her and enabling his father to deliver the lamb more easily. The bull allowed him to run around its legs and swing its tail, whereas when others came near it would snort and paw the ground. Ffion's hens always clustered around Ifan, clucking and allowing him to caress them, but they ran away from everyone else unless they had food to scatter. Strangely, though, the farm dogs would have nothing to do with him, backing away and growling as he approached, baring their teeth if he came too close.

The boy had a wonderful childhood with loving parents, a 'sister' of his own age for company and freedom to wander the farm to do what he wanted, whenever he wanted. Because he was labelled by the authorities as unsuitable for mainstream schooling the 'backward' lad was allocated a personal tutor for two hours a day, which left him plenty of time for his own pursuits. Although an attentive pupil he made little progress and learned neither to read nor write.

There was a big age gap between Ifan and the boy's brothers and sisters and by the time he was twelve, they had all left home, the sons off to the towns, the girls to live locally. At about the same time Sean decided it was time for Cassie to return to her real family for she was old enough now to cook the meals, do the housework and generally become a useful asset to the household.

This was when Ifan began to wander. He would disappear for three or four days at a time and, on his return, would give no account of where he had been or what he had been doing. At first this worried his parents but he came to no harm and, eventually, they accepted it, just as they accepted everything else about their unusual son, knowing it would be just like him to follow in the tracks of a young fox or another wild animal, for he knew the surrounding land as well as the interior of his own home.

Cynan and Ffion lived hard lives and were becoming frail as they worked their way through their sixties. They found the bitter winters hard to bear and both were racked with arthritis. Then, one particularly cold February, when snow and ice had been around for weeks on end, both succumbed to the influenza that was claiming many lives and Ifan was left an orphan. Sean, well aware that he owed his neighbours a debt of gratitude, agreed to run the farm while Ifan continued living in the wooden shack of a farmhouse. He was quite capable of looking after himself now, though his sisters brought him the odd casserole or pie and did his washing and ironing.

Over the next few years Ifan's wanderings lasted longer – a month, two months – and nobody knew where he went or what he did, but his siblings were busy people and had little time to worry about him. Cassie, meanwhile, had left school and her father was insisting she help out with the farming, as well as running the house, while she decided what she wanted to do with her life. In fact, she intended to marry her boy friend, Huw, and be a wife and mother rather than have a career outside the home.

She was a pretty girl, curly brown hair bouncing around her comely face, big brown eyes and full lips, invariably widened by a smile. Her developing figure, with curving hips and tiny waist, held the promise of an eventually voluptuous body. Ifan became entranced by her. He would follow Cassie as she went about her work, feeling strange stirrings in his body as he watched her. Then, one spring morning, he cornered the unsuspecting girl in the barn, pressing himself against her and pulling at her clothes.

Shocked and alarmed Cassie tried to push him off, 'Stop it, Ifan! Go away! You mustn't do this!'

He silenced her with his hot, moist lips and forced her down onto a fallen hay bale, his huge hands ripping her garments. Ifan knew nothing about sex, other than what he had learned from animals or watched on television, but instinct took over and, almost without realising what he was doing, he raped the struggling girl. When he let her go she was violently sick and ran off, clutching her clothes around her.

Cassie was no stranger to lovemaking but what had happened between her and Ifan had been disgusting and she vomited again at the remembrance of it. What should she do? Suppose she became pregnant? She and Huw always had protected sex and the thought of having a child of Ifan's made her throw up yet again.

Should she tell anyone? Her father would go ballistic and suspect she had encouraged him as, indeed, might her boyfriend. No! She must sort this out herself. She would borrow her brother's car and go to town. There she could get the morning after pill and then at least she would be safe from an unwanted and unexplainable pregnancy.

For the next few days she feigned illness, for she dreaded going anywhere near Ifan, so her father had to do the various jobs on both farms. 'That boy's made off again,' he said on his return. 'Wonder how long he'll be this time?'

Ifan was away longer than he had ever been before. Though nobody knew where he was nobody worried about him, for it had become too common an occurrence. Cassie went back to working on the farm, hoping Ifan would stay away for ever.

Three months later he was back. Cassie was bending over a small enclosure that had been partitioned off inside the big shed, checking on a sick ewe that had injured herself on some barbed wire. She heard a sound behind her and turned round to see Ifan approaching, arms open, a huge smile on his drooling mouth. She backed away, terrified that he would rape her again, sure this was his intention. 'Ifan! Go away. You hurt me.'

'I liked it, Cassie. I like you,' he said softly and came closer.

She looked around desperately for something with which to fend off the lad and grabbed a discarded fencing stake from the corner of the enclosure. He was almost close enough to grab her and, hardly aware of her actions, Cassie whacked the stake against the side of his head with all the strength she could muster. He faltered but did not fall and was reaching for her when, in desperation, she rained blow upon blow onto his head. A puzzled look crossed his face as he crumpled to the ground, bleeding copiously. Shaking with fright and terrified at what she had done, Cassie ran out of the shed and hid behind a pile of boxes, convinced that Ifan would chase and overtake her if she ran for home. She stayed hidden there for an hour or more but no sound came from the shed and Ifan did not reappear. What should she do? Was he unconscious or just waiting to grab her if she came anywhere near him?

She waited another half hour or more, finally coming out of her hiding place to move quietly to the shed and look through a gap in the wall. There was Ifan lying on the floor exactly as she had left him except that now there was a large patch of blood congealing on the straw. She must have hurt him badly. If she called a doctor or the police she would have to tell them about the rape but she had no proof of this. It would be her word against his and she might be charged with assaulting him. As these thoughts whirled through her mind unconsciously she took in that Ifan did not appear to be breathing and suddenly she realised that he was dead. She had killed him. She was a murderer.

Cassie knew she had to hide the body somehow, or, better still, get rid of it. There were stacks of hay bales all around her but if she hid him behind these eventually they would all be used and the body discovered. A better answer might be to set fire to the shed, contents and all, ensuring an enormous blaze and, hopefully, incinerating the body but the thought of the poor sick ewe stopped her. She could not burn it alive and, anyway, the blaze might be discovered and put out before Ifan's body was ashes. For the moment she must just hide him while she thought up a proper plan.

There was a hay field next to the shed, its already long, thick grass foretelling a good crop. No-one on the farm would venture through it to flatten and spoil the yield at this stage so, as long as she could cover her traces, it would be a good place to hide Ifan's body, temporarily at least. Accordingly, she dragged him far enough into the field so that he could not be seen from the edge and on the way back pulled the flattened stalks upright again so there was no evidence of where she had been. At least now she had time to think, time to plan.

Cassie went into the farmhouse to clean herself up and was about to leave for home when she became aware of kites and crows gathering over the hay field. Of course! Stupid woman! From their aerial view the birds could see the promise of a juicy meal and Cassie knew that as soon as she was out of the way they would be tearing the flesh from the bones. There was only one thing for it, the body must be moved back to the shed.

Sobbing with exhaustion and the sudden realisation of the enormity of her crime she dragged Ifan out again through the hay, its sweet smell mingling with that created by hot sun on dried blood. Ifan's body felt twice as heavy now and it was with some difficulty that she dragged him back into the shed and behind some hay bales. It would just have to do for the time being. She kicked up the track she had left in the hay in a desultory way, too tired to make much of a job of it this time, and left for home.

That evening, alone in her room, Cassie mulled over various options. Should she just bury the body? But there had been a long, dry spell and the ground was rock hard. The sea was some miles away, but she could borrow her brother's car again and throw Ifan over the cliffs into the water, hoping he would be washed out to sea. But what if he were washed straight back again and identified. How could she render him unrecognisable?

Cassie was every inch a farmer's daughter, moreover, a pig farmer's daughter and from an early age she had experienced every aspect of what this entailed, including the illegal undercover slaughter and cutting up of the occasional pig when one was wanted for the family table. Well, she supposed, a human body couldn't be that different. With these thoughts in mind she polished her plan.

The two most recognisable parts of Ifan were his head and his hands, so these she would remove. Then she would take the torso to the coast and pitch it into the sea. Even if it were washed up it could not be identified readily and no-one would suspect it was Ifan, because he would not have been reported missing given that he had disappeared for months at a time on many previous occasions.

The next day, when her father and brothers had gone to market, Cassie gathered together some black plastic bags and the necessary tools and went over to the neighbouring farm, steeling herself to her unpleasant task. In fact, it was much easier than she expected and before long the deed was done – Ifan's torso wrapped in black plastic ready to be transported. She had decided to dispose of the head and hands in different parts of a notorious quagmire some miles away. Whole sheep were known to have been sucked down into the quaking mud, never to be seen again, and she remembered, in her childhood, watching her brothers toss boulders into the mire and seeing them sink under its muddy surface. This would deal with the head and hands, but there was no way she would risk getting close enough to tip in Ifan's torso or she might well vanish into the quagmire alongside it.

First, though, she must clear up and remove all traces of what had happened here. The blood soaked straw, and the blood splashed apron she had worn, Cassie burnt where Ifan sited his occasional bonfires. Then she rolled the wrapped body behind some bales, to be collected in the morning. The head and hands she decided to hide temporarily inside some hay bales. She was a dextrous young woman and it was an easy task for her to hollow out a space in the centre of a couple of bales. She pushed the head inside one and then replaced the hay she had pulled out. Now the bale looked the same as it always had and its contents could stay safely hidden until she got back from the coast. The hands she hid in the same way, satisfied that nothing unusual would be spotted.

To begin with everything went according to plan. She borrowed her brother's car – after telling him she wanted to check out a few hotels in the small seaside town where she and Huw planned to spend their upcoming honeymoon. Very early in the morning she lifted her grisly load into the boot and made for the coast, the dawn promising yet another hot and dry day. Already she was worrying in case the head and hands should begin to stink and attract vermin. It was easier than she'd expected to find a sufficiently secluded spot and tip Ifan's torso over a cliff into the sea when the tide was on the turn. The body sank as it hit the water and she hoped it was never to be seen again.

It had been such an exceptionally hot, dry summer. When you walked across the grass it cracked and broke underfoot, large fissures zigzagged across the pastures, a heavy heat haze hung in the air. How long, Sean wondered, before thunder storms threatened. Surveying his fields he decided the time had come to cut the hay. Early rain had ensured a plentiful crop this year, the sun had brought it to perfection but it had to be cut, turned, baled and brought in before the weather broke. There was the crop on Ifan's neighbouring farm to be dealt with, as well as his own.

Sean knew there was some of last year's crop remaining in Ifan's shed that would have to be cleared out to make room for the fresh, better quality hay. He'd do that first, he decided, it wouldn't take long. He would put aside a few of the best bales but the rest could be piled up somewhere and left to rot down.

Back at the coast, Cassie started for home. Suddenly she realised the speedometer was pointing to zero although she was travelling quite fast. In fact, none of the dials on the dashboard were functioning. In a panic she stopped the car, then turned on the ignition again. Nothing happened.

The alternator had failed. A new one, according to the garage, could be ordered and fitted by the next afternoon. Cassie cursed inwardly at the thought of being stuck here overnight. She phoned home to tell the family, hoping that Huw or her father might drive over to pick her up but they were too busy with haymaking and could not spare the time. Huw suggested she try out one of the hotels, even promised to pay for it as a pre-wedding treat. This she did but slept badly, too worried to enjoy the unaccustomed luxury.

Next day Cassie waited impatiently for the car to be fixed, striding up and down outside the garage, to the mechanic's annoyance, and by the time she set off for home she felt sick with apprehension. As she neared the farm the sweet smell of newly mown hay filled the car. They had probably cut Ifan's too, Cassie thought, and thanked her lucky stars she had changed her mind about leaving any bits of him in the hay field. She decided she would retrieve his head and hands now and drive straight over to the quagmire. Then it would all be over.

Relief turned to shock when she found an empty shed facing her. Where were the bales? Had Ifan's remains been found? Frantically she looked round, then saw bales heaped in a far corner of the yard and realised the impossibility of identifying the ones she had tampered with. She could think of only one way to deal with this. During the night Cassie stole out of the house, taking care not to wake her father and hushing the dog. Crossing to Ifan's yard she set fire to the heap of old bales. The flames took hold quickly and within minutes the stack was blazing beyond the point of no return. Praying Sean would not hear her; she crept back into the house and watched the fire through her bedroom window.

Eventually woken by the barking of dogs and the smell of smoke, which had wafted across the intervening fields, Sean, still groggy from sleep, stumbled across to find that the fire had almost burnt itself out. Fortunately it was a still night and there was nothing flammable nearby so he contented himself with just damping down the embers, thankful that it had happened before this year's hay was in. How it had started remained a mystery, but Sean thought he could make a pretty good guess: 'Bloody kids!'

At last Cassie relaxed, convinced that all traces of her crime had been removed. Now she could get on with life and look forward to her wedding. This euphoria lasted all of a week – until Sean decided to use one of the hay bales he had put aside. His Border Collie bitch, Meg, was due to whelp and was looking around for somewhere to give birth. This time rather than discover she had chosen some inappropriate spot such as the utility room (as happened on a previous whelping when she refused all human entry for several days, causing much inconvenience), the choice would be Sean's. He blocked off a corner of the disused stable with some sturdy planks, placing them low enough for Meg to jump over but high enough to prevent the pups escaping. He decided too that their bed would be of soft hay and not his old jacket, which Meg had purloined last time. Leaning over the planks, he cut the baler twine and shook out the hay. As it tumbled down, out fell Ifan's head, in the early stages of decomposition but still recognisable.

Shocked as he was, Sean had the presence of mind to gather up the head before Meg could get at it. Even his many years as a farmer had not prepared him for anything like this – a pig's head was one thing but a human one, especially that of someone he knew, was something else. He ran to the house, bursting into the kitchen with Ifan's head cradled in his hands, 'Cassie! Get on the phone to the police! Look what I've found!' She turned from the sink and, when she saw what her father held, collapsed in a dead faint. 'Bloody women,' cursed Sean. 'Want something done, do it yourself!' He grabbed the phone and dialled 999 and reported his find to the police.

Cassie revived to see Ifan's face staring at her, blotched and decomposing, his injuries clearly visible, but still wearing the same puzzled expression as when she killed him. She screamed, ran out of the house and across the fields, refusing to come back until after the police had collected Sean's gruesome find.

It was obviously a murder case but little had been found in the way of clues. To Sean's disgust the police insisted on splitting open all the remaining hay bales. Ifan's hands were recovered but no other body parts and, eventually, the investigation came to an end. A coroner gave a verdict of murder by person or persons unknown and gradually everybody pushed it to the backs of their minds. Everybody except Cassie. Each night when she went to bed Ifan's face swam before her eyes as she closed them for sleep. She saw the huge head, the drooling mouth, the mismatched eyes. It was if a haunting was her punishment.

Cassie married her boyfriend, Huw, as planned and soon became pregnant. Perhaps, she thought, when she was busy with a baby to care for she would finally be rid of Ifan and her memories. Huw desperately wanted their first child to be a son, though Cassie was hoping for a little girl. Nevertheless, she was pleased for her husband when a scan showed that the baby was definitely a boy. Cassie went into labour on her due date, having decided to give birth in the comfort of her own home. She was a strong young woman but it soon became obvious that things were not going well. All her strength and determination were insufficient to push out the baby and what she had expected to be an easy labour went on for a long and difficult time. She could see that the midwife was getting worried and was not surprised when the ambulance was summoned and she was whisked into the nearest hospital. There, with Cassie high on gas and air, her baby was born with the aid of a ventouse vacuum extraction and forceps. As he was delivered Cassie was vaguely aware of the midwife saying, 'No wonder he took a long time to pop out, just look at the size of his head! They should have seen this on a scan and booked her in for a caesarean.' Cassie heard, also, Huw's sharp intake of breath as he took his son from the nurse. 'Is he all right?' The doctor led Huw to one side, 'It's a bit early to tell but a long labour like this can sometimes lead to oxygen starvation and brain damage, though try not to worry. He appears to be a strong, healthy baby. Just look at those great big mitts. He'll make a fine farmhand. We'll just run a few little tests...'

Killing the Village Cat

Jan Baker

He hadn't meant to shoot the cat but now that he had he was glad. Month after month of sitting in his wheelchair watching the moggie from the Cat and Fiddle digging holes in his front garden and defaecating in full view of him, had finally had an effect. Iolo Griffiths had been blamed for the cat's demise; everyone in the village of Pont Losin knew of his expertise with an air gun, as Glyn Jones, minus one eye, could blinkingly testify.

It was all the Prince of Wales' fault of course. If he'd had his new knees when they'd promised, instead of using a shortage of beds as an excuse, he might have chased the offending feline off his property without having to resort to guerrilla tactics.

Emlyn Protheroe opened the lid of the window seat; the air gun belonging to his deceased brother Arwel lay out of sight under a tartan rug.

'Bamps, Bamps guess what?' Owen, burst into the room dragging his schoolbag behind him. 'Dad said I can go on the school trip to Austria next January. I'll be skiing, Bamps.'

Emlyn quickly closed the lid and smiled. Owen, with his eager face and dark hair falling into his eyes, stood in front of him hopping from one foot to the other in excitement. The slight feeling of regret he'd had about the cat was replaced by a surge of love so strong that it brought tears to his eyes.

He could see Maria in the boy's eyes. He'd met her when he

139

was stationed in Cyprus during his National Service. Now that she was gone, Owen was his main reason for getting up in the morning.

'Good for you my lad,' Emlyn replied, 'And you can tell your father not to worry about spending money and buying all those fancy clothes you'll need; I'll see to that.'

The boy bent down, slid his arms around his neck and kissed his cheek. A boy smell of school dinners, bubble gum and cheesy socks filled Emlyn's nostrils and his chest swelled with pride.

'Dad said I could help him cut your lawn tomorrow, if it's fine,' Owen said fetching a biscuit and a cup of milk from the kitchen.

'What about school?'

'Incest day,' Owen mumbled, his mouth full of biscuit.

Emlyn was about to correct him, then thought better of it; knowing the villagers as he did maybe he wasn't so far off the mark after all.

Later, he watched Owen running down the path and into the lane, turning, as usual at the gate to wave him goodbye. His schoolbag was fixed to his back like a tortoise's shell and as he ran one sock stayed up whilst the other curled around his ankle like a boa constrictor. After waiting until his dark hair could no longer be seen above the hedge, Emlyn settled down to enjoy his favourite pastime.

The view from the bay window of the bungalow was the main reason Maria and he had bought the place all those years ago. He looked down the garden towards the village. From his perch on the hill he felt like Gulliver; below him stood the church steeple rising towards the sky like an accusing finger, the roof of the Methodist Chapel, grey and uncompromising and beyond it, the Cat and Fiddle's sign swinging in the breeze. He noticed the queue outside the chip shop snaking around the corner and slithering towards the dry cleaners, every detail spread out before him like an animated map. Then, shifting his gaze towards the sea, he watched the waves sliding back on each other like a pile of envelopes tipping towards the shore. Cotton wool clouds drifted on the breeze towards the headland and for a fleeting moment he longed for his youth when he had run along the beach and dived into the sea without a care in the world.

Out of the corner of his eye he saw a red hat and sighed in exasperation. Maggie Morris, fresh from the Methodist mothers' meeting, was walking up his path carrying a cake tin under her arm.

Again he cursed The Prince of Wales. More years than he could remember of paying his National Health contributions and what had he ever got in return? Treatment for piles and an in-growing toenail and a lot of good that had done him, he thought bitterly. He'd had an infected toenail for nearly three months after the op, and as for his piles, he preferred not to think about that indignity; suffice to say that he couldn't look at a bunch of grapes without wincing.

'Mr Protheroe, it's only me. Let myself in shall I?'

He silently cursed the key that was sheltering under the flowerpot near the front door and whose resting place was known throughout the village. Gritting his teeth he bemoaned the fact that, if he'd had his new knees, he wouldn't have been a captive audience for the likes of Maggie Morris.

'Mrs Morris,' he said, even though she kept insisting that he call her Maggie; somehow he couldn't quite bring himself to attempt that familiarity fearing what doors it might open. 'And what can I do for you?'

She was like an overstuffed sofa. Mounds of floppy floral-covered flesh protruded from the confines of her jacket thrusting their way over the waistband of her pleated skirt.

She'd set her cap at him after they'd buried Maria. It had

begun with the cakes. She'd baked so many that, had he eaten them all, he'd have had more than his knees to worry about. Then there were her regular visits, each one becoming more prolonged and cloyingly familiar than the last.

Maggie put the kettle on; he wished she wasn't quite so accustomed to his kitchen; then with a slice of cake in one hand and a cup of tea in the other, she sat opposite him 'for a chat'.

'How are we today Em?'

She made it sound like a threat; he could see the trap a mile away. If he said he was under the weather she'd take it upon herself to cook and clean for him; he shuddered at the prospect, imagining her poking into his cupboards or worse, finding what was hidden in the window seat. On the other hand, if he said that he was feeling fine then she was certain to suggest a day out, which would include a trip to the Chapel, where she would show him off to any straggling members of the flock who might be lingering inside its walls, followed by a vigorous push along the prom. A fate worse than death in his opinion.

'I'm as well as can be expected Mrs Morris.' Emlyn answered with caution. 'Of course I can't answer for you now, can I?'

Maggie didn't do irony, he thought – ironically.

He took the plate she offered him and sank his teeth into a slice of fruit cake, the consistency of which would have been the envy of the council workers repairing the pot holes in the lane. He felt it clinging to his back teeth, the rock hard raisins slipping under his plate like pellets. Easing his false teeth from the roof of his mouth with the tip of his tongue, he surreptitiously dislodged the intruders.

'How's the cake?' Maggie asked.

'Up to your usual standard Mrs Morris', he replied sucking his teeth back into place and leaving the rest of the cake uneaten on his plate.

'Have you heard the latest about that Catherine Thomas?'

As she spoke, Emlyn noticed crumbs of fruitcake clinging to the coarse grey hairs above her upper lip like the barnacles on the bottom of Tom Eynon's boat. He watched transfixed, waiting for them to fall. Her lips, devoid of lipstick, smacked against each other; two thin desiccated lines, as unattractive as it was possible for a woman's lips to be.

'She's been shortchanging the verger again.'

Emlyn refused to be drawn into stating the obvious.

'And she had the cheek to call you 'Em'. I said to her, "Mr Protheroe to you; only his friends and family are allowed to call him Em."'

He spluttered into his teacup imagining what Catherine's reply would be to that.

When she had finished her character assassinations of his friends and neighbours, Maggie left him. He watched her red hat disappearing down the lane and was surprised, soon after, to see another figure stop at his gate, raise her hand to him, hitch her mini skirt up an inch or two, then trot up his path, high heels clacking like castanets.

Catherine Thomas sat in the chair so recently warmed by Maggie's rear end and leaned forward, treating Emlyn to an uninterrupted view of her cleavage and the lace on her new 'push-me-up' bra that she'd bought from the catalogue.

'Fancy a pint in the Cat?' she asked. 'I've got the rest of the afternoon off.'

It was her usual opening gambit followed by what she knew his reply would be: 'Maybe next week when the weather improves', after which, as usual, he propelled his wheelchair to the cabinet where he kept a bottle of his best malt whisky. Emlyn was no fool; he knew she'd never any intention of wheeling him to the pub.

She was what his Maria would have called, 'a flighty piece'.

Past her best, it was true, but still a looker. Eyes put in with a smutty finger, black rimmed and promising; long legs encased in shimmering black tights, covering age scars and broken veins. If you ignored the myriad lines around her eyes and mouth and the black-rooted blonde hair, she could pass for forty-five.

In a way the subject matter of Catherine's conversation resembled Maggie's but that was where all traces of similarity ended. 'I spent all yesterday afternoon at the infirmary with that bad tempered old devil from next door,' she said. 'He'd fallen off a ladder trying to clean his windows – too mean to pay for a window cleaner.' She drained her glass and held it out for a refill. 'I did laugh though; when the nurse asked him to name his next of kin, he said "Jesus Christ".'

Emlyn felt laughter bubbling up inside like a volcano threatening to erupt; laughter that had been in short supply since Maria's death.

Sensing her audience was primed Catherine said, 'The nurse was writing it down – actually writing it down, before she realized.'

Emlyn was still chuckling half an hour later as he watched Catherine leave, swinging her hips as she teetered down his path. He knew she was doing it for effect and she was bang on target.

The next day, when Emlyn had another visit from Owen, he was shocked to see a large bruise and a cut above his grandson's eye. The full extent of the boy's injuries becoming apparent as Owen came closer. 'Good heavens lad, what have you been up to?'

Owen was evasive, muttering something about a disagreement, but Emlyn knew there was more to it; the lad was subdued and in no time made an excuse about having to do homework. His grandson's visit left a bad taste in his mouth.

Anguish allied itself to his frustration, leaving him determined to seek an explanation for Owen's battered condition. But as it turned out, revelation was to come from a totally unexpected source.

It was later that day, Emlyn's heart sinking as he watched Maggie Morris striding towards his front door (thankfully minus her cake tin), determination in every step. It was beginning to rain and, as she sat in the chair opposite him, he noticed a fine layer of drizzle, like a cobweb covering her grey hair.

Emlyn groaned inwardly as he anticipated the sniping that was bound to come, directed no doubt at her neighbours and fellow Chapel members, acid flowing and arrows flying in all directions. But to his surprise she said, 'I bet you were mad; she's gone too far this time.'

'Mad?'

'That Catherine Thomas wants flaying alive for what she did to your Owen.'

His usual disinterest in her conversation was set aside at the sound of his grandson's name. He sat forward in his wheelchair.

'Owen?' he queried at the risk of sounding like a simpleton.

'I saw her laying in to him in the alleyway at the back of the chip shop. I was cleaning the window in my back passage, so I saw it all. I couldn't believe how vicious she was. She punched and pushed him against the wall and then she gave him such a kick on his shins as he tried to get away. Those heels of hers are lethal at the best of times; they don't call them stilettos for nothing. I opened the window and shouted but it was no use, she wasn't going to stop for anyone…'

The rest of her conversation floated above his head as a black cloud gathered and a knot tightened in his insides forcing bile into the back of his throat.

The next day, Emlyn telephoned his son.

'Ask Owen to pop in on his way home from school, Gareth.

I'd like to give him the money I promised him, for his school trip.'

He silenced Gareth's protestations and went to find his cheque book.

The sun was casting elongated shadows across the lawn when he heard his front door open. Owen's bruised eye was now a dull shade of purple and at the sight of him, the knot in Emlyn's stomach twisted and tightened until he thought he could bear the pain no longer.

'Right my lad: I know who did this to you!' He waved a hand in the region of Owen's injuries. 'And now I want your version.'

Owen glanced at the floor, the window, the ceiling and back again. If he was thinking about lying the glint in his grandfather's eyes decided him against it.

'She was out the back of the chip shop with Gwen, that mate of hers,' he said. 'It was incest day and so we were playing about in the village. Huw had kicked our ball over the wall and I was going to get it. They were shouting. I thought they were arguing at first. Then I heard her say: "I can wind him around my little finger." Owen shifted from one foot to the other. Then she said, "If I have my way I'll be married to him by Christmas and I'll get my hands on that bungalow." He hung his head. 'She said, "He won't last long. Not if I have anything to do with it." And then they both started to laugh.' Owen hesitated, waiting for some sort of response.

'Go on.'

'But I got really mad when she talked about Grammy Maria.' The boy sat on the window seat, his face turned away from Emlyn. 'She said that one of the first things she'd do would be to get rid of that horrible collection of china figures and that chair that was like a throne. "His wife had terrible taste but I'll soon change that; I'll go on a spending spree after the wedding,

146

he's bound to be loaded," she said. I couldn't stand it. I told her not to speak like that. I hate her Bamps. I hate that tom cat.'

'Don't let her hear you calling her that or she might finish off what she started, my lad.'

Emlyn tried to make light of it for the boy's sake but afterwards, when Owen was standing at the gate waving goodbye, the anger that had been torturing him since Maggie's visit erupted like a red mist before his eyes.

That night he had a dream. On waking it hung at the edges of his consciousness like a bad smell. He'd been watching the cat from the chip shop laying into Owen; its fur was standing on end and its teeth sank into the young boy's flesh as if it was biting through butter. As it raised its head it morphed into Catherine Thomas and he heard Maria's voice: 'You've got to do something, Em.'

He heard the voice again later that day as he sat at the window. Gareth had trimmed his lawn and tidied the borders earlier that week and beyond, in the lane, the hedges stood proudly displaying their summer greenery. In the village the church steeple rose to meet the evening sun that dappled the roof of the Methodist chapel, fingered the fruit and veg spread out in front of the grocer's shop and glinted off the metal rungs of the window cleaner's ladder as he hoisted it over his shoulder. The chip shop stood in shadow but the figure of Catherine Thomas was unmistakable as she tottered past. Soon he heard the clatter of heels coming up his path.

She sat on the edge of Maria's chair and cast a contemptuous gaze over the collection of china figurines; Emlyn wondered why he hadn't noticed it before. Then she leaned forward and said slyly, 'I've always loved this view, Em.'

His knees might need attention but there was nothing wrong with his eyesight or the aim he'd perfected during his National Service. No one knew of the air gun he kept hidden

147

in the window seat.

'I've got something for you,' he said. 'A present. It's on the table in the kitchen – would you like to go and get it?'

The following day Emlyn decided the time had come to charge up the motorised disability scooter that was in the garage. He hadn't liked to use it before. It reminded him of Maria and the problems she'd had after the accident. He couldn't wait any longer for the Prince of Wales to get their act together and needs must when the devil drives, he thought.

Later, he parked the scooter in the garage and went to bed exhausted. He was still tired the next morning and had been dozing in his chair when he heard a commotion in the hallway. Owen, red faced and out of breath, burst into the room.

'Owen! What are you doing here?' Emlyn glanced at his watch. It was mid-day.

'I had to come, Bamps. You didn't kill her did you? You didn't kill that tom cat?'

Emlyn sighed, 'Of course I didn't kill her. I might be mad but I'm not crazy. What makes you think I'd do such a thing? Go down for a bag of chips then you'll see her, large as life.'

'I won't. She's dead. They found her in the alleyway behind the Chapel. Dad's been up all night. He said CID were coming down from Cardiff and he didn't want there to be any foul-ups.'

'And you thought I'd killed her?'

'I knew you were mad after I told you what she said and Dad said only the other day that you were a crack shot in the army.' Owen sat down in a heap, relief shining out of his dark eyes.

'Make us a drink and cut some cake, then you must go back to school.' Emlyn said, trying to appear normal.

He bided his time, knowing that Gareth would have his

hands full; then the next day he drove into the village. Gareth was getting into a police car outside the station. He looked harassed. Emlyn waited until he'd driven out of sight and then continued on towards the Methodist Chapel.

He guessed that Maggie had been too busy gossiping about Catherine's death to find the time to climb up the hill to see him. He knew to expect a visit by the weekend but had decided to take matters into his own hands.

She was talking to one of her cronies on the chapel steps when Emlyn drew up at her side.

'Mrs. Morris, I wonder if you could spare me a moment of your precious time?' he asked.

An astonished Maggie turned away from her friend. 'Em! You've got transport!'

'It would seem so. Perhaps you'd like to join me in the coffee shop on the sea front – in half an hour?'

He noticed that she flushed with pleasure, her status immediately elevated in the eyes of any onlookers in general and her friend in particular.

'If you wait I'll push...'

'No need Mrs. Morris,' he cut her short. 'As you said, I have my own transport.'

Later, a melamine-topped table separating them, Emlyn decided to get to the point sooner rather than later.

'Who d'you think shot Catherine then?' he asked, biting into a jam doughnut.

'Half the men in Pont Losin have reason, that's for sure. If anyone had her mind set on ruining a relationship that one had. I was telling Gwyneth Jenkins from the library that no man was safe from her clutches.' Maggie, showers of sugar falling from her chin, continued: 'Well, you'd know that better than anyone, Em. She had her sights set on you before Maria was cold in the ground.'

Emlyn spluttered and coughed. 'Who in particular, besides

me, did she have on the go?'

'They say she'd been messing around with the window cleaner but I'm not so sure. Guto wouldn't hurt a fly. And he's got more sense than to get mixed up with her. And she'd be at least ten years older than him.'

Emlyn frowned.

'That's a lot of ands to consider.'

Maggie straightened her back.

'How long have you had that?' she asked curling her lip in the direction of his scooter.

'It was Maria's,' he replied.

He could see the implication of him having his own transport had dawned on her; he might no longer need her assistance. Trying to keep her on side he said, 'Anyhow we wouldn't be here enjoying the view without it, would we?'

Brightening somewhat, Maggie said: 'I'll keep my ear to the ground then, Em, shall I? See what I can find out?'

He nodded. 'That's the idea. Now, if you'll excuse me I can see Gareth on the sea front. I need to speak to him urgently.'

He left her outside the coffee shop and drove towards his son as fast as the limitations of his vehicle would allow.

'Hello Dad.' Gareth eyed him with what looked like a mixture of surprise and irritation. 'Owen said you were mobile.'

'Owen also said he thought I'd killed Catherine Thomas.'

'He said *what?*' Gareth spluttered.

'Yes, well never mind that. Tell me what's going on. Have they found anyone yet?'

'Look, Dad, it might have escaped your notice, but I'm on duty. Why don't I stop by at your place when I've finished my shift?'

Emlyn could see he would have to be satisfied with that, so, coaxing his vehicle into completing a full circle, he sped away and up the hill, leaving Gareth shaking his head.

Half way home he saw Gwen Griffiths coming out of the

hairdresser's. Her eyes were red from crying. When she saw him she hung her head.

'Sorry to hear about Catherine,' he said coming to a stop in front of her. 'Bad business.'

Gwen took a hanky from her sleeve and dabbed her eyes. Like Catherine, she had made brave attempts to hold back the tide of time but in the harsh sunlight Emlyn thought she looked every inch her age. She wore a pink overall with the name 'Cute Cuts' embroidered on it. The letters stretched over her well-upholstered chest as she fumbled in her pocket for cigarettes. 'Can't do without these now,' she muttered. 'I'd given them up too.'

'We all need help when we lose someone close.'

Emlyn was thinking about the weeks after Maria's death. Gwen's face screwed up like a discarded tissue. She took two puffs from the cigarette, ground it under her heel then disappeared into the hairdressers.

It was gone eight when Gareth arrived. He looked tired as he slumped in the chair opposite his father. Emlyn poured them both a stiff whisky and listened to Gareth sounding off about the CID officers from Cardiff.

'Do they have any idea who could have done it?' he asked.

'Not really. They've got the forensic boys working on it. But if you ask me it has to be someone local.'

'Why?'

'You know Catherine, Dad; she got up a few people's noses, to say the least.'

'Not enough to kill her though, surely?'

Gareth closed his eyes and sighed. 'No, I expect you're right. Funny though: who would use an air gun with intent to kill? They couldn't be sure of the outcome.'

'Where was she shot?' Emlyn asked.

'In the alley behind the Chapel.' Gareth replied yawning.

'You daft beggar! I know where she was found. What part of her body suffered the fatal shot?'

Gareth gave a wry grin, looking exactly like Owen. Emlyn felt a flutter around his heart. How proud Maria had been when he'd joined the police force. They both had her smile, and when it happened, he felt her presence like a warm breeze stroking his cheek.

'Straight through the brain.' Gareth's words brought Emlyn out of his reverie.

When he was alone Emlyn opened the window seat. He'd been disturbed by what Gareth had said. Unwrapping the air gun from the folds of the tartan rug, he breathed a sigh of relief. Anyone might have found it; Owen, Maggie, old Mrs Evans who cleaned every Tuesday, even Guto Harris the window cleaner. Emlyn always left the latch undone on the bay window so that Guto could clean the inside; the window seat was hardly a million miles away.

The next morning dawned with rain clouds threatening on the horizon. As soon as Emlyn had eaten his breakfast he saw Maggie, depressing as the weather, always the willing bearer of bad news. She'd accosted the paper boy, it seemed, as she was carrying his morning paper under her arm

'Not too early am I?' she asked, not waiting for a reply. 'I've got some news.' She sank into an armchair opposite him. 'I was talking to Millie Beynon about her hysterectomy when I saw the police car stop at number twelve. Guto was frog-marched down his path and into the police car by two plain clothes men, probably the ones from Cardiff.'

Emlyn frowned.

'I hope you'll excuse me, Mrs Morris, there's something I have to do.'

Maggie looked on in astonishment as Emlyn revved up his scooter and disappeared down the drive.

'Bye then,' she called after him.

He had to put things right. Guto Harris was no killer; besides he couldn't hit a barn door, let alone a bull's eye, as Gareth had discovered when, as teenagers, they had both joined an archery club run by their sports master.

Outside Owen's school gates Emlyn waited until morning play time arrived. Catching sight of his grandfather, Owen ran over.

'Like the scooter, Bamps!'

'Owen, tell me: you know the day you heard Catherine and Gwen talking behind the chip shop – the day she gave you a hiding? You said you thought they'd been arguing. Any idea what it was about?'

Owen shrugged. 'Er, it was about Guto Harris. Gwen sounded mad. I think she accused Catherine of messing about with him. I wasn't too bothered about all that until I heard Catherine talking about you. Now that I come to think about it, I suppose she might have been trying to put Gwen off the scent – by saying she was after you, I mean.'

Leaving the school gates, Emlyn drove down the hill to the police station. Gareth was in the car park with Constable Morgan. He walked over to Emlyn, muttering something under his breath. 'Dad,' he said, 'I'm up to my eyes in it here. The Cardiff lot are demanding forensic results, which haven't arrived. Guto Harris has been brought in. There's paperwork to do.'

'You've got the wrong bloke, my lad. You should know better than anyone – Guto's no crack shot. Try talking to Gwen Griffiths. Ask her how she felt about Catherine seeing Guto behind her back. Oh, and ask her if it was her brother Iolo who taught her how to shoot.'

As usual it was Maggie who was the first to tell him that Gwen Griffiths had been charged with the murder of Catherine Thomas, Gareth confirming the fact an hour or so later.

Afterwards Emlyn sat in his favourite chair watching the sun setting over the sea and casting shadows over the rooftops of the village he loved.

He raised the lid of the window seat and smiled. Owen would make a good detective. He was the only one who had guessed.

It was well known in the village of Pont Losin that Iolo Griffiths was a crack shot with an air gun and now it seemed that his sister had followed in his footsteps. The pair had been in their mid-thirties when they'd killed Maria. Gwen had been fooling around with an air gun and was shooting at seagulls on the sea front. They'd said it was an accident. Maria had been shot in the leg. Infection set in. She never did use the disability scooter.

He hadn't meant to shoot the cat but now that he had, he was glad.

The Emerald Earring

Sue Anderson

Swaying on its golden wire, the emerald flashed in the firelight, sending out little sparks. 'So what are you going to do now?' he said. She couldn't see him properly – the firelight had given him a gold halo but his face was in shadow. She thought about it: it hadn't been easy, stealing something so valuable. It took nerve. She couldn't have done it without him.

The trouble with walking to work was that Lizzie's shoes had holes in them and when it rained her feet got wet. That was how she bumped into William – picking her way round the puddles, not looking where she was going. He held her steady, and in that split second took away all rational thought. Then he offered to buy her a coffee and began to change her life. She thought he was wonderful, but wasn't sure she could afford him. And he couldn't afford the coffee: she ended up paying the bill.

'I need to be rich,' he said one afternoon, when she had refused a job from the agency for the second time that month, and they had been window-shopping. 'I'm an aristocrat by nature. I have good connections. It's not my fault my father was stupid with money.'

'What did he do?'

'Made bad business investments. He was gullible, always thought the best of everybody. And he was a sucker for a sob story.'

They were in the bedroom of his shabby little flat. The wallpaper was faded and the curtains didn't meet. 'He's right,' thought Lizzie, 'He doesn't fit here. He's like a great golden lion, stuck in a cage.'

'Never mind,' she said. 'I'm sure something will come along. Like you did for me. It's just a case of surviving.'

William sighed, 'Some people are good at making do, but I'm sick of it – juggling the money, robbing one credit card to pay another.' He rolled over and smoothed her tousled hair.

'Time for desperate measures, my love.'

It was cold and the blankets were scratchy. She pulled the worn silk eiderdown up over her shoulders. 'What on earth do you mean? Are you going to rob a bank?' She was half afraid of the answer, but he shook his head.

'Not a bank, no.' There was a long silence. He looked into her eyes, and just for a second Lizzie had the feeling she was being assessed, like some prize animal in a show. Then he kissed her and the moment passed.

'My darling,' he whispered. 'My lovely, auburn darling. You know I adore you.' Nobody had ever said that to her before. Love was cheap; adoration was rarer.

'What do you want me to do?' she asked.

'Oh, nothing too difficult.' He lay back on the pillow, gathering her into the crook of his arm. 'Let me tell you about it. You see, there's this old woman who lives in a big house just across the park. Mrs Pomeroy, she's called. She's rolling in it, and she'd be so easy to steal from.'

She glanced at him: his golden curls were rumpled and his blue eyes were innocent. He looked like a little boy.

'You are joking, aren't you?'

'I'm perfectly serious. I told you, it's a piece of cake. All you have to do is get in there. Become part of the household.'

A little trickle of panic ran down her spine. 'Me?'

'Yes.' He leaned over towards her, eyes twinkling, full of excitement. 'And I've got the perfect plan.'

'What do you mean?'

'Well it just so happens she's advertising for a dog-walker. I saw it in the local rag. Hang on a minute.' He rolled out of bed, dragging the eiderdown with him, and went into the sitting room. A few seconds later he returned with the paper. 'Now where the hell...? Oh, here it is: "Young person, well-groomed, wanted to exercise pedigree dog. Must be physically fit and of good character. References essential..." You see? You'd be perfect.' He saw her face and frowned. 'It's not as if you have a proper job, is it?'

She was a little offended. Temping was hard work and she'd taken every offer that came her way. At least, she had before she met him.

'Why can't you apply?' she said, 'You don't have a job at all.' It was a silly question. William obviously wasn't cut out to be a hired helper. He was much more at home hanging around in fashionable bars, browsing expensive shops, chatting to people who might possibly buy him dinner.

But his answer was unexpected: 'She wouldn't have me in the house,' he said casually. 'She hates my guts.'

Lizzie gave him a hard stare. 'What reason could she possibly have to hate you? She doesn't even know you.'

He was grinning now, in that way of his which made her stomach flip over. 'Oh but she does. Rather well actually. And I'm afraid she has plenty of reasons.'

'What do you mean?'

'Well, you see, I'm part of the family. Her nephew, to be exact. She's known me since I was a horrible little brat. She used to invite me to tea every other Sunday, and my darling mother insisted I went. I think she was hoping I'd worm my way into Auntie's good books. But I hated it, and being a spoilt little monster, I'd play jokes, put slugs in the cups, plant fake dog-dirt on the carpet, that sort of thing. Must have driven the old girl nuts.' His laugh was not at all remorseful.

'Of course, since Mum died I'm the closest relative. So you see, my love, it all comes to me sooner or later. I'm just anticipating a bit.'

'What about the references?' Lizzie said weakly. 'I'm not sure if the agency will give me any.' She would need time to deal with this. He seemed to think it was all a joke, but for her it was a serious step. She'd never done anything remotely illegal before.

'Oh, don't worry. I'll take care of that. I can write you a testimonial that will knock her socks off. Just give me a few minutes to check your credentials.' He pulled the blankets over them and there was no more talk for a while, just laughter and magic.

The first time Lizzie saw the earring it was on an elegant female with rippling russet hair and wonderful cheekbones, who was reclining on a red velvet sofa. Mrs Pomeroy, squashed like a giant cushion at one end of the same sofa, was feeding her bits of Madeira cake. Even though it was summer the fire was burning and the red velvet curtains were pulled half shut. The sitting-room was crowded with furniture: lacquered cabinets and mahogany sideboards, corner cupboards and little tables littered with china ornaments and photographs in ornate frames. It made the room seem quite small, until you looked upwards and saw the high ceiling with its complicated plasterwork and dusty chandeliers.

'I owe Bella everything,' said Mrs Pomeroy, 'Bella is the only true friend I have in the world.'

'But surely it's cruel to pierce a dog's ear?' Lizzie could have kicked herself. If she offended the old lady she'd never get the job. But Mrs Pomeroy gave her an indulgent smile and scooped a crumb into her mouth with her little finger. 'Nonsense, dear. Look at all the dreadful people who have their animals chopped, chipped, whatever you call it.'

'But surely…'

'Don't repeat yourself, dear.'

Lizzie bit her lip. She held her hand out towards the dog and it growled at her, then rose gracefully to its feet and stalked out of the room. The emerald flashed and disappeared.

'See,' said Mrs Pomeroy, 'you've offended her. But she'll forgive you if you give her one of my special chocolates. She does love them so, but they don't really help her skin condition. And the vet says they might give her fits.'

'But how can you…'

'Oh, it's not definite, dear. He's not sure. And she's so fond of them – it breaks my heart to deny her. Now, when can you start?'

'Don't you want to see my references?' William had been to a lot of trouble, writing three testimonials in different styles. But Mrs Pomeroy just shook her head.

'I fancy I'm a good judge of character. I've learnt the hard way to judge people by their behaviour. And besides, your hair is almost exactly the same colour as Bella's. I'm a great believer in coincidence.' She raised a manicured finger. 'But be warned, young lady. If you let me down, there'll be no second chances.'

So it began. Walking Bella through the green corridors of the park. Finding open spaces where she could run free, for a little while. The dog didn't wear the earring here of course; that was for indoors. The pay was awful. Lizzie was expected to give up evenings and weekends on demand. 'Could you come over dear? The vet says Bella needs more exercise. Her tummy's getting too big. Needs to get out.'

Talking to the old lady was some compensation – drinking expensive tea from china cups and listening to her memories. She'd had an interesting life, travelling the world, marrying rich men. Sometimes she discussed her troubles – friends who'd turned against her, ungrateful relatives, the awful nephew who used to visit sometimes. 'Only when he wanted something, dear. He was nice as pie to my face, but he did wicked things when my back was turned.' Disloyalty was something the old lady couldn't stand.

Sometimes she told Lizzie secrets: how, when she died, Bella would inherit everything; how the earring was a token of love from a very unsuitable man who had stolen her heart and then left her high and dry. 'But he didn't steal my money, dear. I made sure of that. A broken heart is an uncomfortable thing, but it's easier to endure if you still have your little luxuries.'

Summer ended. The walks in the park became wet and muddy. But there were plenty of clean towels with Bella's initial on, and quantities of liver in a porcelain bowl. Lizzie would brush the burrs and mud from the glossy coat and think about her plans. And when the dog was clean and fed, she would take Bella into the living room, where Mrs Pomeroy sat drinking tea. There she would perform the final grooming ceremony, smoothing the auburn coat to a glossy sheen with a special ebony brush.

'Do pour yourself a cup, dear,' Mrs Pomeroy would say, 'Oh, but first, would you get the emerald? Over there on the shelf, next to the ormolu clock.' And Lizzie would take the earring from its velvet case, and gently insert the golden hook into the tiny hole. Then they would both sit back and watch the beautiful animal recline into an elegant pose, firelight catching the gleaming stone.

The idea was that Lizzie should steal small things: ornaments, pieces of china and silver, ornamental boxes, anything that she could slip into a pocket. The old lady was short-sighted and a little deaf. Often she would doze off in the firelight, snoring gently. Taking small items from the many crowded tables and shelves, or even from cabinets and drawers on the ground floor rooms would be no problem at all. William coached Lizzie, gave her a set of old keys he'd picked up from somewhere to try on the locked cabinets, told her what to look for, and gloated over the things she brought – delicate posy vases, silver napkin rings, ornamental spoons. She slipped them into her pockets and unloaded them into the leather bag she left in the hall, with her own towel and comb.

'But won't she miss the stuff eventually? I should have thought she'd have an inventory.'

He laughed. 'Of course she doesn't. She's got some major items of jewellery stashed away in the bank, but apart from that she hasn't a hope of keeping track. Don't forget, there's been stuff coming into that house for generations. Most of the family were travellers, and even more of them were collectors of some sort. Nobody ever bothered to make a proper list.'

'Not even for insurance purposes?'

'Maybe once upon a time, but it's never been kept up to date. Old Auntie's quite willing to spend money on that animal, but she watches the pennies on everything else.' Lizzie didn't ask how he knew all this. Instead she enquired: 'What will you do with the things I steal?'

'Don't you worry your lovely head about it. I've got a few contacts in the trade.' He winked at her and pulled a leather notebook out of his jacket. 'See? It's my little brown book. Telephone numbers. Email addresses. I can dispose of it as fast as you can get it to me.' Seeing her expression, he smiled and put the book back in his pocket. 'Oh, I know what you're thinking, and you're right. I did have a little black book as well, but I threw it away. You're the only girl for me now.' She smiled back at him and lifted her face to be kissed.

The lessons went on: 'That's a damn good box. See the mark underneath? That's Fabergé... I think that miniature could be pretty old. Might even be seventeenth century. Have a look through the bookcases if you get the chance. Anything with a nice binding. Even the small ones can fetch quite a bit, and there must be a few first editions. It's easy to tell which ones they are – I'll show you.'

Every now and then, he'd get a call and go rushing off to meet somebody and make another deal. If he got a bad price he'd come back in a temper. If he thought he'd driven a hard bargain, he'd be full of smiles and charm. But the money was never enough. The goods that Lizzie brought in didn't begin to cover William's expensive tastes. He was buying designer shirts now, drinking fine wine, smoking cigars. Occasionally he brought back presents for her: a silver charm bracelet, a pair of elegant shoes, a beautiful dress. Sometimes he treated her to a meal in a fashionable restaurant.

'Why don't you try exploring a bit more of the house?' He said one night, as they lay on the rug by the fire. The flat was warmer now, but just as shabby, and he still couldn't afford to move. 'It's probably best if you don't take too many things from downstairs. She might notice eventually. And it would be easy to have a good look around. You say she sleeps a lot?'

Lizzie was cautious. 'She dozes. I never know when she's going to wake. I have to keep one ear open all the time. And if she calls I need to get back quickly.'

'You could always make up some story. Say you were upstairs, looking for the loo.'

'There are two cloakrooms downstairs.'

'Well then, say you smelt smoke. She'd swallow that. She's paranoid about fire. I once let off a smoke bomb and she nearly went berserk, puffing around all over the place.'

'That was cruel. You could have given her a heart attack.'

'Not her, she's tough as old boots.' He was grinning at her, so confident. It was annoying. She would have to do this, just to show him she wasn't afraid.

So Lizzie began to take chances, and found she was enjoying it. With her little pocket torch to light the way, she ascended the graceful flight of stairs which led from the main hall, and found long corridors and dark rooms smelling of dust, full of cabinets and tallboys and desks. Other, narrower staircases led to more rooms, with wardrobes full of old furs and chests of drawers stuffed with clothes and jewellery. A lot of the jewels were fake. Lizzie wasn't good at picking out the valuable stuff, especially in the dim light, and William got annoyed if she brought something worthless.

'What's the point of this?' he'd say, holding up a necklace. 'Can't possibly be real. The stones are too big, and they're the wrong colour. And why on earth did you bring this brooch? Who's going to buy this? You can pick them up for a tenner in town.' She didn't argue, just tried again, looking for curiosities – Japanese carvings, art deco cigarette cases, and as time went on she became better at spotting the things of real value. Until eventually it was just as William said – easy as pie, money for old rope, with very little risk.

Once, in a small room piled high with a jumble of furniture, she found a silver photo frame. When she got it home, she realised that the picture was of William, much younger but still recognisable, and looking quite angelic. Across the bottom he'd written, 'To my dearest Auntie, with love and kisses. From your own sweet Will.' Lizzie smiled. He hadn't been completely truthful about his relationship with his Aunt. There were obviously times when he hadn't behaved like a brat at all. But the glass was cracked in a spider web pattern, as though something had hit it very hard. Lizzie took it out, together with the photograph, before she passed the frame on.

Another time, wandering in the gloom, she heard soft footsteps behind her, and turned, her heart beating loudly in the silence. But it was simply Bella, wanting more exercise, interested in exploring. The dog trusted her now. They were almost friends, and after that she often came to find Lizzie and accompanied her through the rooms, like the mistress of the house showing off her possessions to a visitor. It seemed appropriate. Bella wasn't cut out to be a guard dog, Lizzie thought, that wasn't her job. She was far too aristocratic. Hunting was more her style: those long legs and powerful haunches. Someone should invite her out to a country estate for the weekend.

'You think more about that animal than you do about me,' said William one night, when she had not complied with all his wishes.

'I'm just tired, that's all.'

'Well I can't think why. All you have to do is wander round that house and pick up a few nice things. And another thing – you're putting on weight.' He ran his hands over her stomach. 'Must be eating too much chocolate.' He saw the warning in her eyes, and went on quickly, 'What I mean is, you're looking so beautiful these days. Your hair is glossy and your new clothes show your figure off. I don't want you spoiling it.'

She pulled away. 'Mrs Pomeroy lets me give Bella her chocolate that's all, and if I eat it, she doesn't have to. At least she doesn't get sick now.'

William grunted. 'See what I mean? That dog's all you think about these days.'

But he was wrong.

It was true; Lizzie wasn't under William's spell any more. Something else glowed in her dreams now, as brightly as his golden hair once had. The emerald earring had become an obsession. She saw it flashing in the firelight, and wanted it with all her heart.

One night, when they were sitting by the fire, sharing the big leather armchair he'd bought, she said, 'It wasn't just childhood pranks, was it?'

'What do you mean?' He was frowning. 'What are you talking about?'

'The reason your Aunt hates you. You've stolen something

from her before. Something very valuable.'

For a moment she thought he was going to turn on her. Then she felt him relax. 'Clever girl. How did you guess?'

'Oh, I kept my eyes and ears open. Put two and two together. I take it I'm right?'

'Well of course you are.'

'And she found out?'

He sighed. 'I was older then, but a lot more stupid. Got into some serious debt with some very unpleasant people. I asked her to lend me the money and she wouldn't. So I broke in and took a diamond necklace. I figured she'd have it insured.'

'Only she didn't?'

'More fool her.'

'And you were caught.'

He shrugged. 'Somebody turned me in. The guy who bought it from the dealer was a friend of hers. I got hauled before her majesty and made to grovel.'

'Did she call the police?'

He shook his head. 'Didn't want the scandal. Family name besmirched, and all that. Typical of that lot. She said she'd keep quiet about it on condition I got out of her sight and never came near her again.'

'And that was why you had to find somebody else to do your dirty work?'

He stroked her hair. 'Don't be like that, sweetheart. This is for both of us, remember? So we can have a future together. I adore you. We're a pair, you and I.'

When three months had gone by, Lizzie decided the time had come. On the final night, she fed Bella and groomed her, as Mrs Pomeroy, eyes drooping, watched from the sofa. She stroked the ebony brush through the silky fur, singing a soft tune, while the firelight flickered. At last, with the sound of snoring from mistress and dog, she knew she was safe. She gently unhooked the earring, and slipped it into her pocket.

Then she patted Bella's smooth head for the last time and crept out into the hall. As the door clicked behind her, a sudden feeling of loss almost made her cry. But it was too late for tears; she knew that after this, she could never come back.

'What the hell did you do that for?' He glared at the earring dangling from her outstretched hand. Swaying on its golden wire, the emerald flashed in the firelight, sending out little sparks. 'You've ruined it all now. She'll definitely sack you, and don't think she won't call the police. It's not as if you're part of the family. If there's anything my Aunt hates, it's disloyalty.'

'And that's exactly why she hates you,' Lizzie said softly.

He ignored her. He was pacing up and down the room now, the lion in a cage. 'I can't believe you've been so stupid. It's not as if we can sell the thing. It isn't even one of a pair.'

'That's not why I took it. What about Bella? Did you ever consider her? Nobody has the right to do that to a dog – stuff it with food and use it as an ornament.'

'But she adores the bloody thing.'

'And you adore me. Or so you say. But you don't really mean it. And even if you did, love is no excuse. You aren't doing me any good. I'm just a way of getting back at your aunt. Just an accessory. Not one of a pair.'

He threw himself down in the big, new armchair and ran his fingers through his hair. Then he looked up at her. 'So what are you going to do now?'

She couldn't see him properly. The firelight had given him a gold halo but his face was in shadow. She thought about it. It hadn't been easy, stealing something so valuable. It had taken a lot of nerve, at the beginning. She couldn't have done it without him.

But now she was free to do whatever she wanted – change her name, disappear. It wasn't as if anyone would notice. She had very few friends and no relations at all. In all her temporary jobs she'd been efficient, but invisible.

Mrs Pomeroy would miss her, of course. And Bella. They would be disappointed, but they wouldn't be destitute. Mrs Pomeroy would have her little comforts and Bella would have her inheritance. And then there was William. He was watching her, quiet now, waiting for an answer. Or an apology. Lizzie smiled. She'd certainly made an impression on him.

It was a pity really – if he hadn't been so disagreeable, she might have done things differently. She was sure she could have found a way to get him back into his aunt's good books. They could have worked at it together. She might even have considered marrying him, at least for a while, given his improved prospects.

She stared back at him for a second or two, trying to recall the charm he'd once had for her, all those months ago.

'Well?' he said, 'Come on. What are you going to do? You'd better find a way of making it up to me. You've just ruined our whole future.'

The trouble was he hadn't much of a future any more. When Mrs Pomeroy read the letter she'd left propped against the silver teapot, she would learn the whole story – how William had led Lizzie astray, seduced her into a life of crime and broken her heart. The old lady would also have the details of his contacts, which Lizzie had copied lovingly from the little leather-bound notebook while he was asleep. He'd be in everybody's black books very shortly. Given Mrs Pomeroy's strong feelings about disloyalty, there was quite a good chance of him ending up in prison.

Of course, he hadn't seen more than a fraction of the stuff she'd taken from the house. Once Lizzie had learned what to look for she was perfectly able to help herself to as much as she could find. And he would get the blame.

The emerald flashed in the firelight. Carefully, Lizzie fastened it into her ear, sweeping back her long auburn hair, letting it fall in silky waves.

'Don't worry about me,' she said, 'I'm going hunting.'

William leapt out of the chair and took a step towards her. She growled at him, and he froze. Then she turned on her elegant heels and stalked out of the room.

Pork Pies

Maggie Cainen

'Quick, get a move on, Dora, catch all that blood! Come on, come on, it's no different from the pig's. Grab hold of that bucket, you stupid girl!' Blood was fountaining out of the widening gash in the man's throat, splashing on the tiles, hitting the walls and dribbling all over the sink. His booted heels drummed a frantic tattoo on the stone floor; suddenly he lashed out with both feet. One of his flailing boots caught me on my bare leg and threw me against the stone sink, banging my head.

I'm a hundred years old next week but I can still remember the pain of the vast purple bruise that blossomed on my white calf that day. The blow on the head gave a dreamlike quality to everything and some days I can't help wondering whether it all really happened at all.

We little kids were all milling around, desperate to see what was going on but afraid to get too close. All we could see was our pint-sized mother hanging onto that giant's neck as she lugged him towards to the sink. Dora came out of her trance and seized the bucket at last, pushing it under the man's throat. I heard the blood hitting the bottom like our Sam pissing into the guzzunder at night. The smell made me retch; I could feel the vomit in my throat forcing itself out. I stuffed both hands into my mouth trying to keep it in, at the same time trying to avoid the man's flying boots. But there were too many of us in that little back kitchen, all the young ones who were too frightened to stay in the front room and the big ones who were just too nosy to leave. My other big sisters crowded in as well, pushing me out of the way, and I crawled under their legs back into the sitting room. I was crying so hard the whole of my pinny was soaked; I thrust it into my face to mop up the tears and gagged as my mouth, nose and eyes filled with blood. Warm, copper-smelling blood invaded my nostrils, sealed up my eyes and tasted disgustingly salty. I started to gag as my mouth filled up with vomit again. I tore at the stout cotton pinafore strings with both hands but they were too tightly tied behind my back and in my panic I just couldn't free them. Suddenly the pinafore fell off and I saw my big sister Ella thrusting it into the heart of the fire with a poker.

There was always a big coal fire burning in the hearth with a ring of clothes horses full of damp clothes steaming all round it, even on the hottest days. Mum and grandma did most of the cooking on it, and heated up water for Dad's bath and the laundry. Of course, Dad was a miner and so was entitled to free coal for life. We got the cottage, too, at a low rent from the Coal Board but mum had quietly re-annexed the little kitchenless house next door as well after my little sister Clare was born. That made fourteen children, Mum, Dad, Grandma and Aunt Jane – who'd starting living with us shortly after she went blind: eighteen people, all told, in one small cottage.

I was dimly aware that was what Mum and the rent man had been quarrelling about. Mum had been insisting that we should only pay rent on one cottage because Dad and my big brothers Jack and Sam had re-opened the blocked up doorways through into the cottage next door so it made only one cottage again now. Someone had divided it into two a few years previously, probably to make even more money, but no one ever lived there as it had no front door and no kitchen.

I can't remember what the rent for each cottage was, so let's call it one shilling a week. But what I do know is we didn't have two shillings: most weeks we were hard put to find one shilling. In the spring and summer we little ones earned a few pence each week scaring the birds off the crops in the fields behind the houses. Sometimes the lads might get thruppence for holding the gentry's horses but the gentry didn't come into the village much.

The rent man was a bully, we all knew that. He always looked enormous to us, a great brute of a man. We had strict instructions to get out of sight whenever we saw him coming. We got out of his way all right, but we hid and spied on him. There was a dreadful fascination about someone so evil.

He was always trying to get his hand up our skirts. He carried a pocket full of wrapped boiled sweets which he'd proffer to us in a kind of competition which never varied. He'd offer to guess the colour of our knickers and if he guessed right we got a sweetie. Obviously he had to check the colour for himself.

Mum and Grandma had explained to us that we were never, ever, ever, to speak to Fred Smith (not his real name) and we were never to be on our own with him. If he tried backing us into a corner we were to scream as loud as we could.

That day was Friday – our rent day – and Smith had turned up with his hair slicked back with grease and a smarmy grin on his face. He'd decided to overlook the extra rent, he announced in his lordly fashion – probably guessing he'd no chance of collecting it – but he was only prepared to forget it on his conditions, of course.

Now, as I said, all the youngsters had to make themselves scarce. So there we were, hiding in the parlour, all the other little ones, my two brothers and all the big girls. My two biggest sisters, Dora and Ella, were taking it in turns to peer through the keyhole. Dora must have been about fourteen at the time and Ella sixteen. The trouble was we couldn't hear exactly what was going on but at one point we heard Mum shriek.

'Not my Ella, no chance! I'll tell her father, he'll have tha guts for garters for even suggesting that!'

'Them's my terms, tek 'em or leave 'em.'

'Get aht, now. Tek tha shilling and get aht.'

Mum always forgot to talk posh when she was cross. She'd been boning some bits of our pig in the back kitchen when he'd turned up even earlier than usual for the rent. When he'd started blustering we guessed that he'd pushed her into a corner and she'd snatched up her boning knife to defend herself. We presumed that in the struggle that went on before we all piled into the kitchen she'd accidentally ended up slitting his throat. Exactly the same as she did with the pig each year.

I forget: you don't know about the pig, do you?

Well, Mum was always looking for new ways to feed her growing family of girls; we weren't as much use as lads at earning extra money. Jack and Sam were still too young to start work down the pit, which is what all the lads in our village did. They used to go out trapping rabbits and hares and pigeon shooting instead and had been known to go fishing – poaching more like – in the trout ponds up at the big house. Mum never said a word: just gutted and cooked the game and the trout and salted any she couldn't use at once. We had a huge cellar under our cottage where Mum kept all manner of preserves; it was really cool and kept everything nice and fresh. But we needed more to supplement the family income than the boys could bring home – so along came the pig.

Strictly speaking, the pig belonged to everyone on our street – everyone who had a share in it – but it was Mum who was in charge. All of us had jobs; mine was collecting all the household scraps from the shareholders on the street for the pig swill bucket. We kept all the buckets of pig swill down in the cellar. It was the job of two of my big sisters to feed the pig usually, not me.

When all the shouting had died down Mum called Grandma

and Aunt Jane in to help her and sent the rest of us back into the parlour and as a special treat told Ella to give us all a piece of parkin and allow us to read the Sunday books. Those of us who could read that is: the rest just looked at the pictures.

Do you know about Sunday books? Do you still have them today I wonder? All Chapel children knew about Sunday books. On Sundays we had to go to Chapel twice. In the mornings we went to Sunday school where an old lady read us Bible stories and told us morally uplifting tales about brave little children who always did the correct thing. Every class started with her giving each of us a peppermint as a bribe to keep quiet. It was very hot in the side chapel where we had lessons and she had such a boring voice. The boys spent most of the time surreptitiously flicking paper pellets at the girls' necks and knees. All of us had a longstanding competition to see who could make their peppermint last the longest.

In the afternoon, at four o'clock, we had to trek all the way to Chapel again and sing hymns and listen to a very dull sermon. We weren't allowed to play on Sundays but had to sit quietly in the parlour and read the Sunday books. These were bound collections of children's magazines about fifty years old at that time. All the characters in the stories wore very old-fashioned clothes; the girls wore frilly drawers and starched aprons, and the boys wore knickerbockers and nankeen trousers. Do you remember that film *The Railway Children*? Well the children were dressed a bit like that. They seemed to drive around in a pony and trap and got up to wonderful adventures involving smugglers, pirates, buried treasure and hundreds of deadly brigands. The magazines were all bound up in the wrong order so you had to hunt for the next part of the serial stories through several volumes. Each magazine contained ideas for projects to do; making a press for wild flowers was one suggestion and prayers for children and some rather twee little poems. As we were only allowed to read them for an hour on Sundays, it was a great treat to get them on a weekday.

Meanwhile, in the kitchen, we all secretly surmised that Grandma, Mum and even Aunt Jane were carving up the rent man's body. We didn't actually know and none of us dared speak about our fears out loud but over and over again I could see that scarlet fountain of blood hosing down the walls and the kitchen floor. I could see mum's boning knife sticking out of his neck and to prove I wasn't having a nightmare there was the spreading bruise on my calf.

I heard Mum's voice calling to Grandma to fetch the axe which was used for chopping up kindling for the fire. We held our breath as we listened to all the crashing and banging but were all far too frightened to try and get out of the parlour and spy on them. It was almost as though the fact we weren't absolutely certain what we'd seen made it OK. There was bound to be a rational explanation.

Time went past and it was getting icy cold in the parlour without a fire and as we'd missed our midday meal we were all starving hungry too, so we drew lots to see who would creep out and find out what was happening. I think the boys fixed the draw because I was the one who ended up with the smallest piece of paper. When Dad came home from the pit each day he used to beat any miscreants with his big razor strop, a long length of thick leather that left great purple bruises all over our bottoms and thighs. To be fair he didn't beat the girls as often as the boys, who were regularly beaten when the gamekeeper came to complain about his dwindling fish and game stocks. We girls had to do something really bad to get thrashed with the razor strop. I think the big girls and boys chose me to investigate because I was one of the smallest and even if I did get caught they thought he probably wouldn't beat me.

I was cold, hungry and very frightened, my knees wobbled and my mouth felt like cotton wool. I suddenly found I couldn't swallow and needed to pee urgently. During the day we had to go up the yard to our privy which was pretty disgusting and only got emptied twice a year. It was coming up to emptying time again and the smell and the flies were awful. After dark we all used the guzzunders, or chamberpots sometimes known as gerries. On that fateful Friday the boys had crept upstairs and brought down all the empty gerries and they were now all brimming full.

First I went to the closed parlour door and peered through the keyhole. I couldn't see very much, even perched on a chair and then I realised why: someone had put the key in the lock. When I tried the handle it wouldn't open. A huge feeling of relief swept through me. Despite my full bladder, I was so happy that I didn't have to go out again to brave my mother's wrath.

'Don't think you're not going,' said Jack, 'We'll use the window instead.' The cottages were at least two or three hundred years old and had immensely thick walls. It took the combined efforts of both boys and Dora and Ella to unscrew the window locks and get the windows open. Jack and Sam bunked me up onto the window sill and held my hands when I scrambled through. It was still a long way to the ground and I fell, bruising both my knees on the cobbled yard.

We didn't have a garden at all – just a backyard which boasted the only well on the street where we all got our water each day. Tears sprang from my eyes again, blinding me, but I tucked up my skirts and ran for the privy. There was a long row of privies: luckily ours was the nearest. I was usually too frightened to go on my own because it was dark and smelly in there and Jack had told me there was a nest of poisonous spiders. My bladder was bursting but I made it. When I came out I saw our next-door neighbour peering through her curtains at me.

'Hey oop, little lass. Hast tha seen t'rent man? He's late today.'

I don't think she'd bothered to learn any of the girls' names.

175

Everyone knew the two boys of course: 'sons of Satan' was one of the mildest things they called them.

I just shook my head, too frightened to speak, and ran back to our house. I stood outside the open window, jumping up to try to see in, whispering frantically.

'Sam, Jack help me back in!'

Nothing happened. I didn't know what to do; it was starting to get dark. There was nothing to stand on to help me get back inside and all my sisters and brothers had disappeared. Dad would be home at any minute and he was always in a filthy mood on Fridays. Actually he was in a foul temper every day but Fridays were the worst: Friday was payday but he had to hand every penny over to Mum and even then, despite her careful management, we often ended up eating stale bread and scrape on Thursdays.

Most of the miners went to the Working Men's Club on Fridays after work to knock back a few pints of bitter to get the taste of coal dust out of their throats. There weren't any pit head baths in those days so first they had to go home and boil up water on the fire and let their wives scrub them clean in the tin bathtub in the only warm place in the house: in front of the fire.

'Sam, Jack let me in!' My voice was getting louder now. Suddenly the front door opened and there was blind Aunt Jane.

'Come in quick, love. Your mam wants you.'

Sure enough there was Mum with a bucket of pig swill in each hand.

'Get this to the pig before it gets dark, love.'

Down the road I staggered lugging the two brimming buckets of pig swill. They were so heavy I had to keep stopping for a rest. The pig was housed in a sty just down the lane. It was a colossal sow called Bessie which would be slaughtered soon at the end of November and shared out amongst the shareholders.

It grunted when it saw me and smelled the pig swill, then rushed up to the bars, poking its huge snout through, almost making me drop the buckets. The feeding technique was quite straightforward. I'd watched our Dora and Ella do it loads of times. You tipped the swill into the feeding trough then pulled back a lever and slid the whole trough on rollers through to the sow and the shutter dropped automatically back into place, sealing the pen.

I put down one bucket, being extra careful not to knock it over and tipped the first bucket into the trough. It was the usual collection of potato peelings, sprout stumps, rotten vegetables, mouldy apples and some odd-shaped pink lumps which I didn't recognise at first. I hastily tipped the second bucket in, trying to cover up the pink bits. All the time the sow was bellowing at me: it was way past her usual feeding time.

My hands shook as I tried to move the lever but it seemed to be stuck fast. I had a horrible suspicion about what the pink pieces were and I was desperate to get rid of the evidence. Yet more weak tears started to pour down my filthy face. I grabbed the wooden paddle which we used to stir the pig swill with both hands and moved it around in the trough, trying to cover up all the pink lumps. Then, summoning all my strength, I smashed the paddle down on the lever, freeing whatever was jamming it and pushed the trough in to Bessie, who fell on it at once.

I stayed there for what felt like hours, watching her cramming every bit of the food in the trough into her huge jaws, her massive molars clamping down, shredding the pink pieces until not a scrap remained.

Very, very slowly, lugging the two empty buckets, I made my way back up the lane. It was pitch dark by then, no street lighting of course and only gaslights in the houses. My nostrils pricked at the sour smell of the homemade candles some of the poorer families used. As I neared our house I could hear a terrible row going on: my parents' voices were echoing out down the street.

'Calm down, Harry. What's done is done. Least said soonest mended. No one knows, not even the kids. Just keep your trap shut and no one will ever know. Look: here's sixpence; send our Ella up to the club for a jug of ale tonight.'

'No daughter of mine is going near that club! Just as soon as I've had my bath I'll fetch it meself. ' And he did and he shared it with Mum and Grandma and Aunt Jane.

Mum killed Bessie as usual in November and divided her up amongst the shareholders. She carved our portion into great joints of pork and made pies, sausages, brawn and pig's trotters. As none of us fancied pork that year she sold the whole of our share in Sheffield market and bought beef and lamb to salt down instead.

As for us kids, we had a silent pact never to mention what we thought had gone on that day. In fact today, as I approach my hundredth birthday, is the first time I have ever told anybody about it. Everyone's dead except me and most people seem to think that I'm not in my right mind half the time.

What did everyone think had happened to Fred Smith, I hear you ask? Well, no one knew for certain, but there was a rumour that he'd run away to join the army. There were a lot of husbands in the village, the story went, whose wives he'd been tupping and they were all after his blood.

Funny things, pork pies: I've never been able to stomach one since.

Christmas Present

Hilary Bowers

Bubbles (birth name, Lois Clough, lost in the mists of time) left for work earlier than usual that morning, her head full of news about the audacious local post office robbery that had, temporarily, kicked the story of the puzzling recent spate of missing young women into touch. Eager-faced eyewitnesses had just been launching into breathless, and no doubt exaggerated, accounts of events when Bubbles' electricity ran out.

Sixty thousand pounds, she thought, as she huddled deeper into her moth-eaten duffle coat. Who'd have believed that Ribblestone post office carried so much cash, and what wouldn't I give for some of it? Bet they never catch them, either. Wearing silicone facemasks, they'd been; Mickey Mouse, Donald Duck and Popeye. Clever, she called that, showed class. She'd been hanging on to every word when the bloody meter ran out.

Extortion, that's what it was; highway bloody robbery, the price they charged for pre-paid electric. All the programmes said so; fleecing those who could least afford it. And I certainly come into that category, she thought, sharp eyes within the hooded face missing nothing as she walked. By the time she'd paid for essentials; gin, fags and her own drinks in the pubs and clubs where she touted for business (street-walking being a desperate last resort), there was next to nothing left for the lottery, electricity, food... She swallowed thickly, remembering that she hadn't even got coffee and milk in the bedsit, never mind the bloody electricity.

A hawk's senses could not have been more hunger-honed than Bubbles' as she hunted – for the glint of coins on wet pavement or road, a gape of handbag, exposed wallet... Anything, everything, was fair game, but there was nothing this morning, nothing.

Closing predatory eyes in momentary dejection she almost missed him; only glimpsed his slight form as he turned from a shop doorway and scuttled away. Habit made her appraise the man's appearance; five feet six at the most, narrow-shouldered seen from the back, stringy, ginger, over-the-collar hair, grey non-descript clothes, but as he'd turned, a brief, sideways exposure of his face, she'd spotted two unforgettable features, or, rather, one defaced one; a large, bulbous nose, pockmarked with acne, a hideous wedge of nasal moonscape.

Bubbles shuddered; she'd always been repulsed by any form of imperfection, however slight, which was why she usually closed her eyes when earning her living; after all, beggars couldn't be choosers.

Then, as she walked on, her eyes brightened in anticipation; the doorway where the man had been lurking belonged to the local hospice's charity shop, and propped against the door were two black bin bags; one bulging with possibilities, the other sagging with unfulfilled potential. Recently, this had been happening almost daily; ever since Social Services and the Salvation Army had persuaded some of the independent charity shops in the county to act as drop-off points for tinned and dry food, new toys and good quality, warm clothes and bedding to provide Christmas presents, food parcels and bare essentials for low-income families and the homeless during the festive season. Details had been broadcast on regional radio and printed in the county and local newspapers. Now the needy, and Bubbles, would be reaping of the bounty.

She quickly removed a key from her shoulder bag and

unlocked the door before scuttling inside with the half-empty sack. Moments later, after switching on the lights, disarming the alarm and ditching her bag, she returned to collect the other sack, grasped the top with both hands then almost fell backwards, it was so light. Cursing, she pulled it across the carpeted floor into the sorting room at the back of the shop.

Catching her breath, Bubbles looked up at the wall-mounted clock. Thirty minutes before the others were due. Her smile was a cruel baring of small, pointed teeth as she savoured the stupidity of the manageress, the grandiose title earned only because the woman was more ancient than the other old biddies who worked here, for nothing! Bubbles had soon got her sussed; volunteer for everything, however shitty. Result? She was now a trusted key holder, allowed to come and go almost as she pleased.

With eager fingers she tipped the contents of the first bag onto the sorting table and quickly divided them into two piles; 'mine' and 'the rest'.

Besides a few scuffed fashion handbags all the clothes were women's, of varying quality and sizes, which was unusual in such a small collection, but Bubbles' interest was immediately taken by a skinny, fuchsia-pink, roll-neck sweater, a short, black vinyl skirt her Gran would have called a pelmet and a sleeveless faux-fur grey jacket, and for two equally important reasons; they were her size and relatively clean, the latter being a big plus as she didn't posses a washing machine and trips to the laundrette were most definitely at the lower end of her essentials list.

Pulling from her shoulder bag the large Lidl carrier that she always used for her illicit pickings, as it wasn't see-through, she was about to stuff the clothes into it when, remembering her empty purse, she took them into the changing room instead where she quickly transformed herself from a scruffy tramp into a tarty one. She twirled and admired; perfect! The sweater made her breasts look high and proud, her long black boots almost hid the ladder in her fishnets, and the skirt was so minimal the punters wouldn't care less. Great. As soon as she left here she would go to work. Cramming her original clothes into the carrier she hung it on her allotted staff peg, covering it with her duffle coat.

After pushing the remaining clothes to one end of the long sorting table, Bubbles hoisted the second, bulging sack up onto it, and after a few seconds' futile struggle with the over-tightened knot, ripped the bag open with her talon-like fingernails. Soft toys of every size, shape and hue cascaded around her and she sighed with disappointment until…until… like a stranded jellyfish, a rubbery mask lay exposed on the worktop. Breath and belief suspended she poked at it with an index finger, turning it around until its identity was revealed. Mickey Mouse!

And in the same moment she remembered Moonface hunched in the shop doorway.

He was one of the post office robbers. He had to be! Yes! With absolutely no idea of what she would do with this knowledge, only certain that she didn't want to share it, Bubbles buried the mask under the clothes in her carrier, then calmed herself by brewing up one of the perks of this job, free coffee. She also consumed two Kit-Kats in lieu of breakfast before embarking upon another perk of the job, pick-pocketing.

Not that she'd ever wanted this job. Left to her own devices she would not have chosen 'official' work at all. But this bloody government had decided that everyone should be in gainful employment, however thick the person or degrading the task. And now you had to prove that you were actively looking for work. Unfortunately, hooking punters didn't count, unlike in some countries where legalised prozzies were part of the service sector. Bubbles grinned as she imagined straight-laced PM Gordon Brown's reaction to that suggestion. Miserable sod!

Worse still, if you didn't apply for jobs, go for interviews and all that crap, you could lose your benefits.

Faced with this unpalatable truth, Bubbles had, for a few hours each day, pretended to become a model citizen; applying for every job going, (before blowing it by being late for the interview or acting thick), and, following the advice of the know-it-all who ran the Job Club, had also become a volunteer in a charity shop. 'Shows willingness to work to the powers-that-be and retail experience will look good on your CV,' Know-it-All had said.

In the remaining minutes before the other volunteers arrived Bubbles demonstrated her 'willingness' and 'experience' by expertly searching everything she could lay her fingers on; pockets of men's trousers and jackets, ladies' pockets, handbags…

Three pounds and sixty pence the richer, she was just eyeing the donation box when the doorbell pinged and she reacted like one of Pavlov's dogs, immediately adopting a helpful smile combined with an ingratiating posture.

Two mornings and one afternoon a week she had to perform like this, and life was passing her by; she wasn't getting any younger.

Later, displaying her wares in a hole-in-the-wall drinking den, Bubbles nursed a single gin and tonic and tried to look into the future, but saw, all too clearly, that she hadn't one – not even one worth recommending to a beggar.

And then she remembered the mask in her carrier, and with chilling clarity, the man she believed had dumped the bags.

'Double brandy, on my tab, Jim,' she shouted from the safety of her corner seat, hoping he'd forgotten how much she owed. Brandy had always helped her to think.

Patience. That's what it would take. Hold on to the mask and one day…one day she might see Moonface again…and then? Well, if she played her cards right, she would never have to work again.

Gin instead of brandy appeared, brought, not by Jim, but by a regular of hers. She shuddered, knowing she was in for a rough time, but for now, all was laughter as her punter called his mates over. They already had girls attached, limpet-like, and as the afternoon progressed, Bubbles felt the welcome tide of alcoholic anaesthesia wash over her.

Later, one-eyed, she'd been half watching a rugby match on Sky whilst trying to deflect her punter's tackles when Jim switched over to the news channel, ignoring the customers' groans of protest. Snatches of commentary buzzed around her ears.

'...Point. Seven... Two months... Parents of the latest missing young woman wish to—' Bubbles took a large swig of gin and snuggled up against living warmth as the parents begged their errant daughter to come home. Then a policeman, doing the usual 'If anyone...' speech.

The pretty 18 year old, with long, frothy blonde hair, had, apparently, been wearing jeans, a mock-fur gillet and a mauve roll-neck sweater. In answer to a journalist's question the Inspector replied, 'We don't know yet if the disappearances are connected although they were all within a ten-mile radius of Barton Point, but as no bodies have been found this is still a missing persons enquiry.'

'She was only going into town on the bus to get my prescription,' the tearful mother interrupted, but Bubbles ignored her, flicking at her bleached tresses, caressing fur and the sleeves of the fuchsia-pink sweater, enjoying the glances that briefly came her way. She'd been noticed!

'And now for the latest update on the Ribblestone post office robbery...' Bubbles had no difficulty in hearing that, but then could hardly believe her ears as she listened to the eyewitness accounts that she'd missed that morning because of her power failure.

'Big, stockily built blokes, all of 'em,' said one octogenarian who'd been collecting his pension at the time.

'Balls!' Bubbles shouted. 'You must be blind, you silly old git!' Then, as she felt every eye in the bar swivelling towards her she remembered that her secret was supposed to be – secret! – and giggled. 'Eye witness! You can see...hic...he can't...can't see straight...hic!'

'That makes two of you!' someone shouted, and Bubbles, whose vision was beginning to blur, nodded happily and downed her gin.

'It's fucking boring here,' one of the other girls slurred.

Bubbles, ever happy for a change of scene, agreed. 'Let's go somewhere exciting!'

She was rewarded with the silence of drunken apathy.

'Le's go...le's go...to that place where those girls disappeared.' Her memory was fogged by gin fumes. 'You know...oh... wherever! I look eighteen.'

This statement was met by howls of derision but she ignored them.

'I've got blonde hair, a fur jacket, a purple sweater. We can barhop. People might think I'm her, call the police. The fucking cops'll be running round like headless bloody chickens all night!'

Her idea met with unanimous approval.

It isn't easy, willing yourself to be eighteen when you're on the wrong side of forty and feel like dying. Bubbles opened one eye, very slowly, unwilling to discover where she was, or who she was with...

The empty bed lulled her into a false sense of security. She had just decided that the unfamiliar sound torturing her eardrums and aching eyeballs was that of seagulls...seagulls?... when her overnight companion (God, how had she ended up with him? She hadn't started out with him) emerged from

185

the bathroom and subjected her to another form of torture, although she was so desensitised that one part of her brain observed the proceedings dispassionately, marvelling anew at how unimaginative, repetitive and boring men really were. Even as he abused her she stifled a yawn.

Later, she had difficulty opening one eye as it was swollen; a love tap the punter had said, laughing as he dropped a ten pound note onto her belly before leaving, adding, 'Bus fare, and count yourself lucky. Your performance wasn't worth what I spent on you last night, even without condoms.'

She almost left the carrier bag behind, assuming it was full of rubbish from the night's bacchanalia, but her insatiable curiosity and greed made her peer cautiously inside, synapses fired randomly and sufficient memory returned to allow recognition of her own clothes. What a downer! She was still swallowing her disappointment as she crept out of the fleapit B&B, just in case the punter hadn't paid the bill.

Bubbles always carried sunglasses, large sunglasses; and this morning they weren't just required for camouflage. Bright winter sunlight struck low-angled molten beams from almost every surface; damp roads and pavements glared like pewter ribbons, white-painted walls of shops and cottages flared like snow-fire; and when her meanderings took her to the promenade she gasped as a riot of sensations assaulted her; thrum of surf as an onshore wind drove the sea up a steeply shelving beach, curtains of spray that stung her cheeks and filled her lungs with ozone…oh, how wonderful it all felt, smelt, tasted. She opened her eyes and added to the feast; white mares'-tail clouds streaming across a blueness of sky no artist had ever recreated, sand muted by moisture but still golden in contrast to the jagged, up-ended strata of black rocks that fringed the bay like prehistoric gills…breathing…breathing…

She swayed and grabbed the rust-pocked guard rail. Too much breathing, not enough drinking, she decided, but although she longed for alcohol realised that coffee and painkillers were more urgent requirements.

She discovered which town she was in as she passed an optimistically open candy and rock stall during her hunt for a cheap café.

Barton Point, inscribed in black through psychedelic-hued sticks of rock, caused memory to stir. Laughter, out for a good time, an endless supply of drinks, groping hands...and suddenly, a party, all diving into taxis for a trip. But why here? It was hardly Blackpool.

She blinked as a stab of sunlight glanced off a shop window and penetrated her sunglasses. The Gull's Nest café looked as weather-beaten as she felt. Her sunglasses steamed up as soon as she entered, and the enveloping fug, redolent of rancid cooking oil, over-brewed tea and frying bacon made her stomach growl. The singing Christmas tree by the door, galvanised into action by her entrance, made her head throb rhythmically to its rendition of 'Jingle Bells'.

Wearily she sank into a window seat, removed her glasses and, after checking her purse, ordered coffee and toast.

Seven quid, a screwed up envelope, (brown, been there for days unopened, probably a bill), five fags and a disposable lighter, and that's my lot, she thought, as she lit a cigarette in direct contravention of the nearby notice: 'It is against the law to smoke in these premises'. Fuck this interfering government, she thought. She'd be dead long before the fags got her, with all this worry. 'And fuck you,' she shouted to the prat behind the counter as he gesticulated at the sign. 'Payback for the fucking tree.'

God knew how much the bus fare home would be, and what was she going back to? No money for booze or fags, nothing; and she needed a drink now. She looked at her watch, which indicated one o'clock, and reached a conclusion. She had two choices. Take the bus back, which would leave her broke, removing any possibility of going into a pub, buying a couple of drinks and picking up a punter, thus reducing her to street-walking on a cold winter's night... She shivered and swallowed the lukewarm dregs of her coffee. Or, she could find a suitable pub in Barton Point and have a few drinks; more chance of a pull here as the men didn't know her...and if the worst came to the worst, well, she could always thumb a lift back with a friendly wagon driver.

The second choice, offering immediate alcoholic consolation, won.

Minutes later, wriggling her still-aching body into the stained plush upholstery of the Fishermen's Rest bar, Bubbles waited for the first greedy gulps of a double gin and tonic to restore her, carry her away into that other, happier world, but it took ever more alcohol to achieve that these days and all she felt was a desperate craving for more. She needed a punter, quickly. Her voracious eyes swept the bar although she knew she was wasting her time. One-thirty on a mid-December weekday; the only men drinking were either pensioners eking out a half of shandy or unemployed yobs doing the same with a pint of bitter. Poor pickings indeed.

Then her ears picked up the sound of the outer door opening and the barman calling out, 'Double scotch as usual, Pete?' Swift as a bat she had him located, pulling a wing chair around closer to the spluttering open fire but seated before she could gain an impression of him. But what did it matter? If he had money for scotch he might have money for her.

'Quick break or are you taking time off for a change?' the barman asked casually as he carried the drink over to the man. 'You work more hours than I do, and that's saying something!' The man's reply was an unintelligible mutter.

Bubbles gave him time to settle, sucked up the dregs of her drink, grabbed the carrier bag, assumed a nonchalant air, and holding her empty glass, sauntered towards him.

He was engrossed in a newspaper as she approached, so, placing the hand holding the carrier on one hip, she struck a provocative pose in front of him and proffered her empty glass towards him.

'Hello, Pete. Care to fill this?' she rasped in what she fondly imagined was a sexy purr.

The next moment her glass was slipping through nerveless fingers as he lowered the newspaper slowly, as if doing a weird striptease, revealing his nose … recognition and the glass's resounding smash were simultaneous; it was Moonface!

Even as she wracked her brain, trying to remember why he was so important, she was taking in the colour draining from his cheeks as he stared at her in horror, although a part of her was annoyed that he wasn't looking at her face, he appeared fascinated by her sweater. OK she wasn't too well-endowed in that region, but still…

She arched her back, pointing her breasts at him…and froze as an almost photographic flash illuminated another memory. Licking her lips, as a fox might on seeing an open chicken-coop door, she switched off her hooker's smile and slid into the chair opposite him, impaling him with her eyes. He appeared to be totally transfixed.

'I know what you did,' she whispered, and rejoiced as he flinched. 'Now buy me a drink and let's talk business.'

The barman was already on his way with dustpan and brush; a few moments later, after Moonface's reluctantly placed order, Bubbles was drinking deeply of a double measure of her elixir of life.

As she lifted her head he met her eyes, and she felt some of the precious, alcohol-induced euphoria leeching away as he stared at her. She couldn't at first pinpoint what it was about him that unsettled her. He appeared so ordinary. Stringy, ginger hair that hung limply over the grubby collar of his yellow parka; yes, she remembered that, his hair; double confirmation that it was him. She finished her drink in a courage-building gulp. He appeared thin to the point of emaciation with an almost skeletal face, so nothing threatening there. What was it about him that troubled her, apart from his hideous nose? Then he removed his glasses to polish them with his handkerchief, and his face was transformed. Whilst wearing the thick-lensed spectacles his eyes had appeared normal; grey, a bit bloodshot, just eyes; but now that the enlarging effect of the jam-jar lenses had been removed, he was glaring at her with tiny, vicious, piggy eyes; eyes that radiated hate and…

He slipped the glasses and his other persona on as the barman walked by with a plate of sandwiches. 'Same again,' she shouted, holding out her glass whilst kicking Moonface's ankle.

Moonface didn't react overtly, merely raised his eyebrows and sipped fastidiously at his barely tasted whisky. Instead of heeding the warning and keeping quiet, Bubble's gin-loosened tongue began to brag.

'I saw you. Outside the shop. And I've got proof.'

His eyes dropped to her chest again, and, worried that he was not taking her seriously, Bubbles played her ace.

Rummaging in the carrier she dragged out the mask and laid it on the table, shielding it from the rest of the bar with his newspaper. 'See? You left this outside the charity shop where I work. I saw you. You're one of the gang that robbed Ribblestone post office, and I want a share of that sixty thousand pounds to keep my mouth shut.'

What he did next, as she snatched back the mask, shocked her. He began to smile, stretching lips that seemed pinkly, obscenely full in his gaunt face, and then his entire body began to shake with silent laughter.

Fielding her next gin from the arriving barman Bubbles fortified herself against his mirth before adding, 'I've not told anyone yet, but you'll be laughing on the other side of your face if I go to the police.'

This statement had the desired effect. His lips thinned, pouted, and then his voice, light as a woman's but more searing than a Saharan wind, asked, 'How much?'

That's more like it, Bubbles thought, feeling in control once more despite a fit of shivers. 'Half of your share of the cash today,' she replied, still not quite believing this was happening, 'and then a regular income.'

He didn't respond, merely continued to stare. 'Don't forget, I know what you look like without the mask, and I've a good eye for detail, I'll make a perfect witness,' she taunted.

He stared at her silently for long moments then thrust his head forward aggressively, eyes narrowing, and Bubbles bit her lip. She'd faced many tricky situations involving men during her career but nothing and no-one like this. She sensed, without understanding, unspoken menace but chose to ignore it. The stakes were too high. 'Well?' she hectored, inching her face closer to his.

He appeared to shrivel. 'All right,' he hissed, eyes downcast, 'but we can't talk here.'

Bubbles relaxed, she was used to bargaining. 'OK,' she whispered. 'So tell me where.'

'Play along,' he muttered, then, in a louder voice, 'Not interested, but I'll buy you one more drink.'

Bubbles pretended to scowl, enjoying the game.

Moonface glanced up at the bar-room clock, then, holding a hand over his mouth whilst avoiding her eye, said, 'Sophia Gardens, main gate, three thirty. Get a taxi.'

Bubbles fumbled for her handbag.

'No!' he rasped. 'Don't write it down. Just listen. Walk through the park to the children's playground, it's well signposted. There's a side gate, by the roundabout. Go through it. They lock it at four so don't be late. Across the road you'll see railway arches made into lock-up garages. Go to the furthest one on your right. Understand?'

Confused, Bubbles said, 'All I understand is that I can't wait here 'til then without money for drinks and the taxi.'

The look Moonface directed at her made Bubbles wish she was safely back in her cockroach-infested bedsit as, once more, the newspaper was used as a shield. Bubbles snatched at the proffered ten pound notes greedily. 'How much will the taxi cost?' she asked, having already calculated that she would require at least four more drinks to while away the time.

'No idea,' Moonface muttered. Bubbles chose to down her drink and look away from the rage that made his entire body tremble as he slid over another tenner. 'Just remember those directions,' he warned as he suddenly stood up.

Bubbles gave him a loose-lipped smile. Of course she would remember; she was brilliant! 'The garage on the left,' she replied in a stage whisper.

'Right,' he hissed. 'Right!'

'Right? Yeah…right!' Bubbles teased, surrendering to a fit of giggles as he turned, ramrod-stiff, and walked to the bar, where he exchanged a few words with the barman, who shrugged his shoulders in reply before Moonface left the pub. Moments later the barman was hovering by Bubbles' shoulder, placing a large gin and tonic on the table.

'You were wasting your time there, love,' he said, grinning. Remembering her role, Bubbles laughed and said, 'Yeah, he made that clear.'

The barman turned loquacious. 'He's always been a mummy's boy, if you know what I mean, and since she died in October, nasty fall, that, all he's interested in is work. The hours he puts in, he must be worth a bob or two.'

Bubbles thought, you bet he is! but still remembered to play the game. 'Well, he's not sharing it with me. I'll have to make do with another gin,' at which she downed her drink in one gulp and held out her empty glass to the barman, who leered at her.

'I get off at half past nine,' he said optimistically.

'And I'm going home at half past three,' Bubbles replied, pushing the glass into his hand. 'Have you got a telephone and a number for a taxi?'

The barman scribbled on a beer mat with a pencil stub then silently pointed towards a door opening onto a passageway before retiring sulkily to replenish her drink.

Moments later Bubbles was in heaven. The log fire was warming, the tawdry Christmas decorations twinkled cheerfully and her supply of drink was guaranteed. This is how I'm going to spend the rest of my life, she thought dreamily, safely ensconced in an armchair. Christmas every day. No work, no need to go out at all, have everything delivered. Just warmth, comfort, idleness, booze and fags, amazing what a bit of blackmail could do...

For once she couldn't even be bothered to break the no smoking rule. She felt too contented. With gin and a log fire she could do without fags; well, just for a while.

She dreamed her way through the remaining time, tantalising herself with visions of cruises, wealthy old men who would marry her and then conveniently drop dead.

'Taxi's here!' the barman shouted, shattering her reverie. As she passed him, following the taxi driver, she wiggled her fingers and said, 'Thanks for everything.'

'Any time, love,' the barman replied. 'You know where to find me if you want a good time.'

Bubbles giggled and blew him a kiss, shouting, 'You won't be seeing me again!' before floating on an alcoholic cloud to the pub doorway, where reality, in the form of cold, rain-filled dusk, greeted her.

Soon be over, she reminded herself as she stumbled into the taxi. Then I'll be able to afford a taxi all the way home; but after she'd paid the driver her nerve failed her. The gardens, seen through the railings, were ill lit, and sobriety threatened.

An off-licence glowed its promise on a nearby street corner and Bubbles ran for it, her remaining coins securing her a half bottle of gin.

Much bolstered by this she swigged and smoked her way through the Sophia Gardens, arriving at the side gate just as a man was about to padlock it.

'Near thing, love,' the man said kindly. 'You wouldn't want to be stuck in here after dark. Dangerous place, even though we lock it.'

Bubbles heard the gate clang behind her, followed by the rattling of a chain as the man secured the padlock. Then silence. Nothing but silence and the growing realisation that it was now totally dark.

Through a misty veil of rain she could see diffused points of light across the road. As her eyes adjusted to the paltry illumination Bubbles could discern the vague shapes of archways, each with a lamp above closed double doors; except that on the far right there seemed to be another archway, unlit. And he'd said, 'Right,' and she'd joked, 'Right? Right!'

As the enormity of what she was trying to pull off hit her, she gripped her bag of evidence more tightly and downed some more gin. He wouldn't dare double-cross her, she told herself. She knew what he looked like.

Again she hesitated, assailed by a sense of something…a subliminal warning of something amiss…but what about the money?

Suddenly, all she wanted was the safety of home, even if she had to walk all the bloody way there. Turning left she strode out for eight, nine steps…then stopped. Which was the right way?

Follow the railings, she decided. Eventually I'll get back to bright lights, a busy road, the chance of a lift…

Then, ahead and to her left, through the railings, she could see the colourful change of traffic lights, red and white gem studded ribbons of vehicle lights beckoned, and she was quickening her step when she heard a vehicle approaching from behind. Keeping her eyes fixed straight ahead she willed it to pass her, to go away, but the engine slowed, and then a large, dark van with hinged side shutters was pulling into the kerb, only feet in front of her. The nearside passenger door opened and an all-too-familiar voice hissed, 'I said "right", you stupid bitch. Now get in!'

Bubbles wanted to run but all the strength had suddenly drained from her legs, so she gritted her teeth instead and smiled, as she had so many times before. Go with the flow, she told herself. You've endured worse, and this time you'll come out of it rich.

'Sorry,' she said as she stumbled up into the van. 'I'm a bit muddled.'

Moonface made no reply, and Bubbles, after one quick glance at his disturbing, shadowy features, kept her gaze fixed on the view outside her window as the van speeded up, infrequent pools of light becoming worryingly more scarce until they disappeared altogether, and once she had no external distraction she gradually became more aware of the unpleasant atmosphere within the van, a faint, sickly-sweet ammoniac smell combined with an all-pervading coldness.

'Can't you turn the heating up?' she demanded, as a growing unease along with the stench made her stomach churn.

'No,' he replied tersely. 'I'm on my way to pick up more stock.'

'Sod the stock!' Bubbles exploded. 'I want out of here. Give me my money. Now!'

'Oh, you'll get that, and more, in a minute,' he crooned, and Bubbles began to shiver, chilled by the pleasure in his voice.

'Please, just let me out,' she pleaded.

'All in good time,' he soothed, braking gently.

Bubbles looked around wildly, but all she could see was a

black void, broken only by the distant soft glow of arc lights that dissolved in a sudden squall of rain. Sweat brought on by panic and nausea prickled her skin and she wound down the window quickly, dragging in deep draughts of cold, damp air, but it was so thickened with a smell that she could almost chew it. Her gorge rose and she rapidly wound up the window again.

'What is that place?' she gasped.

'Just a processing plant,' he replied, switching off the engine, and with the dousing of the dashboard lights, reduced the interior of the van to Stygian darkness.

'I can't see!' Bubbles complained.

'You don't need to, for this,' he whispered, and she gasped as ice-cold fingers fumbled with then grasped her hand.

'What...?'

'Come on,' he urged in his quiet, high-pitched voice. 'Don't play the blushing virgin with me.'

At this Bubbles muttered, 'Well, life is full of surprises,' smiling as she began to relax. Really, men were all the same when it came down to it. 'Where?' she asked, practically, squeezing his hand.

'In the back,' he whispered. 'Wait there a minute.'

Bubbles sat, quiescent, looking over her shoulder. She could vaguely make out his form, flesh of face and hands paler than the night, their movements coinciding with the sound of a door sliding on metal runners.

'You first,' he said, tugging at her hand. Standing up gingerly, she obeyed the pressure of his hands as he encircled her waist and pushed her gently through the door.

'Keep going,' he murmured, and Bubbles yelped as first one hip bone then the other struck solid objects.

'What is this...?' she began.

'Sh!' he ordered, pushing her further along the narrow aisle. Her hands, in an attempt to keep herself upright, slid along contrasting surfaces; on her right, a smooth plastic surface; she peered at it, through it, and as her eyes adjusted to the faint wash of light from the distant lamps she could vaguely discern the outline of metal trays. She looked up; glass windows gleamed blankly, shuttered from the outside world…

She gasped in pain as a sliver of something pierced the soft flesh at the base of her left thumb. She tested the surface with her fingertips…it felt wooden. She raised her eyes and saw the glinting tips of sharply pointed metal hooks.

'Just here,' he grunted, pulling her firmly against him.

'Any way you like, darling,' she purred, rubbing her buttocks against his disappointingly flaccid penis.

'This I like,' he whispered, as the fingers of one hand began to caress her neck, pattering up and down like tiny feet.

'Ooh, I love a massage,' Bubbles cooed, leaning into the pressure. 'You're so good at it. What is it you do for a living?'

She barely registered the pricking sensation.

'I'm a butcher,' he whispered hotly into her ear whilst simultaneously thrusting the tip of a lethally honed boning knife between the first and second vertebrae of her neck, severing the spinal cord.

After collecting the carcasses of two pigs, three lambs and a side of beef from the 'processing plant', the mummy's boy drove his mobile shop to the rear of his premises. If anyone had been watching they would have observed nothing particularly unusual; one slightly limp, plastic-shrouded burden amongst the brutishly naked stiff ones carried into the shop. The late burning of lights glimpsed through the small, opaque window weren't unusual. Everyone knew Pete lived for his work.

He revelled in this recently discovered broadening of his pleasure horizon, one only dreamt of until his beloved mother was finally out of the way.

Smiling, he began preparing meticulously for his evening's enjoyment, which commenced with the ceremonial removal of all his clothes. Shivering with pleasure as the cool air caressed his naked flesh he began to prepare the latest in a series of secret ingredients for his prize-winning sausages and pies, accompanied by an occasional soft groan as his own fluids melded with hers.

His ultimate pleasure was still to come.

Once he'd returned the butchery room to its usual pristine condition of gleaming white tiles and glittering stainless steel he showered, scrubbing himself with a loofah and nailbrush until no trace of his endeavours was left. Then he dried himself vigorously, wrapped himself in a towelling robe, poured himself a tumbler of neat whisky, sat in his mother's armchair in front of the gas fire and began to tip the contents of Bubbles' handbag onto a low coffee table. This was the best moment of all, invading their tawdry privacies.

That there was no-one to grieve for the woman, even less to report her missing, soon became gratifyingly clear. A diary, labelled as free with a popular magazine, contained no names, addresses or phone numbers, apart from that of a doctor, and a pencilled-in appointment; 'clinic – 10.30', three weeks previously. There were no condoms, unlike the others. He laughed aloud at this…no whore in her right mind had unprotected sex these days.

Then he discovered the crumpled official looking envelope, an unexplored treat so full of promise that, after opening it, he began to masturbate.

Surely he was reading this all wrong… 'Sorry… Results: Positive… Counselling…'

Within a Whisker

Beryl Roberts

They say you're never more than a foot away from a rat in downtown Johannesburg. I reckon that's a conservative estimate, given that the largest city in South Africa is the mother of all cesspits, the undisputed arsehole of the universe.

The particular rat I fleetingly shared the gutter with there was certainly less than a foot away, its covering of hair sleek and ebony black, its eyes shining like mahogany beads, sizing me up as so many mega-bites. It had watched me hit the tarmac at a pedestrian crossing and lie stretched full out under the number plate of a metallic grey stationary car, before scuttling forward, full of curiosity, whiskers twitching, eager to identify my scent and flavour. As I eyeballed the rodent, I realised that if my plans backfired, I'd soon be reduced to tyre-tread, and the rat would get a large portion of freshly pulped nibbles.

My musing was cut short when I felt a sharp kick against the sole of my shoe and heard a cry of, 'Hoof it, bass ! Fast! Fast!'

'Sorry, not this time, pal,' I whispered, apologetically, to the rat, 'though you were just within a whisker.' It blinked back at me accusingly, its whole face twitching with hungry disappointment.

I scrambled onto the pavement on all fours, just in time to see the grey car disappearing down the road, the two close-cropped, negroid heads of my accomplices silhouetted through the rear window. Then I became aware of the crunch of glass from a pair of broken spectacles under my feet and an anguished cry for help coming from a writhing bundle of clothes on the grass verge. I was in the middle of a crime scene and the only witness.

I sprinted half a block without stopping then I dodged up a side street and flung myself into a warehouse doorway. Sitting on the bare concrete step, waiting for my jolting heart to subside, I felt the sweat of my exertions set on my skin like a coating of lard. I had half an hour to kill. Time to reflect on our perfectly executed car-jack.

My exit-visa out of hell.

Hell for the last month had been a rat-infested bolt hole in the northern suburbs of Jo'burg; scruffy lodgings in an untidy ribbon development that linked the black township overspill of Berea with the downwardly mobile, white trash of Parkville. In the decade and a half since the collapse of apartheid, it had changed from a no man's land into a virtual everyman's land, a haven for drifters, drug dealers and drunks, besides attracting the usual sprinkling of do-gooders who yearned to mix and match the rag-bag of human riff-raff there and meld it into a microcosm of the new rainbow state. Quaintly described in fringe magazines as 'the sanitised squat of les nouveaux pauvres', the district was a ghetto of fast food joints, pawnshop-cum-money-lenders and sleazy, backroom bars that catered for conceptions, abortions and every type of in-between sexual and narcotic pleasure-fix devised by man. It also spawned seedy boarding houses and two star hotels, patronised by struggling travelling salesmen and those with reasons to hide.

It was in the bar of one of these, the Gold Nugget, that I had first met two recruits from Shabo township, the Kekana brothers, who had once fished a crumpled tourist map of London from a waste-bin and set their hearts and sights on a single ticket to Camden.

By employing brothers driven by a dream, I reckoned I'd keep the minds of both focused. If one of them looked like screwing up, I'd threaten the other with the soup kitchen, or worse. Tribal and family loyalty among location relations is strong and binding, so I knew both would be working in unison, intent upon doing me over – though ultimately, I'd be the one wielding the spanner.

There's a thriving criminal subculture in all third world cities and Jo'burg's no exception. Deprivation and despair ensure a ready supply of raw recruits prepared to obey orders blindly, with a reckless disregard for their own skins. But, however dangerous and dedicated they are, these amateurs remain cat's paws and never get to taste the cream or to enjoy even one of a cat's nine lives. Their criminal careers are as short lived as they are squalid, because, lacking contacts, they get found in possession of hot goods or weapons they can't unload, or for concocting fanciful alibis they have to bully others to substantiate.

The Kekana brothers were typical of this breed of fall guy and I'd had no conscience about exploiting them. I'd already made certain that all the cerebral work had been done before involving them, so all one brother had to do was to act dumb, and all the other had to do was to drive fast.

The connoisseurs of sophisticated crime were the craftsmen of North Korea, sweating at their humid printing presses thousands of miles away, rolling off faultless works of art: virgin-pure rand banknotes, crackling to be exchanged for shabby but genuine dollar, sterling and euro notes.

Transported in sampans via the bustling waterways of Pyongyang, sacks full of counterfeit banknotes had already been shipped across the South China Sea and the Indian Ocean and had landed on the East African coast, disguised as safety packaging and stuffed inside containers full of cane furniture, bound for Durban's riviera hotels. Whilst the furniture was dumped unceremoniously inside dockside warehouses, the more valuable waste by-product was trucked across miles of dirt track and delivered in crates to my front door. Rotten money is easier to sell than ripe oranges.

I'd spent a month dossing down at Jo'burg's international airport terminals, wringing from pliable luggage handlers details of where tourists were heading, then way-laying them in hotel foyers and lounges, bribing couriers, and hanging around bars and casinos, bamboozling boozers and losers with dud notes. I offered large cash loans at give-away exchange rates, swapping millions of Commie-red rands for mint-cool greenbacks, raking it in.

But success breeds envy.

Rival fraudsters registered their disapproval by torching my Chevy and threatening me with instant cremation if I tried to leave town without sharing my good fortune. The syndicate ran all the taxi and car hire companies in the city and, with copies of my photo pinned on every windscreen, there was healthy competition amongst the drivers to be the one to hand me over and collect the ransom.

Like the city's rats, I kept to the back streets and gutters after dusk and lived by night amongst filth and rubble.

During my initial business transactions, the Kekana brothers stayed physically close to me, like a pair of outsize shoulder-pads, looking menacing, but actually doing nothing. Then I needed to get myself and my money out of Jo'burg fast and, to do that, I needed a car.

Anyone would imagine a large and populous city to be full of them – there for the taking! Not so Jo'burg.

Property owners in Jo'burg live under conditions of continuous curfew and permanent siege behind the plush, drawn curtains of their urban mansions. Black, white and mixed-race upper-class residents, who want to keep what they own, are forced to live, discreetly armed, inside virtual castles, fortified by barred windows, locked doors and padlocked gates. Their cars are never parked trustingly on public roads but stand immobilised by alarms on private drives, bordered by gardens patrolled by guards and vicious dogs, and screened from the road by electronically operated gates – all major obstacles, when you need to borrow a set of wheels.

Fortunately, though, there's another phenomenon unique to Jo'burg – black 'kerb kulture'. Hawkers hang around traffic robots waiting for the red light that will bring to a grinding halt a captive market of around twenty drivers every few minutes. Then, natives swoop like ravens from the shadows to tap at driver and passenger windows, holding out bargains for sale, like economy packs of black plastic refuse bags, 'designer' sunglasses, watches, or cheap Taiwan toys.

When the lights turn green and drivers lift their hand-brakes, there's a mad rush to jump clear, because some motorists think running jaywalkers down in cold blood is fair game. Sometimes, drivers roar off clutching goods they haven't paid for but, more often, sellers deliberately fumble with customers' change and are left holding it, gesticulating innocently into the rear mirror that it's not their fault red's turned to green and they've been left with double their asking price.

I was fairly confident that my local knowledge of Jo'burg and its eccentricities would get me that car. Only the street-savvy and rats survive and thrive in Jo' burg.

D-Day – Departure Day – arrived.

The brothers met me in fading light at Smuts Street robots. Alpheus was carrying a reproduction art deco cigarette lighter, a gilt monstrosity shaped like Ali Baba's lamp, stuck unsteadily onto a fake onyx base. He seemed unsure in which hand to hold it. Right. Left. Right. Now thrown up in the air then caught with both hands. He looked anxious, nervously hopping from one leg to the other as if he wanted to relieve himself. His whole body language was arrestable. By comparison, Gladman looked confident and in full control of himself and the situation. He was chewing gum nonchalantly and even dared to wink at me. I acknowledged their presence silently then positioned myself at the kerb as if waiting to cross the busy main street. Smartly dressed and carrying my flight bag crammed tight with high denomination banknotes, I looked like any other anonymous office worker on his way home.

Suddenly, the lights blinked red and a metallic grey car with a single, elderly driver drew up alongside us. There was no car immediately behind him, which suggested that he had probably drifted mindlessly through the previous lights. I coughed and we sprang into action. While Alpheus engaged the driver's attention, pestering him to buy the 'designer' cigarette lighter at bargain price and flicking it on and off to demonstrate its working order, I dropped onto the tarmac, rolled level with the number plate, and made my brief acquaintanceship with the rat.

Gladman, as rehearsed, threw a fit, motioning to the driver that there was a suicidal maniac lying under his wheels and Alpheus joined in the rumpus. Predictably, the harassed driver left the engine running while he got out to investigate. I took my leave of the rat, scrambled onto the pavement and brushed myself down, just in time to catch sight of Gladman flooring the elderly driver with a few well-aimed body blows, before taking possession of the BMW.

It was time to move from my cover and rejoin the Kekanas. I felt confident that the stolen car was now safely housed in the underground car park of the Gold Nugget, where I had reserved a room for one night. Once I had settled my final debt with the brothers, and snatched a few hours' kip, Gladman could chauffeur me to the airport and take ownership of the car as his tip for a job satisfactorily completed. By avoiding using either a hired taxi or a rented car, I would have neatly side-stepped the gangland death threats, but it would only be when I was safe on board the night flight to Cape Town, that I'd be able to relax and look forward to receiving my next cargo of 'gift-wrap' for recycling. By then the Kekana brothers would probably be in custody and the stolen BMW so many spare parts. Tough.

Room 9 was basic, containing two single beds, a television, a mini-bar and a small bathroom. Once inside, the brothers, feeling dehydrated and with adrenalin levels running high, helped themselves to drinks from the mini-bar. I suggested they chilled out on the beds, or watched television, while I calculated their pay. Then, when darkness fell, we could leave from the underground car park and join the convoy of traffic streaming to the airport and there say our fond farewells.

The hotel room lacked air-conditioning, so when Alpheus mentioned that he had a blinding headache, I gave him the aspirins I'd reserved for my flight. Then Gladman grumbled that the car snatch had made him hungry and asked if he could go out and fetch us a take-away meal. The hotel itself offered no dining facilities, because of the glut of native restaurants nearby serving exotic African dishes, like ostrich and kudu, as well as foreign food outlets, including Thai, Indian and Portuguese, that amply catered for all of Jo'burg's cosmopolitan gourmets. In addition, to satisfy the cravings of fast food junkies, there were also burger bars, hot-dog stalls and fish and chip kiosks, wafting their pungent fumes of onions, oil and spices into the air, all adding to the city's humidity and stench.

Gladman was making me nervous, sighing dramatically and pacing about the small room, so I gave him a few hundred rand and told him to get me a salami baguette and whatever he and his brother fancied.

I regretted, later, that I'd put it like that, because he took me literally.

The brothers conferred in native gibberish, to the effect that they didn't trust me as banker, so it was proposed that Alpheus should stay with me, while Gladman went foraging around outside.

Next, Alpheus couldn't decide what to eat. He'd lived his whole life in a township, where the staple diet was mealie pap, a stiff maize porridge, supplemented with chunks of dry bread. What would he know of à la carte menus and haute cuisine?

Being white and carnivorous, I couldn't guess where Gladman would find mealie pap in the city and I didn't give a rat's rectum anyway. With his boozing, his headache and now his finicky appetite, Alpheus was getting on my tits, so I informed his brother there were umpteen vegetarian outlets nearby, including a Thai take-away, which, incidentally, employed a very tasty waitress.

Gladman left his brother watching television and me counting the money and within twenty minutes he'd returned with my baguette and two cartons of Thai Mixed Vegetable Noodles for Alpheus. I asked him what he had found to tickle his tastebuds and he said he fancied sampling a portion of the Thai appetizer who had served him the noodles. He had change in his pocket now to pay to get rid of the roe simmering in his balls like so much dim sum. He reckoned he'd only be gone an hour, but just in case I developed ideas of going solo, he'd take the car keys with him, as a precaution. I told him only a cynical, kaffir bastard could think like that.

'It only fair, bass,' he said, laughing. 'After all, BMW stands for Black Men's Wheels and dis car's nearly mine.' He dangled the car keys hypnotically in front of me, pocketed them and left.

In truth, I found playing for time in that cramped rat-hole more comfortable with one sweating native than two. Alpheus and I sat propped up on each of the twin beds, scoffing our snacks, him by now half-pissed with the mixture of drinks he'd been taking from the mini-bar. Then he lay back, stretched out and began breathing deeply, as if practising relaxation. Poor sod, I thought, I bet he's been used to lying on bare boards all his life. Soon he started to snore loudly, so I took the flight bag of money into the bathroom, locked the door and shat, showered and shaved to save me valuable time later. When I emerged after thirty minutes, I felt de-toxed as well as decriminalised. I could even feel the Jo'burg jitters evaporating through my pores and a perverse nostalgia for the god-forsaken place seeping through me.

Alpheus was still lying on the bed, surrounded by the empty food cartons but now I noticed that he was breathing irregularly and jerking his skinny limbs, as if re-enacting a nightmare. To ignore the convulsions, I switched on the television – just as the Bafana-Bafana Premier League striker headed a winning home goal into the back of the net – but I had to turn it straight off, distracted by the gasping and rhythmic twitching coming from the adjacent bed.

Did I have an epileptic on my hands?

Whatever happened, I resolved not to give him the kiss of life in case he enjoyed it.

Suddenly, Alpheus, draped in a white sheet like a reviving corpse, jack-knifed into a sitting position, frightening the shit out of me. His whole body heaved violently and his mouth gaped open, as if he was going to scream at the top of his voice. Instead, khaki-coloured vomit spouted from deep in his throat, down his clothes and onto the bedding. He gasped and coughed, struggling for breath, his arms flailing about wildly. I ran into the bathroom and grabbed the wet towel. When I reached Alpheus with it, I found him groaning, and retching, his torso overhanging the bed and his head hovering limply above the pool of congealing, mottled vomit on the floor.

'What's up with you, man?' I yelled. 'Are you out of your tiny mind? Look at this fucking mess. The place smells like a sewer! I've paid big money to have a few hours' shut-eye in here, you selfish sod.'

As Alpheus groaned, tears streamed from his bloodshot eyes and fell in cascades down his face. Then, he lay back, exhausted. For the first time in my life, I realised that negroes can turn ashen. Better let him sleep it off, I thought. My mind raced up several blind alleys. Where the hell was Gladman? What would he do when he came in and saw this stretcher-case? What if he took it into his devious mind that I'd been manhandling Alpheus and turned savage? Even worse, how could I rely on this pair of rats' arses to get me out of here tonight in time to catch a plane?

As Alpheus's panting subsided, it was my turn to hyperventilate. Even if I bolted and survived a taxi journey to the airport, Gladman, as designated chauffeur, knew my flight details. He'd follow for his cut, perhaps even involve the police and convince them that I'd assaulted his brother. Bunking off would confirm my guilt, lead to my bags being searched and get me arrested. I had no choice but to sit it out.

The smell of the acrid vomit was unbearable. Just how many exotic Thai dishes was Gladman getting stuck into?

There came a light tap on the door. I dashed to open it, half suspecting that it was Gladman trying to tease me into a temper, but it was a young chambermaid standing there, her hair sleek and black, her eyes glistening like mahogany beads.

'I'se come to turn over yo' bed covers,' she said.

'I don't think it would be wise to disturb my friend when he's sleeping,' I answered, preparing to close the door. 'But thank you, anyway.' Then an idea struck me and I called after her retreating figure. 'I don't suppose you'd have a vacuum cleaner handy, would you?'

'It's in de cupboard at de end of de corridor,' she said returning. 'Why? Has you spilt somet'ing?'

'My friend's been sick,' I said. 'I tried mopping it up but

I've probably made it worse. I've got to stay here for a few more hours, before catching a night flight. If you're not doing anything else now, I'll pay you to clean up the room.'

The maid nodded and bustled off.

I picked up the brothers' pay packets and my flight bag and laid them, for maximum security, under and alongside Alpheus's lank body, tucking the heavy coverlet underneath and all around, so that man and money were enclosed in a tight cocoon of padded cloth.

The maid returned, dragging a vacuum cleaner and holding fresh bed linen.

'Bless you,' I said, handing her a fifty rand note.

'T'ank you, sir,' she said, obviously taken aback by the sum.

I pointed to the mess on the bed and floor, embarrassed, and glanced back at her to gauge her reaction. Her beady eyes glistened and her nose twitched as she breathed in the vile stench.

'Now, you jus' keep out of de way, sir.'

Relieved, I disappeared into the bathroom and sat on the loo with the door open. I could hear the portly maid grunting as she bent to pick up the food cartons and soiled tissues and expressing disgust when she found the sick-encrusted towel. I heard her muttering, probably incanting a tribal curse, as she sorted out the vacuum heads, before plugging the machine into the wall socket.

She knocked on the bathroom door and peeped in.

' Your frien' has a fever, sir. I t'ink he needs a doctor.'

'Doctors take hours to answer a call. I'm just waiting for his brother to come back then we'll all push off.'

'He don't look good, sir.'

'That's his brother's problem,' I said. ' I've paid for the room.'

Despite the generous tip I had given her, a day's wage in current terms, the maid looked reproachfully at me under drooping eyelids and shook her head.

'There'll be extra, if you're quick,' I urged.

The maid hurried into the bedroom and I returned to the loo seat. I could hear she was making a thorough job of cleaning the room; the mechanised nozzles buzzing as they penetrated the carpet fibres, sucking up all the fetid food particles. I decided the filthy job was worth another twenty rand, when she'd finished.

Suddenly, the bathroom doorway darkened with the sinuous profile of Gladman. He looked down at me sitting tensely on the loo seat, his skinny fingers twitching the crotch of his shapeless trousers suggestively, a silly grin spread across his face.

'What de fuck's been goin' on in 'ere?' he asked. He sounded cocky and looked refreshed. It was obvious how he'd spent the last hour and I hated him for getting one up on me.

'Your brother's been honking his guts up non-stop, since you left,' I said cuttingly. 'The maid's clearing up the mess he's made. I'll deduct her hundred rand fee out of his pay packet.'

I rose from the toilet seat and went to examine Alpheus. He was where I had left him an hour before, in deep sleep, motionless. But the coverlet I'd wrapped tightly around him had been loosened and thrown back, as if in a feverish frenzy, and the flight bag and the two envelopes of money had gone.

Near the door, the abandoned vacuum cleaner lay roaring with life on the carpet, unmanned and sucking away noisily at nothing.

'Where's the maid?' I yelled.

'I pass her outside, climbing in de taxi wit' bags, baas. I t'ink she go on holiday. She wave to me an' smile.'

'I bet she did,' I said, between clenched teeth. 'The cunning ratbag's cleaned us right out.'

I explained to Gladman where I had hidden the money. Of course, being a cynical primitive, he didn't believe me. Thought

I was cheating him. Accused me of being in cahoots with the maid, who was obviously waiting for me at the airport. When he said that, it occurred to me that it would have been a brilliant idea – if he hadn't confiscated the car keys. Now, besides being broke and being in possession of a stolen car, we had a casualty on our hands.

Someone knocked on the bedroom door and, for one crazy moment, I thought the chocolate-eyed charmer had scuttled back, racked with guilt at chiselling a punter, who had paid her over-generously for work she hadn't even done.

Instead, a thin, wiry-haired Jew stood in the doorway, clutching a Gladstone bag.

'You called a doctor?' he asked, sliding through the doorway, like an eel. 'Hotel reception contacted me minutes ago. Fortunately I had my cellphone on and I was passing. Where's the patient?'

He seemed to know the layout of the room and, by the time I had checked the corridor for snoopers and closed the door, he had glided past Gladman and was struggling to rouse Alpheus, by first tapping his face, then pounding his chest. I moved into the bathroom to think and Gladman followed me.

'How we go pay a real doctor wit' no money, bass?' he whispered, his eyes rolling.

'The same way we're going to pay the hotel bill,' I answered, out of the corner of my mouth. 'By doing a runner.'

The doctor called out, 'What's this man eaten recently?'

'Thai noodles, sir,' Gladman shouted.

'With meat?' yelled the doctor.

'No, sir. Just veggies,' yelled back Gladman.

'Definitely Thai?'

'Def'ni'ly, sir.'

I pushed Gladman into the bedroom to stop the shouting, in case the management arrived to complain. Walls in these doss houses are as porous as sponges and some clients expect to sleep during evenings, to prepare them for their nocturnal activities.

'And drink?'

'Plenty,' I said, indicating the waste bin full of discarded bottles and cans.

'Drugs?'

'A few headache pills.'

'Headache pills?' the doctor queried.

'Aspirin.'

'Hm. As I suspected. The classic lethal cocktail,' said the doctor. 'Alcohol, aspirin and peanuts.'

'Peanuts?' I echoed, convinced everyone was going ape. 'Peanuts?'

'A staple ingredient of Thai cooking,' said the doctor. 'I'm afraid there's nothing I can do for this young man, beyond issuing him with a death certificate. The cause of death is peanut anaphylaxis. With more time, I could have tried epinephrine injections, but there's a good chance he'd have died of respiratory failure anyway. Chronic TB is a natural hazard of living in a township and a post mortem is certain to prove that his lungs were about as useful as a pair of lace doilies inside his chest.' The doctor snapped his bag shut. 'I'll leave my bill at reception to be added to your tab. Would you like the mortuary contacted?'

Tears and sweat mingled on Gladman's contorted face.

'No, t'anks, sir. I take my brudder home,' he said weakly. 'No money for dead parlours, or t'ings like dat. I go take him home.'

I nodded my agreement and showed the doctor out.

Gladman looked broken, so I put my arm around his shoulders.

'No money and no brudder to go to Camden wit', baas,' he murmured thickly. 'And all dat work for nuttin'.'

'Within a whisker,' I said in a daze. 'We came just within

a whisker. It was nothing we did wrong, Gladman. Blame the Jo'burg jinx. And the local rats. The female ones are real mean killers.'

The Visitor

Delphine Richards

I was hoovering the hallway when I saw a man standing in my dining room.

You know the feeling. It's probably happened to you a hundred times. You think you saw something. You go back to look and see that a curtain hook has broken or something and the sagging material is the same shape as a person's outline.

I took two quick backward steps to the dining room door. And there was a man in there!

'Oh!' said a high pitched noise which came out of my mouth, though I didn't have any conscious knowledge of having produced it.

The man looked around and I saw that he was holding a garden fork. Not a small one but the type that stands about three foot high and you have to put your foot on the back of it to get the spikes into the ground. I was acutely aware that something had dropped off it onto my clean carpet.

Fear injected a burst of images into my mind and I had a swift vision of the newspaper headlines: 'Woman, 32, Stabbed in Farmhouse' and a picture of me taken on holiday in Tenerife where I look as if I've stood on something sharp. That was the moment I had seen Gareth and Siân betraying me as they waited at the bar.

I told myself to stop being a drama queen and that there was probably a reasonable explanation for the presence of my

215

impromptu visitor.

'Were you looking for my husband?' I asked.

I knew it was a stupid thing to say. I could see that the man just didn't look right.

'The Ziggles are coming,' he said.

His eyes looked hazy and confused. Just like the sheepdog looked when we had to have his leg amputated after Gareth accidentally drove over him in the tractor. He'd had a sedative first and I had to wait with him until he was woozy enough for the vet to take him away.

'The Ziggles?' I said.

His eyes changed to fear and alarm. I didn't know who the Ziggles were. One of the Polish families we have in the village maybe…

'They leave footsteps of blood,' he said, looking around as if he could see bloody footsteps on my carpet.

'Oh no,' I said sympathetically. Then, in a flash of inspiration, 'They won't be coming here.'

He shook the garden fork and more stuff drifted on to the carpet. I hoped it wouldn't stain. It was important, on such a momentous day, that the house was spotless. I didn't want to give anyone an opportunity to say that Beth Price kept a dirty house.

'It's not purple, you know,' he said

'I see,' I replied. There didn't seem to be an answer to that. I was trying to work out how to get to the phone. It would mean calling the police and I hadn't really wanted them around and interfering. Well, not at that point anyway…

'Do you want a cup of tea?' he said, suddenly brighter.

'Good idea,' I said. 'I'll go and put the kettle on, shall I?'

I turned away from the doorway and instantly heard him shout out some unintelligible word. I stopped dead. He was looking at my feet.

'Look at the blood!' he said, eyes wide with fear.

I looked down. He sounded so convincing that I really expected to see blood around my feet. Of course, all I saw were the caramel coloured fibres of the carpet.

'I think it's better in here,' I said, gesturing towards the kitchen.

I turned away from him again and started to walk to the kitchen. Immediately, he was behind me. I increased my pace and turned to face him as soon as I had cleared the kitchen doorway.

'Shall we have some tea now?' I suggested. I recognised my tone of voice as one I would have used to distract a young child. It's what I call my 'Shall we watch *Jungle Book* again?' voice. A tone I probably would have used to my own child had things been different.

He walked towards the kitchen table, pulled out a chair and sat down. He still held the garden fork; its tines facing up towards the ceiling and almost level with his face.

'Is that in your way?' I asked. 'Shall I put it outside?'

I reached out my hand for the fork and he gave it to me. I breathed out quietly and turned towards the door. If I could only get outside I could run to the barn where the quad bike was kept with its keys always in the ignition.

I hadn't even got to the kitchen door, never mind the utility room beyond, when he let out a fearsome yell. 'By the fence! By the fence!'

He was pointing at the cupboards where the units jut out as a partial division between the cooking area and the table.

'You want me to put it there?' I asked.

'By the fence,' he said again.

I leaned the fork against the units. It slid down the smooth tiles and I tried to re-adjust it, but that only seemed to make him more agitated so I laid it flat on the floor.

He watched me closely.

'I'd better get the kettle on.' I went over to the sink. He

got up and stood by the fork. Mindful of the fact that he was between me and the utility room door, I went off again into *Jungle Book* mode. 'Cups or mugs? Mugs are better, I think. More tea in them. Which one would you like? There's a huge Mr Men mug or a—' I stopped suddenly. I had been about to say 'a Give Blood – Play Rugby mug'.

He came to stand behind me. Panic reared up with flailing hooves.

'Oops! 'Scuse me. Let me get out of your way. You choose a mug that you want.' I said all this in one breath and scuttled out of his way. He just stood there as if deep in thought, hands hanging at his side.

'If you just open that cupboard you can get a mug each for us.' I waved my hand in the direction of the cupboard.

Quick as a flash, he had my hand held in his. His grip was like a child's. As if he was waiting for me to help him across the road.

'You come and sit down, then,' I coaxed. I led the way and, to my relief, he followed like a little boy. This pseudo-maternal role was something I was used to: in my marriage I had been more of a mother to Gareth than a wife – a mother and farm manager rolled into one.

'OK. You just sit there and I'll get the tea,' I said while prising his hand off mine. I went back to the sink and, with my body turned slightly towards him, went through the automatic task of filling the teapot and stirring it.

'Do you take milk and sugar?'

He didn't reply. I realised that he hadn't actually said anything for a while.

'And maybe we can have a piece of cake, too,' I said. The *Jungle Book* voice had completely taken over. I took some deep breaths and pictured myself cutting a piece of cake. With a knife. Maybe not...

'Or a biscuit. Less filling so that you don't spoil your lunch.'

Bloody hell, I thought, where had that little gem come from? I must have sounded like his grandmother.

He still didn't say anything. I took the milk out of the fridge and took it over to the table. He put his hand on the blue plastic cap.

'It's sensible,' he said and then patted it.

I had no idea what he meant so I went back to get the sugar, spoons and some biscuits on a plate. Somewhere in the back of my mind a little know-it-all data bank warned me that giving him caffeine and sugar was a bad idea. Too late. He had picked up an orange cream biscuit. The data bank added 'artificial colours' to its warning list.

I watched him take a bite out of the biscuit while I went to get the teapot and mugs. He looked as if he was on his own in the room. He made no attempt to watch me or communicate.

I sat down at the table and poured the tea with lots of nonsensical, nervous comments like 'Oops,' and 'There you are,' and, God forbid, 'Nothing like a nice cup of tea, is there?'

I poured milk into his Mr Men mug and automatically added and stirred a spoonful of sugar. He picked up the mug and took a sip before twitching slightly and put it down.

'Careful! It's a bit hot.' I wondered why I was considering his welfare when he had made such mess of my day.

Still no answer. I wondered how on earth I was going to get rid of him. On that day, of all days, I needed the house to myself. Where was he from? He couldn't be local. Everyone knew everyone else in Pwll y Coed. Even if you didn't know someone's name you categorised them by faces or as 'the people who bought Dai the Wood's old place' or whatever. He didn't look abnormal in any way. He had a trendy haircut and the serviceable clothes of a labourer of some sort. I could see smudges of oil or something similar on them. In different circumstances I supposed I would have described him as 'tasty'.

While he remained in his trance-like state, I checked my

gilet pocket for my mobile phone, realising as I felt for it that I had left it upstairs with all the other equipment needed for later in the day. In a way, it was a relief. I fully intended to go through with my plans. Having people turn up before I was ready for them would ruin everything.

The man looked at the calendar on the wall by the table. Clearly marked on the day's date was 'Leominster Cob Sale'. I hoped that he wouldn't connect the information with the absence of my husband and realise that I was on my own for the whole day. Though, of course, that was not where Gareth was, the fact remained that he was not going walk through the door at any moment to see if lunch was ready.

The man ran his hand down the calendar.

'Birthday,' he said. 'Is it your birthday, today?'

He looked at me as if he had forgotten I was there.

'Penblwydd Hapus!' I said, wondering if speaking in Welsh to him would make him more communicative. He looked at me as if I'd uttered something in Urdu.

I became aware of a slight draught around my feet which signalled the way he had come into the house. I could even hear the low tapping of the utility room door against its frame. 'Perhaps I should shut that door,' I suggested. 'It's a bit draughty. Are you cold?'

He looked at me in surprise and I got up and walked purposefully across the kitchen. His chair scraped against the tiles as he leapt to his feet and came after me. His longer legs and obvious panic gave him the advantage and he grabbed my upper arm as I started to run. I raised my other arm over my head and started screaming 'OK, OK, OK...'

He swung me round to face him and hauled my arm upwards making me wail in pain.

'Fucking bitch!' he snarled and dug harder into my arm.

'Please don't hurt me, please! Please let go, you're hurting me!' I sobbed.

His face was close to mine and I could smell his bitter breath mingled with orange cream biscuits. There was also a faint smell of petrol on his clothes. My arm felt pinched and sore where he was holding me. His eyes started to lose their concentration again.

'Please let go!' I begged. My tears had stopped but my cheeks were still wet.

'Fucking bitch took them,' he said. 'No way! No way!'

'I'm sorry you're upset, but please don't hurt me. I haven't done anything to you…' I pleaded again.

His gaze faded out and his grip slackened.

'Cheryl took them.'

'What did Cheryl do?' I asked cautiously.

He looked at me as if I was lacking a brain.

'She took them away,' he repeated. 'They're my children too! She's a bitch!'

It started to make sense to me. I felt a sort of compassion for him. He was obviously the victim of an unreasonable spouse. I knew all about that. Though, if his behaviour so far was anything to go by, I wasn't entirely surprised by his wife's actions.

'Let's sit down, shall we?' I suggested.

He looked around him as if he was wondering where the chair had gone. He turned and went back to his seat. I felt my mind, but not my eyes, veer in the direction of the utility room and escape. I couldn't risk it. I went over to sit at the table with him. There was a puddle of tea where the mug had spilt its contents when he'd jumped up to follow me. The perfectionist in me wanted to fetch a cloth to wipe it. My intention to have the house spotless before the police and Scenes of Crime Officers arrived was being thwarted at every turn.

'I'm Beth. What's your name?' I asked.

Silence from him.

'I'm Elizabeth really, but no-one calls me that. Well, my

grandmother used to – when I was about four. She died when I was nine.' I realised that I was babbling due to nerves.

'Have you finished your tea?' I asked. 'I expect you're running late now.'

'It's too late,' he said.

An uneasy chill prickled through my back at his words. I was afraid to ask him what he meant so we both sat there, staring at the table.

It occurred to me then that within personal relationships people are split into two types – those who are doers and those who are done by. The doers are people like Gareth, who please themselves regardless of what anguish they cause their partners. The 'done bys' are like me – trying to adjust their lives to make others pleased with them. And when you're a 'done by', you're born like that. Sometimes, when you are young, you get a glimpse of this destiny. That moment happened to me when I was nine years old and I had missed a day at school to go to my grandmother's funeral. The following day I caught Emyr Bowen kissing Siân Davies behind the toilet block. Yes, the same Siân! The day before the funeral he had kissed me and said he would marry me when we were grown up. Siân said that he had told her he would marry her when they were grown up. They didn't, of course. Things change when you grow up. The thing that hadn't changed was the presence of my best friend, Siân, in my life. And Siân herself obviously hadn't changed. Emyr Bowen went on to marry another local girl. Neither Siân nor myself would have looked twice at him as an adult. Not with his old-fashioned hairstyle and clothes. I still see him around the sheep sales sometimes – a nice man but not my type. Siân, meanwhile, became a local celebrity – a tragic young thing with her career as an MP ahead of her and a handsome young solicitor husband who died of leukaemia three years after they got married. Despite the tragedy, Siân was a 'doer'. When it came to my husband, she was most certainly a 'doer'! I wondered who would have become the 'done by' in their relationship if I had not decided to intervene. My way had them both condemned.

'Where's the toilet?' said the stranger sitting at my kitchen table.

I looked at him and wondered if the phrase was more gobbledegook or whether he really did need to go to the toilet.

'You need the toilet? It's through there.' I pointed towards the utility room door. My mind considered sending him upstairs but then he would see things I preferred him not to see. And while he was up there, what could I have done? I had decided that leaving the house was not a good idea. Having planned the day to the last detail, it was imperative that I followed my own script.

He got up and stood uncertainly next to me.

'This way,' I said and got up to show him where the door was.

He followed me to the utility room, then turned and waved his hand at me.

'I'll wait in the kitchen,' I said and obediently returned to my chair.

He must have left the toilet door open because I soon heard the frothy flow of urine. With slight embarrassment, I turned on the radio on the windowsill. Scissor Sisters were singing that they didn't feel like dancing. Me neither, I thought.

I heard the toilet flush, then the tap being turned on. At least he was house-trained, I thought. Pity about the unfortunate habit of implanting himself in strange houses – I really needed to think of a way to get him to leave.

He came back to sit at the table without speaking and took a small jewellery box out of his pocket. I watched as he opened it. There was a little silver charm lying on a blue bed of velvet. It looked like some kind of flower.

'That's nice,' I said, 'Is it a present for someone?'

He leaned forward over the box and didn't answer.

'It's very nice,' I said again.

He made some noise that I couldn't understand. Then, as I was about to ask him to repeat it, I saw that he was crying.

'Oh, don't be upset,' I said, reaching out and gently rubbing his arm.

That seemed to act as a release valve and he began to sob like a child.

'I'll never see them,' he said.

'Oh, I'm sure you will,' I replied, 'A good solicitor will make sure that you have regular access.'

I hoped that this was true and that there was no other reason, his mental state for instance, that would influence the amount of contact he had. I didn't even know for certain that he was talking about his children. I decided to shut up.

The utility room door continued its gentle tapping and the room got colder as the April chill worked its way indoors. I wondered if I could get up to turn on the central heating dial in the hallway without provoking an extreme reaction from him. I watched his face to see if I could catch his eye and tell him what I wanted to do. He carried on sniffing and looking downwards.

I briskly rolled my shoulders to try to warm up but the arm he had grabbed me by was sore and stiffening. It was typical, I thought, that you could never rely on a hormonal hot flush when you needed one. But then again, I thought bitterly, if I had been a normal woman with normal fertility reaching menopause at a normal age perhaps I could have conjured up some body heat. I felt the beginnings of self pity seep into my mind. Why? All I had wanted was a family. Just one child would have been fine. It just wasn't fair how irresponsible women seemed to breed like rabbits when they didn't particularly want more children and I couldn't even have one.

The consultant had been very kind to me after they had

done the emergency hysterectomy the previous summer. 'This doesn't mean the end of your hopes for a family,' he'd said. 'When you have recovered and we've got you stabilised on HRT, maybe you'll think about adoption. I'm sorry that we had no option but to remove your womb. All those miscarriages have weakened your uterus and damaged the blood supply to the surrounding tissues…' I remembered his words exactly. They had been a pinprick of hope in an otherwise desperately sad situation for me.

The HRT had never agreed with me and, eventually, I had given up on it. My physical recovery had been slow and painful but I'd almost welcomed it as a tangible symptom of the heartache I felt. By September I was well enough – bodily at least – for our friends to suggest a holiday for several of us in Tenerife in October. Included in the crowd, of course, was Siân – she who always had to be considered because of her tragic loss. It was Siân who had to set the date for the holiday as an MP's time is apparently more important than a sheep farmer's. She suggested certain hotels, activities and even who was going to look after the farm while we were gone. We didn't mind her being in charge. After all, she had seen a lot more life than the rest of us who had rarely strayed out of Wales. In the end it was the old crowd of Gareth, me, Carys, Tony, Gwenda, Mike, Siân and Christine who went to Tenerife. Christine's husband looked after our farm as he hated sunny resorts and had bargained with her so that he could go with the boys to watch all the rugby internationals when that time of year came around.

At the time, I remember thinking that Gareth was behaving strangely. He was unusually quiet and I stupidly put it down to concern about me and the fact that I couldn't have children. I realise now that people like him don't have real feeling for anyone else. Stupid me. But nothing would have changed. Our destiny was set and I know now that I was about to be written out of Gareth's cast.

By the date we flew to Tenerife, he was his old self. At the airport he was buoyant and animated – filling the role of designated comedian for our circle of friends. Even Mike, who can be irritating in his cheeriness, kept shaking his head in disbelief.

By the time we arrived at the hotel in Tenerife, Gwenda had developed a spectacular stomach bug and that was the last anyone saw of her for two days. I was the next one to catch it, followed closely by Mike. The virus seemed to bypass the others as far as I know. Gareth has never been able to cope with ill people so he stayed out of my way as I made the very regular route from our bed to the en-suite bathroom. By the third day, I felt that eating was a possibility again and I started to explore the hotel. It was lunchtime and I thought that I could manage something light. As I walked into the hotel dining room I saw Christine and Gwenda sitting at a table together trying to master Christine's new camera.

As I got closer, Gwenda said: 'That's it. Try it now!' and Christine pointed the lens at me and a big flash of light went off. I've never worked out if the flash of light was from the camera or in my head as the truth of the situation hit me.

Behind Christine and Gwenda's table was an elaborate archway into the bar area. Through the archway I could see Gareth and Siân waiting to be served. I could see their lips move as they spoke to each other. Then, Gareth raised his hand and gently stroked down the inside of Siân's arm. She smiled and ran her index finger around his hairline over his ear. It was the intimacy of the action that stunned me. As a crowd of friends, we could be very touchy-feely, but it was always done in front of each other. Gwenda would grab Tony's buttocks and make a rude remark or Mike would lick the side of someone's face while the victim screamed with laughter and disgust.

I sat down heavily next to Christine.

'Are you OK?' she asked. 'You still look a bit yuk.'

'I think I'll go back to the room,' I said. 'I thought I felt better but…' I got up and started to leave. As I pushed the chair back I noticed Gwenda glancing nervously towards the bar. Great! So all my friends knew about their seedy little affair too! And as Gwenda had spent the first two days of the holiday in bed and would therefore have missed any new developments, it seemed likely that she had known about them before we even got to Tenerife.

I went up to our room, my heart beating so fast and hard that I'm sure people could see and hear it. My mind whirled and somersaulted with possibilities. One moment I wanted to confront them, the next I wanted to sit it out and wait for the affair to end. I was too valuable to Gareth. He couldn't afford to lose me. I ran the farm like clockwork – paperwork and DEFRA matters, breeding programmes, show entries, sales – everything. Gareth was efficient enough at the physical stuff but the reputation he had gained for his livestock was down to my management. Apart from anything else, I had loved him. I had always known that I loved him more than he loved me. The previous months had only highlighted my precarious position in Gareth's life. I had often felt relegated to the same category as the non-breeders in our pedigree sheep flock and our Welsh Cobs. Once a breeding female proved to be unable to reproduce, she would be sent on her way to the sale.

I had sat on the bed in the hotel room and cried.

'Crocodile tears!' snarled the stranger in my kitchen. I jumped. I had forgotten where I was. The bitter past months had called me back for a cruel re-run of events. I realised that I had tears running down my face. That happened often now. The experts called it Post Menopausal Depression. I preferred to call it the result of a cheating, lying, bastard of a husband.

'Yes, crocodile tears,' I said, wiping my face. 'Nothing

important enough to get upset about.'

He was watching me carefully and it made me uneasy.

On the radio, Pamela Jones from Llanelli was live on the phone telling the presenter how to keep cats away from the garden by using a mixture of washing-up liquid and white vinegar. I wondered if Pamela Jones had any magic solutions for keeping strange men out of your house. And while she was at it, some tips on how to keep the ones you wanted. A bit late for me but…

Pamela rang off and we returned to music instead.

'Thank you, Pamela,' I said. 'Very helpful, I don't think!'

The man started and looked nervously at me. I suddenly wanted to laugh. Did he think he had exclusive rights to insanity! I could be as insane as anyone when I wanted to be! According to Gareth, I had completely lost the plot. When he told me about him and Siân I had reacted pretty extremely and had tipped the contents of the teapot over his head. Unfortunately, the tea was still hot and he was scalded. He must have been a little ashamed of himself because he didn't go to A and E, though I'm sure that his personal MP rendered first aid. I told him that MP obviously stood for Mistress Personified and, unbelievably, he leapt to Siân's defence saying that it was due to her morals that he and I were having that conversation.

'Siân wants to do this the right way,' he said

'That's very big of her,' I had snarled back at him.

Then he went on to say that everything had to be done properly, as they wanted to be together and start a family! That was when I tipped the tea over his thick head. The memory of doing that will always feel right to me. I could feel a vengeful smirk appearing on my face.

The stranger at my table stared at me again and made a surprised noise in his throat.

'Sorry, just daydreaming,' I muttered, but he continued to look as if someone had poured a bucketful of ice over him.

I realised that he wasn't actually looking at me but over my shoulder towards the windowsill. I glanced backwards, but could see no sign of anything.

'What's wrong?' I asked and jumped as he hit his hands down on the table.

I froze and held my breath. I couldn't hear anything except the radio. The local news was being read.

'...despite the police having set up roadblocks there has been no fresh sighting of Rogers. However, Maesymynydd is on the regular route used by ferry traffic so it is possible that he could be anywhere in the UK by now.'

I remembered to breathe and then held my breath again.

'...The three victims of the arson attack are still in a critical condition in hospital. It's thought that he may have set fire to Briar Cottage in the belief that his wife was still living there, but the house was occupied by a woman and two children who have no connection whatsoever to Barry Rogers...'

The man at my table jumped slightly.

I jumped too.

'...Police have warned the public to be vigilant but not to approach Rogers, who is reported to have suffered mental problems since the separation. A neighbour has told us that he was obsessed with the idea that an alien force was taking away his children...'

I continued to listen while watching him for a reaction or sudden movement.

'...and can call this number at the Incident Room at Maesymynydd Police Station...'

Oh, Barry, I thought. Oh my God, Barry!

Maesymynydd was about thirty miles from Pwll y Coed, but I assumed that he had hitchhiked in a very random direction. I could see no reason for him wanting to come to our village or the farm other than to get away from the scene of the arson.

I began to think things through.

'Barry,' I said.

He jumped a little.

'You heard what they said on the radio. The police are looking for you. Those people at the cottage weren't Cheryl and the children. You made a mistake. If you go to the police they'll understand. You can't stay here.'

He lowered his head and started to cry again.

He put his head on his arms and cried and muttered for a very long time. I tried to talk to him and get a response but he had withdrawn completely into himself.

Eventually, he straightened up. The look on his face was strange – unlike the expression he had worn since being in my house – more calculating, less vague. More dangerous...

He sat like that for about two hours while I sat opposite him, too scared to do anything else. Meanwhile the radio gave us regular reports on the news programme.

Then, I heard a car engine.

Barry stood up suddenly. Defensively, I pushed my chair away from him and back against the window sill. I missed seeing the car but Barry had obviously seen it.

'They're here,' he said loudly and looked around him as if searching for something.

'The police? Is it the police?' I asked in a hoarse voice.

Barry's eyes had their wild expression again.

'The Ziggles are here!' he said and grabbed my arm. 'They're here!'

He started to cry again.

'It's OK. It's OK.' I said trying to calm him down.

Then I glanced out of the window and glimpsed a patterned sweatshirt passing the window. A sweatshirt with a cartoon sheepdog and a cluster of sheep on the front. Underneath the cartoon were some words. The glimpse was too quick for either of us to read the words, but I knew they said 'Let's Get The Flock Out Of Here'. I knew because I had bought it.

I got up with Barry still gripping my arm.

'You're right,' I sighed, 'the Ziggles are here. Here comes the bad guy.'

Barry roared a cry and let go of my arm. He whirled around and bent down. The garden fork! He held the fork in both hands as I heard the utility room door click shut and a familiar voice call hesitantly 'Beth? I just want to collect some things. OK?'

'The Ziggles are here!' I yelled at Barry.

Gareth didn't stand a chance. Barry plunged the fork into his stomach as he came through the door. I screamed and ran the other way.

For a long time everything was quiet. I crept out of my hiding place in the dining room and carefully, step by step, went to the kitchen. Poor Gareth lay on his side in a pool of blood, his mouth open, his eyes staring but not seeing. Just like so many sheep I had seen dead over the years. The fork was still implanted in his stomach. Barry appeared to have gone.

I needed to phone the police, but first I went upstairs. I removed the noose from the landing and the plastic sheeting, Stanley knife and box of paracetamol from the bathroom. I had not intended leaving anything to chance. Mine was not just going to be a suicide attempt. I picked up the folder with the whole sordid story written inside it. Then I went to the spare bedroom and deleted the email that was waiting to be sent to the Western Mail explaining why one of our MPs had been the cause of my suicide. A mere marriage split would not have been enough to ruin her, but a full investigation into a death would have finished her.

Barry, however, had saved me from my personal sacrifice. A murder would be just as effective in getting the story told.

My mobile phone had already been set to 999, but I decided to wait another five minutes, to give him a chance to get away, before I called the police.

Without a Trace

Imogen Rhia Herrad

There were two of them, a man and a woman, ringing my doorbell. I'd got home from work not long before and was standing in the kitchen wondering about dinner. My heart sank when I saw them through the peephole. They looked grave. They looked like bad news.

I opened the door.

'Yes,' I said and cleared my throat.

'Police.' They showed their ID, introduced themselves, and all the while I was wondering what it was they'd come to tell me.

'Isobel Jenkins?'

I nodded.

'Would you mind if we came in?'

'Yes', I said. 'I mean, no, come in, I don't mind.'

I opened the door, led them to the living room, my brain whizzing in overtime.

I sat, they sat, and it was all horribly unreal, like a scene on TV.

'Is your father Peter Jenkins?'

'Yes. Yes, he is.' I thought of Dad – coming home from work when I was growing up; sometimes he was tired and sometimes bubbling over with stories. Unbidden, an image rose before my eyes, of Dad as I'd seen him on my last visit: his face so pink against his grey hair; sitting at his desk with the new computer, writing, surrounded by stacks of books.

'Why?' I asked. Nervous, wanting to know, not wanting to know; afraid to hear what they'd come to tell me.

She gave me a small smile. Maybe it was meant to look reassuring. 'We will be able to tell you that in a minute. For now, we have to ask you just to answer that question. When did you last see your father?'

'A fortnight ago,' I said. 'I went up for the weekend then. Please, tell me. Has something happened?'

'How were your parents when you last saw them?'

My stomach clenched. I don't know why, but that question really got to me. I could imagine what they were going to tell me next. I tried to swallow the rising fear.

'As always,' I said, striving for calm, in answer to the question. 'They were fine. I was there for the weekend – got there that Friday evening and left on Sunday after dinner. It – they... everything was just as always. They were fine. Something's happened to them, hasn't it?'

'What illnesses are there in the family?'

I shook my head, slowly, surprised. 'I'm not sure... Nothing serious, my mother has rheumatism and a stomach ulcer, and my father high blood pressure, but nothing worse than that; and quite normal for their ages. No cancer or anything like that.'

What on earth made me think of cancer I couldn't have said. Maybe because the pair of them looked so serious; and because I was worried, and thinking of worst-case scenarios. But the police don't come to your house to tell you that your dad has cancer.

'Has either of them ever suffered any seizures, dizzy spells, fainted?'

'No, no – nothing like that. Why? Please, tell me!'

The woman officer exchanged a glance with her colleague, a slight nod. I braced myself.

'I am afraid there is some bad news. You mother has died. She was found earlier today at the bottom of the staircase. She appears to have fallen down the stairs and hit her head.'

I swallowed. Of course. That must be why they had asked about seizures. But I had never known Mum even to feel as much as giddy.

'She must have tripped,' I said, and even while I said it, I realised that I was shaking my head. No, no, no. Mum. Dead. I reached out blindly for somewhere to support myself. Dead. Suddenly, the word was horribly real.

The walls swayed briefly.

Not the walls, me.

Hot tears rose into my eyes. I fought them down. Later. There would be time later, when I was alone. To digest it all. To think about Mum.

Later. Not now.

I stared at my hand, which was braced against the table. Glass table. I'd actually dusted it the other day, and its surface was clear as water. Two figures were reflected in it, sitting upside down. My gaze travelled from the reflections in the glass to the two police officers. I felt as though I'd fainted, but I was still sitting reasonably upright, so it seemed unlikely that I had. I blinked, slowly. Not real, I thought; nightmare. But it was all real. A tear rolled town my cheek, and I brushed it away, and swallowed, and found my voice again.

'Dad,' I said. 'How is he? I must go and see him.'

The two police officers exchanged another look.

'I'm afraid that won't be possible,' the man said. He hadn't spoken so far. His voice was odd, much lower-pitched than I would have expected. The surprise of his voice took me aback for a moment. Then his words registered.

'Why not? Has something happened to him as well? Did he find her? Is he suffering from shock? Did he have a heart attack? Tell me!'

My voice had risen. I was sitting on the edge of the sofa, my hands clenched.

I turned my head away, struggled to breathe.

'I'm sorry,' I said. 'I'm sorry, I didn't mean to shout at you. I'm so worried and you're not telling me...please, I need to know. What's happened to Dad?'

'We don't know,' said the woman officer.

'You don't *know?*'

'I'm sorry,' she said. 'We can't find your father anywhere. We wondered whether he might have come to you. He's disappeared. A neighbour found your mother.'

I stared at her.

'But...' I said. 'What... I mean – has something happened to him too? Was the house – could it have been a burglar?' Seizures, fainted, she had said. 'Do you think he might have seen her fall and had a shock and is confused now, and has run away or something?'

That would never happen. Not Dad, who was always so in control. Never confused, never unsure. He always knew what to do. Never in doubt.

'At the moment, we just don't know,' she said. 'We're looking for your father. We had wondered whether he might have come here. Or contacted you.'

'Me?' I said, stupidly. 'No – no, I would have told you. I haven't heard from him since I saw them both a fortnight ago.'

'Did you speak to them since?' the male officer asked. 'Even if you just rang or texted them to let them know that you'd got back safely. It's quite a way from Flint.'

I shook my head. 'They don't believe in mobile phones. I've been trying to get them to get one for years – just to have one in case of emergencies...'

Would it have made a difference, Mum having a mobile phone on hand? Punching 999 as she fell?

Stop it, I told myself and tried to wrench my thoughts away.

'And you didn't ring them either?' the policeman persisted.

They were probably trained to deal with the newly bereaved. Did it every day. I tried to pull myself together.

That was one of Mum's phrases. *'Pull yourself together,'* she'd told me a hundred times when I was small. And *'Don't make a fuss.' 'Come on, Isobel.'* Always Isobel. Never *Izzy*, or *Is*. She'd never say it again. Never say anything again.

I shook my head again. I wasn't functioning very well.

'Sorry,' I said, looking up. 'I...could you say that again?'

They smiled, both of them. Small smiles, polite, without warmth.

'Don't worry, that's quite normal. You've had a shock,' he said. 'I wanted to know whether you'd rung your parents after you got back here – perhaps last Sunday evening to let them know that you'd got back home safely?'

I shook my head.

'Is that usual?'

It took me a moment to get it. 'That I don't ring to say I've got home? Yes.'

'You're their only child, aren't you?'

I nodded. Only me.

Another thought fought its way through my cotton-wool brain. 'When... I mean...' I clenched my hands together tightly, dug my nails into my palms. 'When did Mum... Do you know when it happened?'

'A neighbour found her earlier today, around noon. Neither of your parents had been seen for a few days, and the neighbours assumed that they had gone away, for a short break perhaps.'

I nodded like one of those dogs in the backs of cars. Down and up. Down and up. 'Yes, they do...they did that quite often. They like travelling.' I was getting all my tenses mixed up. How do you talk about your parents when one of them is dead and the other has disappeared?

I don't know why grammar should matter so much at

a moment like this, but I really wanted to get it right. Dad had taught English before his retirement. He was always very concerned about correctness. He never allowed me to get away with mistakes, always insisted on the correct tense, the correct plural, *fewer* flowers not *less*, that sort of thing. He'd taught me all the rules.

'The neighbour noticed that your parents' cat seemed to be hungry – it came to be fed with hers, which I gather it doesn't usually do.' The police officer consulted his notes. 'She said that normally when they go away, they ask the neighbour on the other side to come in and feed it.'

'Napoleon,' I said, with a stab. White, with just two black patches on his back and one on his head. He would have been so confused with no one there to look after him. Poor, orphaned cat. I swallowed down rising tears, pulled myself together. Why on earth did the thought of the cat, of all things, make me cry? 'Mrs Lewis from number 11 has a key, she pops in to feed him when they go away.'

'You're sure your father hasn't contacted you?' The woman officer asked, abruptly.

'What? No, no, of course not. I haven't heard from him. You said he was missing...'

There was something in the way she said it. It took me a few moments to compute her meaning.

'You don't mean...you can't be saying—' I stared at her. 'No! Are you saying you think he's run away? You think he might have something to do with...'

I couldn't say it.

'We're not thinking anything at the moment,' she said, and for a terrible moment, I had to fight a nervous giggle.

Sloppy use of language, Dad was saying in my head.

'He didn't,' I said flatly. 'There is no way.'

They said nothing. Used to it, I supposed. People never believe their fathers or husbands or brothers would do something bad.

'If he does contact you, please let us know directly,' the woman said.

'Yes, of course I will. He's *missing*. I *want* him to be found. He's over sixty, he's an old man, for all I know he's wandering about somewhere, confused, or he's had an accident, or a fall...' I'd never called Dad an old man before. Never thought of him as one. He'd always been Dad, big, strong, invincible. Now, an old man. Missing. Under suspicion from the police, possibly. And Mum, dead at the bottom of the stairs.

The world had turned upside down.

Belatedly, something in what I had just thought caught my attention. *Accident.*

'Has he taken the car?' I asked. 'Maybe he tried to go for help. Maybe he's had an accident and...'

But the woman officer shook her head. 'The car is in the garage. Just one, but there's room for two.'

It was a statement, but she made it a question.

I answered it. 'Mum...used to drive, but she decided to stop a few years ago, when her eyesight got worse. She – she was in a near collision, and it gave her a bad scare. They sold her car after that.' I swallowed. 'Dad drives a white Toyota... I don't know the model, but it's a few years old, and looks sort of boxy. Square.'

They looked at each other, and the man nodded. 'It's a white Toyota in the garage.'

'You are looking for him, aren't you? I mean, you've got people out...in case something's happened to him?'

'Yes,' said the woman. 'We're looking for him.' She said it so blandly, with no inflection at all, that it sounded oddly threatening. As though what she meant was, *'We're looking for him all right.'*

They went soon after that. Left a card with their contact details, and admonitions to ring them straight away if I heard from Dad, or if I could think of anything that might help. And then they were gone, and I sat there in the living room with the silence ringing in my ears.

Suddenly tears were running down my face. Pain caught in my throat, bulky and hard and impossible to swallow.

I just sat there and cried. Now, suddenly, I could cry about Mum. Mum lying at the bottom of the stairs, dead. Dead. Mum who would never move again, never look at me again, never draw another breath, dead, gone, gone. I cried and cried.

I hadn't thought anything could hurt so much. Mum, gone. Forever.

I cried like I never had in my life. Cried and cried and couldn't stop. Where did all the tears come from?

And then I just sat, slumped on the sofa, eyes burning, nose clogged; my head hurting.

Finally, I got up, went to the bathroom on unsteady legs and splashed cold water in my face.

In the mirror, my face looked pink and swollen.

All those tears for Mum.

Not Dad.

But Dad was still alive.

I thought about him as I went into the kitchen and put the kettle on. I'd been about to make dinner earlier, but now just the thought of food made me feel ill.

Dad, missing, with the police looking for him. What would they find? What did they really think? They couldn't really be suspecting him, could they?

The phone rang.

I nearly jumped out of my skin, off-balance from shock and grief.

Who?

What if it was...

It continued to ring, shrilly. The sound stabbed into my ears.

I snatched it off the hook.

'Hello?'

'Isobel? Oh my dear, the police have been here to say that you mother has passed... I can hardly believe it. I am so sorry.'

It was my parents' next-door neighbour.

'The police have been to see me too, Mrs Lewis. They just left. It's terrible.'

'They've been to every house in the street, asking if anybody's seen your father. Oh, it's awful, awful. I expect he's wandering lost somewhere, poor man.'

'The police say nobody's seen them lately?'

'Well, I certainly haven't. Not since last week, I don't think. I had a chat with your mother last Friday, but then I went away for a family celebration on Anglesey, you see, and I didn't get back till the day before yesterday. Monday. I did notice that the lights went on at night in your parents' house, but as I told the police, I know that your father has these timed switches for when they go away, doesn't he? So proud of them, he was, when he got them installed. Impossible, he said, for anybody to tell whether someone's actually in or not. So now I don't know what to think...'

'I know,' I said. My voice was unsteady. I cleared my throat. 'I know, Mrs Lewis, it's terrible. Like a nightmare. It doesn't feel real at all.'

She told me again how sorry she was; and that she'd look after Napoleon.

'Until your Dad comes back,' she said firmly. 'He's had a shock, hasn't he. I'm sure they'll find him soon.'

'I hope so,' I said. 'Oh, I hope so. I'm so worried.'

'They were here,' I told him. 'Looking for you, fishing to see if I was hiding you. I think they suspect you. Mrs Lewis-next-door thinks you're wandering about somewhere, dazed because you've had a shock. I don't believe the police think that. They wouldn't say, but I got the impression they think maybe you did it.'

I listened to him breathing. Wondered what went through his mind.

'Don't worry,' I said. 'They won't find you. I'm not going to let them.'

I made a cup of tea and went and sat in the sitting room. The tea was hot and strong and sweet like they say you should take after you've had a shock. I thought of the weekend: the last time I'd seen my parents.

The last time, ever, that I'd seen Mum.

Just that thought made the tears start again. They ran down my face, unstoppable.

It was the strangest feeling, as though I was melting from the inside.

I never cried.

I couldn't even remember crying as a child. Mum hadn't liked it. It made her feel unhappy, she'd said.

I hated the idea of Mum being unhappy. I loved her. She was all I had.

I had learnt early on that there was no relying on Dad.

I'd admired Dad. He knew everything. He knew what was right and what was wrong. There was never any doubt with him. I wanted to be like that.

He never hit me in anger, like Mum.

I could understand anger.

When Dad didn't like something, he went as cold as ice. He wasn't there at all. He didn't even look at you. He would freeze you to death, until you'd apologised and backed off and made yourself small and made amends. And even then, he'd never forget. He'd let you know from time to time that he remembered. You couldn't ever settle a score with Dad. He always won.

Mum had been different. Mum had always been human. She reacted. Things got to her. I didn't know what I would have done without Mum. I always felt that she'd kept me sane. Without her, life would have been even worse.

I'd finished the tea, and I didn't feel like having another one. I needed something different. Something stronger.

I got the Bailey's out. Someone had given it to me for my birthday. Not my kind of thing, really, but it was at hand.

And actually, it wasn't so bad, a bit on the sweet side, but they do say sugar is good for your nerves.

So I sat and sipped sweet thick whisky, and thought about Mum.

She'd been brittle and fragile, so much in the shadow of Dad. So, so different from Dad.

My tears were flowing again.

She'd had so many flaws, but somehow, that had made me love her more. Dad had been perfect. Like a landscape covered in snow.

Mum hadn't. Mum had been human.

She'd lash out at you when you'd done something wrong. Or when she thought you had. And then she was sorry. Often. Crying upset her then. Made it worse for her, because she could see that she'd hurt you.

So you'd learn not to cry, to help her not feel bad.

I wanted Mum to feel good. I loved her. She was all I had. I stayed at home much longer than I would have otherwise, because of her. I didn't want to leave her. She'd be alone with Dad. I was afraid for her. I wanted to protect her, because she couldn't protect herself.

Couldn't protect me, when Dad started to ask me into his study. To supervise my schoolwork, to help me with things I didn't understand.

To punish me when I made mistakes. Not in anger. He was always very particular about that. He never struck me in anger.

Anger was weakness.

That's how I first learnt that Mum was weak. She allowed herself to be governed by her anger.

Dad would never allow anything to govern him.

He handed out precise punishments. He would hit me three times for a minor mistake. For something more grave, make me take my skirt and knickers off and stand like that for five minutes exactly.

There were also rewards. Sometimes for me: money, or a sweet. At other times rewards for him, because he was working very hard to make me understand my homework. He would touch me when my knickers were off; and teach me to touch him.

I was not to tell any of this to Mum.

It would upset her. It would make her feel bad.

It was the hardest thing in my life not to tell Mum. The things that happened in Dad's study made me feel that I was slowly going empty, like a balloon that's losing air. I wanted him to stop. I wanted to tell someone.

But if I told Mum, she would feel as terrible as I did, and worse, because she wouldn't be able to do anything to help me. She wouldn't be able to stop him.

I protected Mum, and that made me feel a little bit better.

All through my life, the knowledge that I had protected Mum from the worst had sustained me.

Until last Sunday afternoon.

I'd gone up to see them again. I'd been worried about Mum. The weekend before, she'd seemed odd. On edge, somehow. So I went up to Flint again on the Saturday to make sure she was all right. Funny really, when you think how it all came out.

So there I was, about to leave. Mum had been as always, after all. I must have been imagining things. I was a bit irritated with myself for overreacting. But mostly I was relieved that everything was all right.

My overnight bag was already packed and in the car, but I'd forgotten my handbag upstairs. Dad was in his study across the hallway, working; I'd go in to say good-bye to him in a minute. I just stood and surveyed the spare room, my old room, to make sure I had everything. Stood a moment longer to look at the view from the window, towards the estuary.

I heard Mum coming up the stairs and thought she would come to call me, but she went into Dad's study instead. 'Isobel is about to leave,' I heard her say. 'She's putting her bags into the car.'

Dad said he'd be down in a minute. Computer keys clacked.

'Shut that thing off before you go,' Mum said. 'I don't want Isobel coming in here for some reason and seeing you looking at pictures of little girls on your internet.'

I thought, even then, that that moment would stay with me for the rest of my life: standing by the door with the bag dangling from my hand, and Mum's voice ringing in my ears, and the world crashing all around me.

She knew.

She knew about Dad.

I didn't think. I got up and opened the door and went through it and met Mum at the top of the stairs.

'Mum,' I said.

'Isobel.' She looked surprised.

You'd think I'd have been upset, but I wasn't. I was as calm as calm.

'Mum, what you just said to Dad... About little girls on his computer. I heard you.'

'Rubbish,' she said. But something in her face changed. It went still, and nervous, at the same time. As though she'd slipped a mask on in a hurry and it wasn't sitting right.

'You knew. About Dad and me, when I was little? About what he did? You knew!'

Her face changed again. She looked nervous now, but also

sly. She passed the tip of her tongue over dry lips. Said nothing.

'Mum?'

'You were a difficult child, Isobel,' she said, finally. 'Quite precocious. He was trying to teach you some discipline, some restraint. Perhaps he went a little far sometimes. I'm sure it never did you any harm.'

She turned away and made as though to go back down the stairs.

'Wait,' I said and put my hand on her arm. 'Did you know that he made me take my clothes off sometimes and...made me do...things with him?'

I couldn't say the words I had wanted to say. I couldn't bring myself to pronounce them. I didn't want their taste on my tongue. I thought I was going to be sick.

Mum looked back at me, unmoving. 'Some men are like that,' she said. 'Perhaps it's good to learn that sooner rather than later.'

'You could have stopped him,' I said. I was tugging at her arm, as though to tug her to his study, to show her what he was doing. But it was too late; far, far too late. 'You could have stopped him!'

'I wish you didn't make such a fuss, Isobel,' she said. 'I'm sure it wasn't that bad. He said you quite enjoyed some of it.'

Even if I live to be a hundred years old, I will never regret that I pushed her then. I hadn't meant to. I hadn't meant to do anything, other than make those words unsaid, or at least make her stop, now, now, this minute. But while my head was still trying to make sense of what she said, my arms seized her and pushed her away from me, with all the strength in my body. And I saw her stumble backwards, her feet touching air, her arms flailing for something to hold on to. Finding nothing.

She was falling, and she knew that she was falling because her face was sheer terror.

I'd always tried to protect her from the horrors of life, and instead in the end I killed her.

She must have screamed, too, although I didn't register the scream until I saw her lying at the foot of the stairs, her leg twitching a little but the rest of her very still. There was a lot of blood, mostly on the floor and some on the walls and the stairs.

I was quite glad at that moment that she hadn't got a mobile phone despite the fact that I had tried to convince her to get one. What would I have done if she'd held it in her hand just then, if she'd managed to call 999 in the last moments of her life?

I suppose I could always have said that it was an accident, but it would have been very awkward.

Dad had heard the fall and the scream. He must have heard our conversation before that too. But the noise of the fall and the scream brought him out of his study.

I had been afraid of him all my life.

Until that moment. Suddenly, I wasn't afraid of him any more.

'I could kill you now,' I told him, as he stood there, staring down at Mum's body, still twitching. Mum's blood. 'One shove, and you'd be down there with her. But that would be too quick. Do you remember how you made me take my clothes off and just stand there and wait? I hated that waiting. Hated it. Now you're going to see how it feels.'

It was the crowning moment of my life. I was big and he was small now. It felt good, good.

I tied his hands with a belt and gagged him and made him go downstairs. We had to step over Mum's body, and I was careful not to put my feet on any of the blood spots. And then I took his shoes off and put them on and went back upstairs wearing them, and packed a bag for Dad with some clothes and underwear and his shaving things, and his wallet and his keys. I went into his study and shut the computer down. I used a pen to press the keys. It was the only place where I worried about leaving fingerprints. I am proud that I remembered to think about fingerprints at that moment.

There was a connecting door from the house to the garage. My car was parked next to his, in the space where Mum's car had used to be. I made him lie on the back seat. He didn't put up much resistance. He seemed frightened of me.

As soon as he was in the car, I tied his feet as well, and I put a coat over him. I even remembered to set the timer for the lights.

I don't think anybody saw me. I'd arrived lateish on the Saturday evening, and when I left on Sunday it was already dark. I like driving late. The roads are much clearer at night, and it's just me and the car and the radio, cutting through the dark. Mum had told me that Mrs Lewis was away. My car had been in the garage and we hadn't gone out, so there was no reason for anyone to have seen me. I was careful not to turn the headlights on until I turned on to the main road.

But I forgot all about poor Napoleon. Once the police told me about him, I thought of how confused he must have been, not understanding why nobody came to feed him and stroke him. I wish I had remembered to put some food out for him. He's probably the only one who misses Mum.

Although that's not true.

I miss her, dreadfully.

I miss the Mum I always thought I had; the one who would have protected me and stopped Dad. I miss the Mum who loved me and cared about me. But she's gone. She never was.

Even so, I miss her.

I'm crying for her.

I'm not sure why I didn't just kill Dad too. I don't think I'd miss him. But perhaps losing both of them at once would have been too much.

* * *

There's a crawl space under the floorboards of the front room of my house. I never knew it was there until I took the carpet up last year. It's the strangest thing, you lift a trap door in the corner of the room and there, four feet down, is the soil. And some electrical cables I think, but mostly just soil.

Dad is down there as well now. Tied hand and foot, and gagged, with a heavy rug over him so he won't make any noise. He's learning what it's like to wait. Every day, I lift the trap door and tell him what it was like for me, in his study when I was small and he was powerful. He's learning. He watches me and listens. There's nothing else he can do.

The police are still looking for him. When he's dead, I'll throw his body in the river, and write a note saying that he killed Mum, and how he couldn't live with it.

I haven't told him that yet.

I'm saving it up.

Author Biographies

Yasmin Ali has worked in higher education and professional training, in relation to which she has contributed to a number of books and journals on social policy and citizenship. She is now a website editor and freelance consultant and lives in Aberystwyth.

Sue Anderson is a teacher. She always meant to write, but it was only when she came to Wales twenty-odd years ago that she actually began. She says she has the Welsh air to thank for that, and Honno, who have published three of her pieces so far, in the anthologies *Mirror Mirror*, *Coming up Roses* and *In Her Element*. She's won a few writing competitions, had poems and articles published and attempted the odd novella. Her current project is a full-length novel and her dream, of course, is to see it in print. She's taking long, deep breaths of Welsh air.

Jan Baker was born in Mumbles, educated in Swansea and now lives in Penarth where, after taking early retirement, she concentrates on her writing. She also works as an 'extra' for film and TV. Her main interest lies in writing crime fiction and thrillers. She is in the process of completing a novel entitled *Murder on the Mumbles Train* using the characters first formulated in the short story published in this anthology. She has written for *Cambrensis* and has had articles published in several local papers. In collaboration with another local writer, she has written a sit-com script and produced a short film, which they are in the process of submitting to production companies. She attends creative writing classes and workshops and is a member of Cardiff Writers Circle, where she currently holds the Muriel Ross Trophy Prize donated for the winner of their annual competition for article writing.

Hilary Bowers is fifty-nine years old, divorced and, until recently, lived near the beautiful coastal university town of Aberystwyth where she attended creative writing classes for several years and helped set up a writers and artists' support group which still meets regularly. She was also an active member of Arts Centre based community theatre group, Castaways. She is a charity shop manager and while in Aberystwyth she worked for the Salvation Army in that capacity. She now lives near the wonderful city of Wells in Somerset where she works for Barnardo's. Since moving, she has become a member of Wells Little Theatre and is training to be a bell ringer. One day she hopes to ring in Wells cathedral. She is a novelist by inclination but also enjoys writing short stories, one of which was published by Honno last year in the anthology *Coming Up Roses*. She also writes book reviews for the Welsh Books Council.

Maggie Cainen went to university in Manchester, London and Swansea and recently did an MA in Creative Writing at Swansea. She has taught in universities, FE's, grammar schools and comprehensives and lectured extensively on teaching training. She is interested in everyone and everything from current affairs, politics and religion to gardening, childcare and cooking. She reads very widely and belongs to two reading groups and a play reading circle. She has worked as: a chef, a waitress, an au pair for a princess, a simultaneous interpreter, a first aider, a life guard and a play leader in French holiday colonies. She adores adrenaline sports, is an instructor in half a dozen water sports and has written for scuba magazines for the last seven years. She has also been published in magazines, newspapers, online, in a BBC book and recently in Honno's anthology *In Her Element*. She does regular book reviews for Tesco and just started reviewing for *Woman's Weekly*.

Caroline Clark was born in the Midlands but has lived in Aberystwyth for twenty-seven years, married to Alan, a university librarian. A former member of the Shakespeare Institute, she has contributed to publications on Shakespeare and Ovid. Having always written poetry, with some success over the years in magazines, local and national competitions, she is presently working on a collection of poems inspired by the landscape and history of north Ceredigion. Most of her short story writing has been in fantasy genres. While living in Wales she has been involved with theatre and dance groups: costuming, performing and directing. She has worked in wardrobe for Aberystwyth University's Theatre Department and has been active for many years in the Drama Association of Wales. More recently she has been an advisor on Welsh Arts Council committees. However, family commitments have meant that for the past four years she has been a full-time carer at home.

Val Douglas moved from rural Kent to a farm in West Wales six years ago and has never regretted it, having met with nothing but kindness there and stunned by the wonderful countryside on a daily basis. She has spent a lifetime in education, the last ten years of her career as headteacher of two schools in socially deprived areas of Kent. Now retired, she spends most of her time writing and walking as well as studying for an MA in Creative Writing at Aberystwyth University which, she says, has given her a new lease of life. She has had two non-fiction books published and hopes to have some more short stories and a novel published in the next few years.

Imogen Rhia Herrad is a freelance writer and broadcaster currently based in Cardiff and Cologne. She is German originally and has also lived in London and Argentina. Her first book, *The Woman who loved an Octopus and other Saints' Tales*, was published by Seren Books in 2007. She is now working on a novel set in ancient Rome and Wales.

Helen Lewis was born and brought up in Hampshire on the edge of the New Forest. She originally trained as a Graphic Designer at Southampton College of Art. Having completed the four-year course she worked in studios in Southampton and then London before finally going freelance, which she still dabbles in. In 2006 she moved with her husband and two sons to Pembrokeshire. She began writing shortly after they arrived and has had short stories published in national magazines. Having finished her first novel she is currently collecting ideas for a second.

Kate Kinnersley was born in the Potteries. She left grammar school to work as 'cub' reporter on the local weekly paper. She graduated to evening papers and then Fleet Street journalism before running a 'slip' edition newspaper. She works as a freelancer and holds workshops in creative writing. Now she travels the world researching and is currently working on two crime novels. Kate is an extrovert, fun loving personality always looking for new challenges. She writes erotic stories under the name SEKSI.

Delphine Richards was born and raised in Llandysul and now lives near Llandeilo. She served for thirteen years as a police officer with Dyfed Powys Police before a complicated brain tumour enforced her retirement. She then took a freelance journalism course and subsequently ran her own tongue-in-cheek column in the *Carmarthen Journal* for twelve years. She also contributed to a variety of other newspapers and magazines. Drawing on police experience, she co-wrote *Humour in the Police Force* with a Canadian writer. Along with her husband, she was commissioned to write *Newfoundlands Today* as part of a 'Book of the Breed' series for Ringpress Books. This followed their involvement in showing and judging the Newfoundland dog all over the world. She claims that walking the dogs gives her the best ideas for short stories.

Beryl Roberts was born in the Rhondda and graduated from UCW Aberystwyth. On her retirement from teaching, she completed an MA in Creative Writing at Bath Spa University. Her short story *A Touch of Gloss* was broadcast on BBC Radio 4 and others have won national competitions and been published. She spent six months of each year between 2003-7 in South Africa, travelling extensively and teaching English to black township teenagers. She has recently completed two novels set in Wales and is currently looking for a publisher.

Anita Rowe (née Smalley) was born in Pwllheli, Gwynedd, educated at Pwllheli Grammar School, Bangor Normal College and London University, and writes in both English and Welsh as well as teaching creative writing. After nearly 40 years teaching in England she has now returned to her roots on the Llŷn Peninsula. She has written three teenage novels (for Pan Books, Severn House and Terrapin) which have been translated into German, Dutch and Slovenian, all under the name Anita Davies. She has contributed news features to local and national newspapers and had short stories, fiction serials and articles published in several teenage and women's magazines. Some of her poems have been published in *Envoi* and she has contributed to a previous Honno anthology. She is currently working on a novel set on the Llŷn Peninsula at the beginning of the last century and studying for an M.A. in Writing at the University of Wales, Bangor.

Kay Sheard was born in Bradford, West Yorkshire in the 1970s and is a graduate of Cambridge University. After teaching Latin, Greek, Classical Civilisation and History for several years, she spent a year writing for the Cambridge Online Latin Project before leaving to start a family. Long drawn to Wales by tales of her Welsh great-grandmother, who died before she was born, she moved to Denbighshire eight years ago. Kay now lives next to a babbling little river deep in the Clwydian Hills with her husband, four-year-old daughter and three cats, and divides her time between writing and home-educating her little girl. Her short story in this anthology is her first piece of published fiction.

Joy Tucker is a Scottish writer who has lived in Wales for many years. Her first short story was published in the 1960s and she has been writing ever since. A former columnist and feature-writer with *The (Glasgow) Herald*, her short stories have been published in anthologies, newspapers and magazines throughout Britain. Some have been broadcast on BBC Radio 4, and her radio credits include children's stories and poems. Joy also writes one-act plays, several of which have now had successful productions by amateur companies in South Wales, North Devon and West Sussex. Joy lives on the Gower Peninsula with her Welsh husband.

About the Editors

Lindsay Ashford is the author of five crime novels, one of which, *Strange Blood*, was shortlisted for the Theakston's Old Peculier Crime Novel of the Year Award. A former BBC journalist, she was the first woman to graduate from Queens' College Cambridge, where she studied Criminology. Currently working on a sixth novel, she has also had short stories published in magazines and broadcast on BBC Radio 4. She lives on the Welsh coast near Aberystwyth.

Caroline Oakley has edited one previous collection of short stories for Honno – *Coming up Roses*. Before joining Honno as editor she worked at the Centre for Alternative Technology, publishing titles on everything from ecological sewage treatment to sustainable architecture, and before that as Editorial Director at Orion Books in London. She has been editing crime fiction since the late eighties and hopes to continue doing so for a good while to come.

The Megan Rhys Crime series

by Lindsay Ashford

The Killer Inside, by Lindsay Ashford

Forensic psychologist Megan is investigating the unusually high suicide rate among prisoners at the grim Victorian Balsall Gate jail in Birmingham. While she is there yet another death occurs. The police are uninterested. To them this is just another drug overdose. But Megan is not convinced. Carl Kelly died in agony from something even more lethal than heroin, telling his cell mate he was being haunted by the ghost of a man he'd stabbed to death. Megan believes that Kelly himself has now been murdered.

The fourth title in the Megan Rhys crime series.

978 1 870206 92 1
£6.99

Death Studies, by Lindsay Ashford

Some secrets haunt the living and the dead... A windswept seaside strip in West Wales – sleepy enough, until three bodies turn up within as many days. A shocking coincidence or a serial killer? Forensic psychologist Megan Rhys is supposed to be on holiday but she can't ignore the body in her backyard... Her journalist sister Ceri is being held to ransom by an editor eager to steal a march on her national red-top rivals, and the closer the sisters get to the heart of the case the more their careers bring them into potential conflict...

The third title in the Megan Rhys crime series.

978 1 870206 86 0
£6.99

Strange Blood, by Lindsay Ashford

Women are dying with pentagrams carved on their faces. Satanic ritual or cunning deception? Forensic psychologist Megan Rhys is called in to help the police investigate what they believe is a ritual killing. She feels that prejudice is taking the enquiry in the wrong direction and she is suspicious of the media-obsessed police chief in charge of the case. As more women die – and as the press, the police, her boss and her own family turn on her – Megan stakes everything on finding the killer.

The second title in the Megan Rhys crime series.

Shortlisted for the *Theakston's Old Peculier Crime Novel of the Year*, 2005.

978 1 870206 84 6
£6.99

Frozen, by Lindsay Ashford

Megan has been asked to advise on two murders: two young prostitutes, dumped like rubbish, seemingly the victims of two men working together. But there is something wrong the the information the police are giving her. Someone is trying to manipulate her. Or are Megan's own prejudices colouring her judgement? As the killings add up, Megan is being pushed harder and harder towards one solution – and someone is getting into her house. Can she trust her instincts ? Is the killer closer than she realises?

The first title in the Megan Rhys crime series.

"Gritty, streetwise and raw" *Denise Hamilton*, author of the Eve Diamond crime novels

978 1 870206 82 2
£6.99

Other titles from Honno

Girl on the Edge by Rachel V Knox

A chilling story of love, betrayal, secrets and lies…

Just how did her mother die and what did Leila witness on the cliff top, if anything? Leila knows that there's something about her childhood she can't quite remember… that haunts her dreams and sometimes her days. This year she's determined to find out the truth… but someone has tried very hard to keep their secrets and will go to extremes to make sure it stays that way. A compelling psychological thriller set in the moors of North Wales.

9781870206754
£6.99

Skin Deep, by Jacqueline Jacques
In this playful and terrifying thriller, Max is the first successful transplant, after the chilling discovery of six frozen brains in an abandoned cellar. Journalist, Clare, wants to tell the story, get her promotion – perhaps even a new relationship – but she can't see the nightmare she is being drawn into, until it's much too late.

"Terrific thriller, combining violence, psychological suspense and romance"
Women Writers' Network News

9781870206679
£6.99

All Honno titles can be ordered online at www.honno.co.uk,
or by sending a cheque to Honno with free p&p to all UK addresses.

About Honno

Honno Welsh Women's Press was set up in 1986 by a group of women who felt strongly that women in Wales needed wider opportunities to see their writing in print and to become involved in the publishing process. Our aim is to develop the writing talents of women in Wales, give them new and exciting opportunities to see their work published and often to give them their first 'break' as a writer.

Honno is registered as a community co-operative. Any profit that Honno makes is invested in the publishing programme. Women from Wales and around the world have expressed their support for Honno by buying shares in the co-operative. Shareholders' liability is limited to the amount invested and each shareholder has a vote at the Annual General Meeting. To buy shares or to receive further information about forthcoming publications, please write to Honno at the address below, or visit our website: www.honno.co.uk

Honno
Unit 14, Creative Units
Aberystwyth Arts Centre
Penglais Campus
Aberystwyth
Ceredigion SY23 3GL